DERYNI RISING

Volume I in the Chronicles of the Deryni

Katherine Kurtz

A Del Rey Book

BALLANTINE BOOKS • NEW YORK

A Del Rey Book
Published by Ballantine Books

Copyright © 1970 by Katherine Kurtz

ISBN 0-345-27599-3

Manufactured in the United States of America

First Edition: August 1970
Sixth Printing: August 1978

For

CARL M. SELLE

who knew all along that

it would begin this way.

CONTENTS

DERYNI
RISING

CHAPTER ONE

"Lest the hunter become the hunted."

BRION HALDANE, King of Gwynedd, Prince of Meara, and Lord of the Purple March, reined in his horse sharply at the top of the hill and scanned the horizon.

He was not a big man, though regal bearing and a catlike grace had convinced many a would-be adversary that he was. But his enemies rarely had time to notice this technicality.

Dark, lean, with just a trace of grey beginning to show at his temples, in the precise black beard, he commanded instant respect by his mere presence in a room. When he spoke, whether with the crackle of authority or the lower tones of subtle persuasion, men listened and obeyed.

And if fine words could not convince, often the persuasion of cold steel could. The worn scabbard of the broadsword at his side attested to that, as did the slim stiletto in its black suede sheath at his wrist.

The hands that steadied the skittish war horse be-

1

tween his knees were gentle but firm on the red leather reins—the hands of a fighting man, the hands of one accustomed to command.

If one studied him more closely, however, one was forced to revise the original impression of warrior-king. For the wide grey eyes held promise of much more than mere military prowess and expertise. Indeed, they glittered with a shrewd intelligence and wit which were known and admired throughout the Eleven Kingdoms.

And if there were a fleeting aura of mystery, of forbidden magic about this man, that was discussed in whispers, if at all. For at thirty-nine, Brion of Haldane had kept the peace in Gwynedd for nearly fifteen years. The king who now sat his horse at the top of the hill had earned such infrequent moments of pleasure as he now pursued.

Brion slipped his feet from the stirrups and stretched his legs. At mid-morning, the ground fog was just lifting, and the unseasonable cold of the night before still permeated everything. Even the protection of hunting leathers could not wholly prevent the light chain mail beneath Brion's tunic from chilling like ice. And silk beneath the mail was small consolation.

He pulled the crimson wool of his cloak more closely around him, flexed numb fingers in their leather gloves, drew the scarlet hunt cap farther down on his forehead, the white plume floating gently on the still air.

The sounds of voices, barking hounds, the jingle of burnished bits and spurs and other horse noises drifted up on the mist. Turning to look back down the hill, he could catch fleeting glimpses of well-bred horses moving in the fog, their equally well-bred riders resplendent in finely embroidered velvets and polished leather.

Brion smiled at that. For despite the outward show of splendor and self-assurance, he was certain that the riders below were enjoying the jaunt no more than he was. The inclement weather had made the hunt a chore instead of the anticipated pleasure.

Why, oh, why had he promised Jehana there would be venison for her table tonight? He had known, when he said it, that it was too early in the season. Still, one did not break one's promise to a lady—especially when that lady was one's beloved queen and mother of the royal heir.

The low, plaintive call of the hunting horns confirmed his suspicion that the scent was lost, and he sighed resignedly. Unless the weather cleared dramatically, there was little hope of reassembling the scattered pack in anything less than half an hour. And with hounds *this* green, it could be days, even weeks!

He shook his head and chuckled as he thought of Ewan—so proud of his new hounds earlier in the week. He knew that the old Marcher lord would have a lot to say about this morning's performance. But however much he might make excuses, Brion was afraid Ewan deserved all the teasing he was certain to get in the weeks to come. A Duke of Claibourne should have known better than to bring such puppies out in the field this early in the season.

The poor pups have probably never even seen *a deer!*

The sound of closer hoofbeats reached Brion's ears, and he turned in the saddle to see who was approaching. At length, a young rider in scarlet silks and leathers emerged from the fog and urged his bay gelding up the hill. Brion watched with pride as the boy slowed his mount to a walk and reined in at his father's side.

"Lord Ewan says it will be awhile, Sire," the boy reported, his eyes sparkling with the excitement of the chase. "The hounds flushed some rabbits."

"Rabbits!" Brion laughed out loud. "You mean to tell me that after all the boasting we've had to endure for the past week, Ewan's going to make us sit here and freeze while he rounds up his puppy dogs?"

"So it appears, Sire," Kelson grinned. "But if it's any consolation, everyone in the hunt feels exactly the same way."

He has his mother's smile, Brion thought fondly. *But the eyes, the hair, are mine. He seems so young, though. Can it really be nearly fourteen years? Ah, Kelson, if only I could spare you what lies ahead . . .*

Brion dismissed the thought with a smile and a shake of the head. "Well, as long as everybody else is miserable, I suppose I feel a bit better."

He yawned and stretched, then relaxed in the saddle. The polished leather creaked as his weight shifted, and Brion sighed.

"Ah, if Morgan were only here. Fog or no fog, I think he could charm the deer right to the city gates if he chose."

"Really?" Kelson asked.

"Well, perhaps not quite that close," Brion conceded. "But he has a way with animals—and other things." The king grew suddenly distant, and he toyed absently with the riding crop in his gloved hand.

Kelson caught the change of mood, and after a studied pause he moved his horse closer to the older man. His father had not been entirely open about Morgan in the past few weeks. And the absence of conversation about the young general had been keenly felt. Perhaps this was the time to pursue the matter. He decided to be blunt.

"Sire, forgive me if I speak out of turn, but why haven't you recalled Morgan from the border marches?"

Brion felt himself go tense, forced himself to conceal his surprise. How had the boy known that? Morgan's whereabouts had been a closely guarded secret for nearly two months now. Not even the Council knew just where he was, or why. He must tread softly until he could ascertain just how much the boy knew.

"Why do you ask, Son?"

"I don't mean to pry, Sire," the boy replied. "I'm certain you have reasons even the Council isn't aware of. I've missed him, though. And I think you have, too."

Khadasa! The boy was perceptive! It was as though he'd read the unspoken thoughts. If he was to avoid the Morgan question, he would have to steer Kelson away from the subject quickly.

Brion permitted himself a wan smile. "Thanks for your vote of confidence. I'm afraid you and I are among the few who've missed him, however. I'm sure you're aware of the rumors afoot in the past weeks."

"That Morgan is out to depose you?" Kelson replied guardedly. "You don't really believe that, do you? And that isn't the reason he's still at Cardosa, either."

Brion studied the boy out of the corner of his eye, his crop tapping lightly against his right boot where Kelson couldn't see it. Cardosa, even.

The boy certainly had a good source of information, whatever it was. And he was persistent, too. He had deliberately turned the conversation back to Morgan's absence, despite his father's efforts to avoid the issue. Perhaps he'd misjudged the boy. He tended to forget that Kelson was nearly fourteen, of legal age. Brion himself had been only a few years older when he came to the throne.

He decided to release a bit of concrete information and see how the boy would react.

"No, it isn't. I can't go into too much detail right now, Son. But there *is* a major crisis brewing at Cardosa, and Morgan is keeping an eye on it. Wencit of Torenth wants the city, and he's already broken two treaties in his efforts to annex it. By next spring we'll probably be formally at war." He paused. "Does that frighten you?"

Kelson studied the ends of his reins carefully before replying. "I've never known real war," he said slowly, his gaze shifting out across the plain. "As long as I've been alive, there's been peace in the Eleven Kingdoms. One would think men could forget how to fight after fifteen years of peace."

Brion smiled and allowed himself to relax slightly. He seemed to have succeeded in shifting the topic of discussion away from Morgan at last, and that was good.

"They never forget, Kelson. That's part of being human, I'm sorry to say."

"I suppose so," Kelson said. He reached down and patted the bay's neck, smoothed a stray wisp in the mane, turned wide grey eyes squarely on his father's face.

"It's the Shadowed One again, isn't it, Father?"

The insight of that simple statement momentarily rocked Brion's world. He had been prepared for any question, any comment—anything but a mention of the Shadowed One by his son. It was not fair for one so young to have to face such awesome reality! It so unnerved the older man that for an instant he was speechless, open-mouthed.

How had Kelson known about the Shadowed One's threat? By Saint Camber, the boy must have the talent!

"You're not supposed to know about that!" he blurted accusingly, trying desperately to remarshall his thoughts and give a more coherent answer.

Kelson was taken aback by his father's reaction and showed it, but he didn't allow his gaze to waver. There was a touch of challenge, almost defiance in his voice.

"There are a good many things I'm not supposed to know about, Sire. But that hasn't kept me from learning. Would you want it any other way?"

"No," Brion murmured. He dropped his eyes uncertainly, searched for the proper phrasing for what he must ask next, found it.

"Did Morgan tell you?"

Kelson shifted uneasily, suddenly aware that the tables had turned, that he was in deeper than he'd planned. It was his own fault. He'd insisted on pursuing this matter. But now his father would not be satisfied until Kelson followed through. He cleared his throat.

"Yes, he did—before he left," Kelson replied hesitantly. "He was afraid you wouldn't approve." He wet his lips. "He—ah—also mentioned your powers—and the basis for your rule."

Brion frowned. *That Morgan!* He was annoyed he hadn't recognized the signs sooner, for he guessed now what must have happened. Still, the boy had done an admirable job of keeping the knowledge a secret. Perhaps Morgan had been right all along.

"How much did Morgan tell you, Son?" he asked quietly.

"Too much to please you—not enough to satisfy me," the boy admitted with some reluctance. He hazarded a glance at his father's face. "Are you angry, Sire?"

"Angry?"

It was all Brion could do to keep from shouting with relief. Angry? The inferences the boy had made, the guarded queries, the skill with which the boy had played the conversation back and forth, even on the defensive—by God, if not for this, then what had he and Morgan worked for all these years? Angry? By Heaven, how could he be angry?

Brion reached across and slapped Kelson's knee affectionately. "Of course I'm not angry, Kelson," he said. "If only you knew how much you'd put my mind at ease. You gave me a few rough moments, granted.

But I'm more certain than ever, now, that my choice was the right one. I want you to promise me one thing, though."

"Anything, Sire," Kelson agreed hesitantly.

"Not so solemn, Son," Brion objected, smiling and touching Kelson's shoulder again to reassure him. "It isn't a difficult request. But if anything should happen to me, I want you to send for Morgan immediately. He'll be more help to you than any other single person I can think of. Will you do that for me?"

Kelson sighed and smiled, relief written all across his face. "Of course, Sire. That would be my first thought in any event. Morgan knows—about a lot of things."

"On that I would stake my life," Brion smiled.

He straightened in the saddle and gathered the red leather reins in long, gloved fingers. "Look, the sun's coming out. Let's see if Ewan's got those hounds rounded up yet!"

The sky had brightened appreciably as the sun climbed toward the zenith. And now the royal pair cast faint, short shadows before them as they trotted down the hill. It had grown so clear, one could see all the way across the meadow to the forest beyond. Brion's grey eyes scanned the scattered hunting party with interest as he and Kelson approached.

There was Rogier, the Earl of Fallon, in dark green velvet, riding a magnificent grey stallion Brion had never seen before. He seemed to be engaged in a very animated conversation with the fiery young Bishop Arilan and—very interesting—a flash of McLain tartan identified the third rider as Kevin, the younger Lord McLain. Ordinarily, he and Rogier did not get along. (For that matter, few people *did* get along with Rogier.) He wondered what the three had found to talk about.

He did not have time to speculate further. For the loud, booming voice of the Duke of Claibourne drew Brion's attention to the head of the ride. Lord Ewan, his great red beard fairly bristling in the sunlight, was giving someone a royal chewing-out—not an unexpected event in the light of the hunt's success to date.

Brion half-stood in his stirrups for a better look. As he'd suspected, it was one of the whippers-in who was getting the brunt of Ewan's anger. Poor man. It wasn't his fault the hounds weren't performing well. Then, again, he supposed Ewan had to have someone to blame.

Brion smiled and directed Kelson's attention to the situation, indicating that he should rescue the unfortunate huntsman and placate Ewan. As Kelson rode off, Brion continued to scan the assembly. *There* was the man he'd been looking for—over by Rogier.

Touching spurs to his mount, he galloped easily across the turf to hail a tall young man in the purple and white of the House of Fianna. The man was drinking from a finely tooled leather flask.

"Halloo! What's this I see? Young Colin of Fianna drinking up all the best wine, as usual! How about a few drops for your poor, shivering king, my friend?"

He drew rein beside Colin with a flourish and eyed the flask as Colin lowered it from his lips.

Colin smiled and wiped the mouth of the flask on his sleeve, then handed it across with a jovial bow.

"Good morning, Sire. You know my wine is always yours for the asking."

Rogier joined them and deftly backed his stallion a few paces as Brion's black reached out to nip. "Good morrow, My Liege," he said, bowing low in the saddle. "My Lord is most astute to locate the finest brew in the company so early. 'Tis a prodigious feat!"

"Prodigious?" Brion chuckled. "On a morning like

this? Rogier, you have a fantastic gift for understatement."

He threw back his head and took a long swallow from the flask, lowered it and sighed. "Ah, 'tis no secret that Colin's father keeps the finest cellars in all the Eleven Kingdoms. My compliments, as usual, Colin!" He raised the flask and drank again.

Colin smiled mischievously and leaned his forearms against the saddle horn. "Ah, Majesty, now I know you're just trying to flatter me so my father will send you another shipment. That isn't Fianna wine at all. A beautiful lady gave it to me only this morning."

Brion paused in mid-swallow, then lowered the flask with concern. "A lady? Ah, Colin, you should have told me. I would never have asked for your lady's token."

Colin laughed aloud. "She's not my lady, Sire. I never saw her before. She merely gave me the wine. Besides, she'd doubtless be honored should she learn you sampled and enjoyed her brew."

Brion returned the flask and wiped across his moustache and beard with the back of a gloved hand. "Now, no excuses, Colin," he insisted. "It's I who have been amiss. Come and ride at my side. And you shall sit at my right at supper tonight. Even a king must make amends when he trifles with a lady's favor."

Kelson let his mind and eyes wander as he rode back toward the king. Behind him, Ewan and the master-of-hounds had finally reached a tentative agreement as to what had gone wrong, and the hounds seemed to be under control again. The whippers-in were keeping them in a tight pack, waiting for the royal command to proceed. The hounds, though, had their own ideas, which did not include waiting for kings or lords. It was questionable just how long the huntsmen would be able to hold them.

A flash of royal blue to the left caught Kelson's eye as he rode, and he immediately identified it as his uncle, the Duke of Carthmoor.

As brother of the king and ranking peer in the realm, Prince Nigel was responsible in a major way for the training of some thirty young pages of the royal household. As usual, he had some of his charges in tow today, and as usual, he was engaged in one of his seemingly endless battles to teach them something useful. There were only six of them along on the hunt today, and Nigel's own three boys were elsewhere in the entourage, but Kelson could see by Nigel's harried expression that these particular pages were not some of his brighter pupils.

Lord Jared, the McLain patriarch, was offering helpful advice from the sidelines, but the boys simply could not seem to get the hang of what it was Nigel wanted.

"No, no, no," Nigel was saying. "If you ever address an earl simply as 'Sir' in public, he'll have your head, and I won't blame him. And you must *always* remember that a bishop is 'Your Excellency.' Now, Jatham, how would you address a prince of the royal blood?"

Kelson smiled and nodded greeting as he rode on by. It was not so very long ago that *he* had been under the iron tutelage of the Royal Duke, his uncle, and he didn't envy the lads. A Haldane to the core, Nigel neither asked nor gave quarter, whether he was on the field of battle or training pages. But though the training was rigorous, and sometimes seemed over harsh, pages who came through Nigel's schooling made fine squires, and better knights. Kelson was glad to have Nigel on his side.

As Kelson approached, Brion broke off his conversation with Colin and Rogier and raised a hand in greeting. "What's happening up there, Son?"

"I think Lord Ewan about has things under control,

Sire," Kelson replied. "I believe he's waiting for your
signal now."

"That I am, young master!" Ewan's voice boomed,
as he thundered up in Kelson's wake.

Ewan removed his cap of Lincoln green and swept it
before him with a flourish. "Sire, the pack is ready.
And this time, my master-of-hounds assures me that
the scent is true." He replaced the cap on his thick red
hair and tugged at the brim in emphasis. "It'd better
be, or there'll be weeping and wailing in my household
tonight!"

Brion laughed and leaned back in the saddle,
slapped his thigh in mirth. "Ewan, it's only a hunt!
And I want no weeping and wailing on my account.
Let's go!" Still chuckling, he gathered his reins and
began to move forward.

Ewan stood in his stirrups and raised his arm, and
the hunting horns reverberated across the meadow in
reply. Far ahead, the hounds were already giving
tongue in clear, bell-like tones, and the riders began to
move out.

Down the slope, through the rough, across the open
fields in the clear once more, the hunt was off at the
gallop.

In the ensuing excitement of the chase, no one
would notice when one rider at the rear dropped back
and made his way to the edge of the forest. Indeed, he
would not even be missed.

In the stillness of the forest, Yousef the Moor stood
motionless at the edge of a small, dim clearing, his
slim brown hands light and sure on the reins he held,
the four horses quiet behind him.

All around, the leaves of an early autumn blazed
with color, seared to gold and red and brown by the
past week's frost, yet muted here by the play of
shadow and darker gloom among the tree trunks.

Here, beneath tall, dense trees, where sunlight rarely penetrated except in deepest winter, Yousef's black robes merged and blended with those shadows. Black eyes beneath black silk darted swiftly about the clearing, seeking, scanning, yet not really noting what they saw. For Yousef was not watching so much as he was listening. And waiting.

In the clearing itself, three others listened and waited. Two were Moors like Yousef, their dusky faces muffled under the hoods of black velvet juhhas, eyes dark, restless, ever-vigilant.

The taller of the two turned slightly to glance at Yousef across the clearing, then folded his arms across his chest and turned back to repeatedly scan the opposite side. The movement parted the black velvet slightly, and the silver of a richly embossed baldric of command glinted briefly beneath the cloak. At his feet, on a cushion of grey velvet, sat the Lady Charissa, Duchess of Tolan, Lady of the Silver Mists—the Shadowed One.

Head bowed, heavily cloaked and veiled in silver-grey, the lady sat motionless on the pillow, a slight, pale figure shrouded in richest velvet and fur, delicate hands encased in jewelled doeskin gloves and folded primly in her lap. Beneath the grey silken veil, pale blue eyes opened abruptly, searched serenely across the clearing, noted with satisfaction the black-robed Yousef standing guard over the horses.

Without turning her head, she was able to discern the vague, dark shapes of the other two Moors standing behind and to either side of her. She raised her head and spoke, a low musical voice.

"He's coming, Mustafa."

There had been no warning, no rustling betrayal of dried leaves underfoot to announce any approach to the clearing, but the Moors would not have thought of questioning their Lady's word. A brown hand in a flowing black sleeve reached down from the right to help her to her feet. And he who had been to her left moved to a strategic position midway between his mistress and the horses, there to stand vigilant guard with his hand on the hilt of his sword.

With a leisurely motion, Charissa brushed the leaves from her cloak, settled its silver-fox collar more comfortably around her neck. As the muffled crackling of underbrush finally announced the predicted caller, a faint breeze stirred the Lady's silken veil. One of Yousef's horses nickered softly, shuffled its feet, was quickly silenced by the tall Moor.

The rider entered the clearing and drew rein, and the Moors dropped their protective stance. The rider on the sorrel stallion was well-known to them.

The newcomer, too, wore a cape of grey. But it flashed a lining of deepest golden-yellow as he dropped his hood and swung the cloak to the horse's near side. Beneath, a jewelled tunic of grey and gold glittered coldly as he smoothed a windblown lock of chestnut hair with one grey-gloved hand.

Tall, slim, almost ascetic of face and feature, Lord Ian Howell viewed the world through a pair of eyes even deeper brown than his hair. A meticulously-tended beard and moustache framed a rather thin mouth, accentuated the high cheekbones, the slight cant of the round eyes—eyes which outshone the dark jewels that glittered coldly at his throat and ears.

Those eyes darted briefly over the Moor who reached up for his horse's bridle, then came casually to rest on the grey-shrouded form of the woman.

"You're late, Ian," the woman said. There was challenge in her voice, as well as statement of fact, and she met his gaze aloofly through the heavy veil. When Ian made no further move to dismount, she reached slowly to her veil, raised the front, let it cascade back over the pale, coiled hair. Her gaze sharpened, but she said nothing more.

Ian smiled lazily, dismounted with a flourish, crossed lightly to Charissa. He nodded curtly to Mustafa standing slightly behind her, then swirled his cloak around himself in a sweeping bow.

"Well?" Charissa acknowledged.

"No trouble at all, my dear," Ian replied silkily. "The king drank the wine, Colin suspects nothing, and the hunt is now on the false scent. They should be here within the hour."

"Excellent. And Prince Kelson?"

"Oh, he's safe enough," the young lord replied, tugging on the cuff of one grey glove with a studied nonchalance. "But it does seem like a great deal of bother to spare Kelson today simply so he can be killed later. It's not at all like you, Charissa—to show mercy to your enemies." Brown eyes met blue ones, slightly mocking.

"Mercy?" Charissa repeated, measuring the challenge.

She broke eye contact and began strolling casually across the clearing. Ian followed.

"Don't worry, Ian," she continued. "I have plans for our young prince. But I can't lure Morgan to his death without the proper bait, now, can I? And why do you think I've been so carefully planting those rumors for the past months?"

"I'd assumed it was an exercise in malice—not that you need the practice," Ian retorted.

They had reached the edge of the clearing, and Ian stopped in front of her, leaned lazily against a tree trunk, arms folded across his chest. "Of course, Morgan—he does present a special challenge, doesn't he, my pet? Alaric Anthony Morgan. Duke of Corwyn, Lord General of His Majesty's armies—and a half-breed Deryni who is accepted among humans, or *was* accepted. I sometimes think that bothers you most of all."

"Tread softly, Ian," she warned.

"Oh, I beg your Ladyship's pardon!" he demurred, raising a hand in feigned conciliation. "There *is* a slight matter of a murder, too, isn't there? Or was it an execution? I tend to forget."

"That is one thing you would do well *not* to forget, Ian," Charissa replied icily. "Morgan killed my father fifteen years ago, as you well know. We were both hardly more than children then—he but fourteen, I a few years younger—but I can never forgive what he did."

Her voice dropped an octave, hushed to a harsh whisper as she remembered. "He betrayed his Deryni blood and allied himself with Brion instead of us, defied the Camberian Council to side with a mortal. I watched them slay my father Marluk and strip him of his powers. And it was Morgan, with his Deryni cunning, who showed Brion the way. Never forget that, Ian."

Ian shrugged noncommittally. "Don't worry, my pet. I have my own reasons for wanting Morgan dead, remember? The Duchy of Corwyn borders my Eastmarch. I merely wonder how long you intend to let Morgan live."

"He has a few weeks at best," Charissa stated. "And I intend to see that he suffers in the time remaining. Today, Brion will die by Deryni magic, and Morgan will know that it was I. That, in itself, will hurt Morgan more than any other single thing I could do. And then I'll proceed to destroy the others he holds dear."

"And Prince Kelson?" Ian queried.

"Don't be greedy, Ian," she answered, smiling with vicious anticipation. "You shall have your precious Corwyn, all in due time. And I shall rule Gwynedd as my ancestors did. You'll see."

She turned on her heel and crossed the clearing, gestured imperiously to Mustafa, who pulled aside the dense foliage to disclose a break in the underbrush. Beyond and down a gentle slope stretched a wide green meadow, still damp and silent in the weak, late-morning sun.

After a pause, Ian joined Charissa and peered briefly through the hole, then put his arm lightly around her shoulders.

"I must confess, I rather like your little plan, my pet," he murmured. "The deviousness of your lovely mind never fails to intrigue me." He glanced down at her thoughtfully through long, dark lashes. "Are you certain no one besides Morgan will suspect, though? I mean, suppose Brion should detect you?"

Charissa smiled complacently and leaned back against his chest. "You worry too much, Ian," she cooed. "With his mind muddled by the *merasha* in the wine, Brion will feel nothing until my hand clutches at his heart—and then it will be far too late. As for Colin, *merasha* can't affect him unless he has Deryni blood somewhere in his background. And even if he has, he's safe as long as you keep him away from Brion when the time comes."

"Colin will be well out of range; you can depend on that," Ian replied. He idly plucked a stray wisp of grass from her cloak and twirled it between gloved fingers as he continued. "I've been cultivating this particular young nobleman for weeks. And if I do say so myself, he's quite flattered to have come to the favor of yours truly, the Earl of Eastmarch."

Charissa pulled away from him in irritation. "Ian, you begin to bore me. If you insist upon being so pompous, I suggest you return to the company of your royal playmates. The air there is much better suited to the self-praise and stuffy exchange of platitudes you seem to enjoy so much!"

Ian said nothing, but he raised one slim eyebrow as he crossed to his horse and began adjusting the off stirrup. When he had completed the task to his satisfaction, he flicked his glance across the saddle at Charissa.

"Shall I convey your compliments to His Majesty?" he asked, a wry grin pulling at the corners of his mouth.

Charissa smiled slowly, then crossed toward him. Ian came around to the near side, and Charissa took the horse's reins, nodding dismissal to the Moor who had been attending.

"Well?" Ian murmured, as the Moor bowed and backed off.

"I think you need not greet Brion for me this time," she murmured coyly. She ran a gloved hand down the sorrel's neck, adjusted a wayward tassel on the intricate bridle. "You'd best go now. The hunt will be approaching soon."

"I hear and obey, My Lady," Ian said cheerfully, swinging up into the saddle.

He gathered up his reins and looked down at her, then held out his left hand. Wordlessly, Charissa put her gloved hand in his, and he bent to touch his lips to the soft leather.

"Good hunting, My Lady!" he said.

He squeezed her hand lightly and released it, then moved his horse into the underbrush, crashing back the way he had come.

The Shadowed One watched with narrowed eyes until he had disappeared from view, then returned to her silent meadow vigil.

Rejoining the hunt, Ian gradually began working his way toward the royal party. They were cantering easily through lightly wooded terrain now, and he could see the meadow not far ahead. With a perfunctory glance

at his stirrup, he urged his mount closer to Colin and
raised a gloved hand in greeting.

"Lord Ian," Colin acknowledged, as Ian drew
alongside. "Good riding at the rear of the pack?"

Ian flashed a disarming smile at the youth. "Unbe-
lievable, my friend."

He shifted his weight slightly, and there was the resounding pop of leather parting as the right stirrup
gave way.

"Damn!" he swore explosively, as he caught his balance. "That just about finishes the hunt for me!"

He pulled up slowly to let the hunt ride on by, bent
to retrieve the stirrup still hooked on the toe of his
boot, smiled approval as Colin reined in and returned
to join him. When all the riders had passed, he dismounted to inspect the saddle, and Colin watched with
concern.

"I told that pig of a groom to replace this leather
three days ago," Ian fretted, fingering the broken strap.
"I don't suppose you have a spare, Colin?"

"I might," Colin said, as he dismounted.

As Colin rummaged through his saddlebags, Ian
gazed furtively across the meadow. The timing had
been perfect. Even now, the pack was pulling up in the
center of the meadow, the scent lost again.

Any second now . . .

The whippers-in were trying valiantly to bring the
hounds under control, and Brion slapped his riding
crop against his boot in mild vexation.

"Ewan, your pups have done it again," he said,
peering ahead. "Kelson, ride up ahead and try to see
what's happened, will you? They can't have lost the
scent in the middle of an open field. Ewan, you stay."

As Kelson rode off, Ewan stood in his stirrups to get
a better look, then sat back muttering. In the midst of
all the milling hounds and riders, it was impossible to

distinguish anything at this distance, and the fiery old
warrior was obviously on the verge of a tirade.

"The blasted beasties've gone mad!" he growled.
"Just wait till I get my hands on——"

"Now, Ewan, don't get overwrought," Brion interjected smoothly. "We obviously just aren't destined to
——oh!"

Brion suddenly broke off in mid-sentence and froze,
his grey eyes going wide with fear. "Oh, my God!" he
whispered, his eyes closing as he doubled up with pain.
Riding crop and reins dropped from numb fingers as
he clutched at his chest and slumped forward in the
saddle, stifling a moan.

"Sire!" Ewan cried.

As Brion toppled and slid from the saddle, Ewan
and Rogier grabbed simultaneously for his arms and
somehow managed to ease him to the ground between
them. Others nearby dismounted and rushed to his aid.
And Prince Nigel appeared from somewhere to wordlessly cradle his stricken brother's head in his lap.

As Rogier and Ewan knelt anxiously on his left,
Brion was wracked by yet another wave of blinding
pain, and he called out weakly, "Kelson!"

Far ahead with the hounds, Kelson saw rather than
heard the commotion back at the center of the hunt
and returned at the gallop, certain only that something
was seriously wrong. But when he reached the group
gathered noisily around the king, saw his father
sprawled on the ground in agony, he jerked his horse
to a sliding halt on the slick grass, flung himself from
the saddle to push his way through the onlookers.

Brion's breathing was labored, his teeth clenched
tightly against the searing pain which came now at
every heartbeat. His eyes darted back and forth feverishly, trying to locate his son. And he was concertedly
ignoring all efforts of Ewan, or Rogier, or the Bishop
Arilan to comfort him.

All he could see was Kelson as the boy dropped to his knees at his father's right. And he gasped and clutched for Kelson's hand as another wave of pain engulfed him.

"So soon!" he managed to whisper, his hand almost crushing Kelson's in the intensity of its grip. "Kelson, remember what you promised. Remem . . ."

His hand went limp in Kelson's and the eyes half closed. The pain-wracked body relaxed.

As Nigel and Ewan searched frantically for a pulse, some sign of life, Kelson watched in stunned disbelief. But no reassuring sign came. And with a muffled sob, Kelson collapsed to rest his forehead against his sire's hand.

Beside him, Bishop Arilan crossed himself and began reciting the Office for the Dead, his voice low and steady in the terrible stillness. All around, Brion's lords and vassals dropped to their knees, one by one, to echo the bishop.

"Eternal rest grant unto him, O Lord."

"And let perpetual light shine upon him."

"Kyrie eleison."

"Christe eleison . . ."

Kelson let the familiar phrases wash over him, let the cadence lull the sickening, sinking emptiness in the pit of his stomach to a more bearable numbness, willed the tight constriction of his throat to relax. After a long moment, he was able to raise his head and look dazedly around him.

Nigel seemed calm, almost serene, as he knelt with Brion's lifeless head in his lap. Again and again, his long fingers smoothed the straight black hair across the still brow—gently, almost tenderly—his thoughts in some place that only Nigel knew.

And Rogier—Rogier stared unseeing, his eyes following Nigel's fingers, his lips moving automatically in the litany, but not knowing what he saw or said.

But it was Ewan that the young prince would remember later, long after other details of the day had faded mercifully from his mind. From somewhere, Ewan had retrieved Brion's red leather hunt cap, now stained and trampled in the confusion and horror of the past minutes.

By some miracle, the snowy plume on the cap had emerged unscathed, its whiteness unsullied, unbroken. And as Ewan clutched the cap to his breast, the feathered plume trembled almost hypnotically before Kelson's eyes.

Ewan suddenly became aware of Kelson's fascinated stare, and he looked down at the cap, at the waving plume, as though he'd never seen them before. There was a moment of hesitation. And then he slowly took the plume in his huge right hand, bent it until it snapped.

Kelson started.

"The King is dead—Sire," Ewan murmured dully, his face ashen beneath the shaggy red beard and hair.

He opened his hand slowly and watched the broken end of the plume drift gently to rest on Brion's shoulder.

"I know," Kelson replied.

"What is—" Ewan's voice broke with emotion, and he began again. "Is there any—"

He could not go on, and his shoulders shook convulsively as he buried his face in Brion's cap.

Nigel looked up from the face of his dead brother and touched the old warrior's shoulder. "It's all right, Ewan," he said softly. He dropped his hand, glanced at Brion once more, then met the eyes of his brother's son.

"You are King now, Kelson," he said gently. "What is your command?"

Kelson looked down again at the dead king, then disentangled his hand and folded his father's hands on his chest.

"First of all," he said steadily, "send for General Morgan."

CHAPTER TWO

Princes met and talked against me.
Psalms 119:23

NEARLY TWO WEEKS LATER, Morgan and a single blue-cloaked military aide clattered through the north gates of Rhemuth, Brion's capital city. Though it was not yet mid-morning, the horses were lathered and nearly spent, and their ragged breathing shot dense, snowy plumes of condensation into the cold morning air.

It was market day in Rhemuth, and the streets were even more congested than usual. The coronation tomorrow had brought hundreds of additional visitors to the city, travellers from all the Eleven Kingdoms. They were rendering the narrow, cobbled streets almost impassable.

Produce carts and richly curtained sedan chairs, merchants with their pack trains, peddlers hawking over-priced trinkets, bored-looking noblemen with their lavish retinues—all merged and blended in a kaleidoscopic array of color, scent, and sound, vied with the brilliantly decorated buildings and arches of the city itself.

Rhemuth the Beautiful, they called the city. It was easy to see why.

As Morgan guided his weary mount slowly among the milling pedestrains and conveyances, following Lord Derry toward the main palace gate, he glanced wistfully down at his own somber garb, so conspicuous amidst all this garish splendor: dusty black leather covering most of his mail, the heavy black wool and sable cloak enveloping him from helm to knee.

Strange, how quickly the atmosphere of a city could change. A few short weeks ago, he was sure almost all of the gaily clad citizens around him had been similarly dressed, genuinely mourning the loss of their monarch. Now all wore the colors of festival, celebration.

Was it a shorter memory, or the blessed blurring of the senses as the days passed, or simply the excitement of a coronation that let the common people put aside their grief and resume the business of living? Perhaps for these, who had never known Brion, it was simply a matter of changing mental gears, of putting another name after the title "King."

Another name . . . another King . . . a kingdom without Brion . . .

Memories . . . nine long days . . . dusk . . . four travel-worn riders drawing rein in the Cardosa camp . . . the ashen faces of Lord Ralson, Colin, the two guards, as they gasped out the horrible news . . . the anguished futility of trying to reach across the miles and touch a mind which could no longer respond, even if it had been in range . . . the numbness that set in as they began covering the frantic miles to Rhemuth . . . spent horses, changed along the way for new . . . the nightmare of ambush, massacre, from which only he and Derry emerged alive . . . more dulling miles. . . .

And now, the sickening realization that it had all been real, that an era had passed, that he and Brion would never again ride the hills of Gwynedd. . . .

The totality of his grief washed over Morgan like a physical thing, threatening to overwhelm him as it had not in nine long days of riding.

Gasping, he clung to the pommel of his saddle for support.

No!

He must not allow his own emotions to interfere with the work ahead! There was power to be secured, a king to be crowned, a battle to be won.

He forced himself to relax and take a deep, controlled breath, willed the anguish to subside. Later, there would be time enough for private grief—indeed, perhaps no need, if he should fail in his task and join Brion in death. But enough of such thoughts. Right now, grief was a luxury he could ill afford.

The moment past, he was suddenly acutely self-conscious, and he glanced ahead to see whether Derry had noticed his internal struggle.

But Derry hadn't, or at least pretended not to. The young Marcher lord was too busy staying in the saddle and avoiding pedestrians to pay much attention to anything else. And Morgan knew the young man's injuries must be giving him more than a little discomfort, though Derry would never admit it.

Morgan worked his way alongside his companion and was about to speak when the other's horse suddenly stumbled. Morgan grabbed for the reins, and miraculously the animal did not go down, but its rider lurched heavily against the saddle horn and only barely managed to keep his seat.

"Derry, are you all right?" Morgan queried anxiously, shifting his grip from reins to the younger man's shoulder.

They had stopped in the middle of the street, and

Derry slowly sat up, a pained expression etched across what little of his face was visible beneath the crested helmet. Carefully cradling a bandaged left wrist in his right hand, he closed his eyes and took a deep breath, then opened them and nodded weakly.

"I'll be all right, M'lord," he whispered. He eased the injured arm back into a black silk sling and steadied himself with his good hand. "I just banged it against the saddle."

Morgan was clearly skeptical. He started to reach across to check the injured wrist for himself when his action was interrupted by a strident bellowing almost in his ear.

"Make way for the Supreme of Howicce! Way for His Loftiness!" And then, in a lower tone, "Can't you find some other place to hold hands, soldier?"

At the same instant, there was a sharp smack of leather against Morgan's horse's flank. The animal jumped sideways with more energy than Morgan had dreamed possible, crowding Derry's mount into half a dozen shrieking pedestrians.

Derry's eyes flashed angrily as Morgan turned to look, and he was on the verge of a smoking retort when the general kicked him to silence. Morgan arranged his features in what he hoped was a suitably abject expression and signalled Derry to do the same.

For the bellower had been a seven-foot giant of a man, mailed in bronze and garbed in the garish greens and violets of the United Kingdoms of Howicce and Llannedd. And while this alone would have been no deterrent under normal circumstances, the man *was* accompanied by six more just like him. And Derry was wounded. It did alter the odds slightly. Besides, Morgan had no overwhelming desire to get himself arrested and jailed for brawling just now. Too much was at stake.

Morgan watched with unconcealed interest as the

giants rode past. He took careful note of the shaggy black beards and hair; the winged bronze helmets that marked the wearers as Connaiti mercenaries; the barbarically patterned violet and green livery, signed with the badge of Howicce; the longswords at belts and writhing blacksnake whips in hands.

There was no hint as to who or what the Supreme of Howicce might be, though Morgan had his suspicions. The giants were escorting an ornately carved horse-litter, carried by four matched greys. And the tapestried curtains shrouding the litter were embroidered in a headache-inducing design of green, violet, orange, and brilliant rose. Six more of the swarthy giants brought up the rear. And all things considered, Morgan doubted they would approve of him approaching for a closer look.

No matter. Morgan had already made up his mind about anyone with the audacity to style himself "His Loftiness." He would not forget the Supreme of Howicce, or his retainers.

Evidently Derry's thinking had been along similar lines, for as the cortege passed, he leaned toward Morgan with a wicked grin. "By all the devils in hell, what is a Supreme of Howicce?"

"I'm not certain," Morgan replied in a penetrating stage whisper. "But I don't think it's as high as a Quintessence or a Penultimate. Probably some minor ambassador with delusions of his own importance."

Morgan had intended the remark to be overheard, and there was a ripple of nervous laughter around them. The last giant glared in their direction, but Morgan put on his look of innocence and bowed in the saddle. The giant rode on.

"Well, whoever he is," Derry remarked as they moved out again, "he certainly has ill-mannered retainers. Someone should teach them a lesson."

This time it was Morgan's turn to grin wickedly. "I'm working on that," he said.

He pointed down the street where the procession was just about to disappear around the corner. The lead giant with the overactive whip was lashing out with even greater vengeance now that the troop was approaching the palace and there were more important people to be impressed

And then, a strange thing happened. The long black whip the giant was wielding with such obvious relish suddenly seemed to develop a mind of its own. On return from a particularly negligent flick at a scurrying street urchin, it abruptly and inexplicably wrapped itself around the forelegs of the giant's mount.

Before anyone was aware of what had happened, horse and giant went down on the cobblestone street in a thrashing, kicking confusion of shouts and metallic crashes.

As the giant picked himself up, livid with rage and gushing a highly articulate stream of profanity, gales of laughter swept through the spectators. And the giant finally had to cut the thongs of his whip to free his frightened mount.

Morgan had seen enough. Sporting a smugly self-satisfied smile, he beckoned Derry to follow him down a less crowded side alley.

Derry cast a sidelong glance at his commander as they emerged at the other end. "How satisfying for us that the giant managed to get tangled in his own whip, M'lord," Derry commented. There was admiration in his voice. "Rather clumsy of him, wasn't it?"

Morgan raised one eyebrow. "Are you implying that *I* had something to do with his unfortunate accident? Really, Derry. Anyway, I understand giants sometimes have trouble coordinating. I believe it comes of having too small a brain." He added, almost to himself, "Be-

sides, I was never fond of people who flicked other
people with whips."

The main courtyard of the royal palace was more
crowded than Morgan could ever remember having
seen it, even as a boy. It was all he and Derry could
do to work their way through the gates. Heaven knew
what they were going to do with all these people.

Evidently many of the visiting dignitaries for the
coronation tomorrow were being housed in the palace
proper. For the area in front of the main staircase was
glutted with horse-litters, sedan chairs, carriages, and
baggage animals. Everywhere, lords and their ladies
and hordes of servants milled about in seeming confusion. The din and the stench were formidable.

Morgan was amazed that so many of the Eleven
Kingdoms' nobility had deigned to come to the affair.
Not that the coronation of the next Haldane King was
not a noteworthy event—not at all. But that so many
usually dissident lords should be willingly and peacefully gathered in one place was remarkable indeed. He
would be quite surprised if at least one major alterca-
tion didn't develop before the festivities were over.

Already, groups of squires from two of the warring
Forcinn Buffer States were disputing whose master
should have precedence at table tonight. What made it
ludicrous was that they would all take second place to
another lord. For all five of the Buffer States were
under the protection and economic control of the Hort
of Orsal. And the Orsal's banner already flew from
one of the flagstaffs protruding from the main battle-
ment. The Hortic emissary would precede all Forcinn
contenders.

The Orsal himself, who controlled trade in most of
the Southern Sea, had probably not bothered to come.
His relations with R'kassi to the south had not been
too amicable of late. And the old sea lion had proba-

bly deemed it wiser to stay at home and guard his port monopoly. The old Orsal was like that.

But the younger Orsal was there. Over to the right, his sea-green banners waved from four or five standards. A number of servants in the Orsal's livery were busily unloading his extensive baggage train.

Morgan made a mental note to look up the younger Orsal after the coronation tomorrow, if he was still alive, of course. He, too, had been having his troubles with the Forcinn States. Perhaps a mutual agreement could be reached to deal with the problem. At least the Orsal should know how he felt. Corwyn and the Hortic State had always enjoyed excellent relations.

Morgan nodded greeting as the lord high chancellor of Torenth passed, but his mind was no longer on foreign emissaries. It would be the Lords of the Regency Council he would have to deal with before the day was out. He must be on the lookout for local arrivals.

Morgan caught the flash of Lord Ewan's bright orange velvet, topped by the familiar red hair, just entering the main doors at the top of the stairs. The old Earl had Lord Bran Coris and the Earl of Eastmarch in tow. And off to the left, heading toward the royal stables, a page was leading two horses with the Mc-Lain tartan bright on their saddles.

Now, *there* was strong backing he could count on. Lord Jared, his adopted uncle, ruled nearly a fifth of Gwynedd, if you counted his elder son's Earldom of Kierney adjoining his own Cassan. And the Kierney Earl, Kevin, was a long-time friend of Morgan's, soon to be a brother-in-law. That was not even mentioning the third McLain, Duncan, on whom so much would depend later today.

Motioning Derry to follow, Morgan eased his way across the crowded courtyard to the left of the stairway. Derry pulled up to his left, and the two dismounted. After running his hands briefly along his horse's legs, Morgan tossed the reins to Derry and pulled off his helmet, absently ruffling through his matted blond hair as he searched for a familiar face.

"Ah, Richard FitzWilliam!" he called, raising a gloved hand in greeting.

A tall, dark-haired young squire in the royal crimson livery turned at the sound of his name and smiled as he identified the caller. Then the smile faded abruptly to concern as he made his way nervously to Morgan's side.

"Lord Alaric," he murmured, sketching a hurried bow, his eyes dark with apprehension. "Ah, ye shouldn't be here, Your Grace. 'Tis said the Council's out to get ye, body and soul, and that's the literal truth!"

His eyes darted nervously from Morgan to Derry and back again. Derry froze in the act of hooking his helmet over the pommel of his saddle, then resumed fiddling with his gear at a sharp glance from Morgan. Morgan returned his attention to Richard.

"The Council's planning to act against me, Richard?" he asked, feigning innocence. "Whatever for?"

Richard squirmed uncomfortably and tried to avoid Morgan's eyes. He had trained with the young general and admired him tremendously, in spite of what was being said about him, but he wasn't eager to be the one to tell him.

"I—I'm not certain, Your Grace," he stammered. "They—well, ye've heard some o' the rumors, haven't ye?" He eyed Morgan fearfully, as though hoping the general hadn't heard, but Morgan raised a knowing eyebrow.

"Yes, I've heard the rumors, Richard," he sighed. "You don't believe them, do you?"

Richard shook his head timidly.

Morgan slapped his horse's neck in exasperation, and the animal jumped. "Damnation take the lot of them!" Morgan said. "That's what I was afraid of! Derry, do you remember what I told you about the Regency Council?"

Derry grinned and nodded.

"Good," Morgan replied. "Then how would you like to go placate the Lords of the Council while I get to work?"

"Don't you mean *delay*, sir?"

Morgan laughed and clapped him on the shoulder. "Derry, lad, I like your kind of thinking! Remind me to think of a suitable reward."

"Yes, sir."

Morgan turned to Richard and handed him his helmet and the two sets of reins. "Richard, will you see to our horses and gear?"

"Aye, M'lord," the squire replied, eyeing the two smiling men with a look of wonder. "But do be careful, sir—both of ye."

Morgan nodded gravely and patted Richard on the shoulder, then began to make his way resolutely toward the stairs, Derry at his heels.

The staircase and entryway were still crowded with richly garbed lords and ladies, and Morgan was suddenly aware again how he must stand out among them in his dusty black leathers. But there was more to it than that, he realized. As he made his way up the staircase, he noticed that conversation stopped as he passed, especially among the ladies. And when he returned their glances with his usual half-smile and bow, the ladies shrank away from him as though afraid, and the men moved their hands a little closer to their weapons.

Abruptly, he recognized the problem. In spite of his long absence, he was being recognized and connected with the wild Deryni rumors. Someone had certainly gone to a lot of trouble to taint his name. These people

actually believed him to be the evil Deryni sorcerer of
the legends!

Very well. Let them stare. He would play along. If
they wished to see the suave, self-assured, vaguely
menacing Deryni Lord in action, he would oblige!

With a slight swagger to his movements, he paused
on the threshold to slap the dust from his clothes, deliberately positioning himself so that his sword and
mail glittered balefully and his hair glowed like burnished gold in the sunlight. His audience was suitably
impressed.

When he was satisfied that the act had achieved its
desired effect, he allowed his gaze to sweep across his
audience one more time, slowly. Then he turned on his
heel like an insolent boy and swept into the hall. At his
back, Derry glided along like a watchful blue shadow,
his face enigmatic beneath the thick mane of curly
brown hair.

The hall was immense. It had needed to be. For Brion
had been a very great King, with many vassals, and he
kept a court that rewarded faithful service well.

The high-ceilinged hall with its oaken support beams
and dozens of silk-embroidered battle flags was almost
symbolic of the new unity which had come to the
Eleven Kingdoms in the twenty-five years of Brion's
reign. Banners of Carthmoor and Cassan, of Kierney
and the Kheldish Riding, the Free Port of Concaradine, the Meara Protectorate, Howicce, Llannedd, the
Connait, the Hort of Orsal, episcopal banners of most
of the Lords Spiritual in the Eleven Kingdoms—all
hung alike from the high oak beams, their silken and
gold insignias and devices gleaming in the half-light that
poured from the clerestory and from the three immense fireplaces that heated the room.

On the walls, rich tapestries vied with armorial banners for color and splendor. And above the main fire-

place, dominating the hall, the Golden Lion of Gwynedd glittered darkly from its background of deep crimson velvet.

Gules, a lion rampant guardant or, the heralds would blazon the Haldane arms on the hanging above the fireplace. But mere heraldic jargon could not begin to describe the rich embroidery, the priceless artistry and jewel-work which had gone into its creation.

The panel had been commissioned more than fifty years before by Brion's grandfather King Malcolm. Times were harder then, and it had taken nearly three years for the nimble-fingered weavers of the Kheldish Riding to complete the basic design alone. Another five years passed while the gold and jewel artisans of Concaradine plied their arts. And Brion's father, Donal, had finally hung the masterpiece in the great hall.

Morgan remembered the reaction of a small blond boy on seeing the Lion for the first time. For that first impression was indelibly etched on his memory with his first glimpse of Brion, the shining King who had stood before the Lion of Gwynedd and welcomed a shy young page to the royal court.

Morgan savored the memory and scanned the hanging once more, slowly, as he always felt compelled to do after a long absence. Only then did he permit his gaze to slip casually up and to the left, where hung another banner.

Worked in green, on black silk, the Corwyn Gryphon actually defied many of the conventional rules of heraldry, at least where color was concerned. But perhaps that was part of the charm of the Deryni heritage, into whatever disrepute that bloodline had fallen in past decades.

The emerald Gryphon, its wings dripping gold and jewels, rearing up its head and claws in the rampant pose—*segreant,* when applied to gryphons—gleamed darkly, mysteriously, with an almost sinister aura from its background of shining black. Around the edge, a golden bordure—the double tressure flory counter-flory of the old Morgan arms—gave homage to his paternal inheritance.

Morgan tended to forget about his Morgan lands. It was just as well, perhaps. For the two-dozen-or-so estates and manors scattered about the kingdom were his sister Bronwyn's dowry for the most part, capably managed by that shining lady and soon to be joined to the Kierney lands when she married Kevin McLain next spring. Then only the golden tressure on the sable shield would remain of Morgan's paternal birthright—that and the name.

It was the calling of that name that summoned Morgan from his reverie. From a dozen feet away, Lord Rogier was pushing his way through the thronged nobles, his thin face pinched with worry, the slender brown moustache bristling with impatience.

"Morgan, we expected you days ago! What happened?" He glanced nervously at Derry, obviously not recognizing him, but disturbed by his presence nonetheless. "Where are Lord Ralson and Colin?"

Morgan ignored Rogier's question and began moving purposefully down the hall. For he had caught a glimpse of Ewan approaching with Bran Coris and Ian Howell. If he waited until they arrived, he would have to tell the news only once. As it was, it would be painful enough. He and Ralson had been close.

As he reached the three, Kevin McLain appeared at Morgan's left elbow to clap him on the shoulder in silent greeting. Rogier nearly ran them all down in his exasperation.

"But, Morgan!" Rogier was sputtering, "you didn't answer my question. Has something happened to them?"

Morgan bowed greeting to the assembled group.

"I'm afraid so, Rogier. Ralson, Colin, the two guards, three of my best officers—they're all dead."

"Dead!" Ewan gasped.

"Oh, my God!" Kevin whispered. "Alaric, what happened?"

Morgan clasped his hands behind his back and steeled himself for the ordeal. "I was at Cardosa when the news came. I took the escort, Derry, and three of my own men, and we headed back for Rhemuth immediately. Two days out of Cardosa, we were ambushed in a pass—I think it was near Valoret. Ralson and our escort were killed outright. Colin died of his wounds the next day. Derry may lose the use of his left hand, but at least he escaped with his life."

Ian frowned and stroked his beard with feigned concern. "Why, that's ghastly, Morgan. Absolutely ghastly. Ah, how many did you say attacked you?"

"I didn't say," Morgan replied neutrally. He eyed Ian suspiciously and tried to discern a motive for the question. "But I believe there were ten or twelve of them, wouldn't you agree, Derry?"

"We killed eight, M'lord," Derry stated promptly. "But several more got away in the confusion."

"Humph!" Ewan snorted. "Nine Gwynedd men killed only eight of the ruffians? I'd've thought ye could do better than *that,* man!"

"So would I," Ian added, folding his arms casually across a brocaded doublet of golden yellow silk. "I don't pretend to be an expert in these matters like Lord Ewan, but it seems to me that you *did* make a rather poor showing. Of course, none of us was there . . ." He shrugged and let his voice trail off meaningfully.

"That's right," Bran Coris said, his eyes narrowing suspiciously. "None of us was there. How can we be sure it happened the way you say it did? Why didn't you use your precious Deryni powers to save them, Morgan? Or didn't you *want* to save them?"

Morgan stiffened as he whirled to glare at Bran. If the idiot wasn't careful, he was going to start something Morgan would have to finish. And Morgan didn't dare risk a bloody open battle here and now.

Damn! This was the second time today he'd had to back down from a good fight!

"I did not hear that remark," he said pointedly. "I obeyed the command of my King and I came." He turned to the left. "Kevin, do you know where Kelson is now?"

"I'll tell him you're here," Kevin replied, slipping out of Bran's reach before the angry lord could stop him. His bright plaid swung jauntily from his shoulder as he hurried across the room.

Bran dropped his hand to his sword hilt and glared at Morgan. "Smoothly maneuvered, Morgan. But seven deaths—I think that's too high a price to pay for your presence here!"

He started to draw, but Ewan seized his wrist and forced him to return the blade to its sheath.

"Stop it, Bran!" Ewan growled. "And Alaric, I wish ye hadn't come. Frankly, the Queen didn't even want Kelson to send for ye. In any event, I don't think ye should see the lad until ye've talked with Her Majesty."

"I'm well aware of the Queen's feelings about me, Ewan," Morgan replied softly. "Fortunately for my conscience, I don't care *what* she thinks. I made a promise to the boy's father, and I intend to keep it." He glanced casually around him. "And I'm not at all certain Brion would approve of my being the agenda for today's Council meeting. That *is* why you're all gathered here, isn't it, gentlemen?"

The Lords of the Council exchanged furtive glances and tried to decide which one had told Morgan about their plans. Across the room, Morgan saw Prince Nigel exchange a few words with the exiting Kevin and head toward Morgan and his companions.

"You must understand, Morgan," Rogier was saying. "None of us has anything against you personally. But the Queen—well, she hasn't taken Brion's death well at all."

"Neither have I, Rogier," Morgan replied evenly, his grey eyes flashing.

Nigel stepped deftly between Rogier and Ewan and took Morgan's arm. "Alaric, I'm delighted to see you. And Lord Derry, I believe."

Derry bowed acknowledgement, obviously pleased to have been recognized by the royal Duke, and grateful for the interruption of hostilities. Around him, the others also bowed.

"I have a favor to ask, though," Nigel continued, playing the part of perfect host to the hilt. "Would you mind sitting in at Alaric's place in Council, Derry? He has some important matters to take care of for me."

"It would be my pleasure, Your Highness."

"Excellent," Nigel said, beginning to edge himself and Morgan in the direction Kevin had disappeared. "You'll excuse us, won't you, gentlemen?"

As Nigel and Morgan moved off and disappeared in the direction of the royal apartments, Ian mentally congratulated Nigel on the smoothness of the rescue. Not that it would matter in the end. Even if Morgan did talk to Kelson, and there was no way he could have stopped it at this point, there would still be a few unexpected surprises for the Deryni lord.

Meanwhile, there was the matter of this Lord Derry of Morgan's. And Bran Coris—that had been a surprise. He had known that Morgan's strength in Council would be lessened by at least one vote. Ralson's timely end had assured that. But now it appeared that Bran Coris had defected, too. It would be interesting to find out what had prompted the change. Bran had always been carefully neutral in the past.

As he and Nigel left the great hall, Morgan was amazed at the change which had come over Brion's younger brother in the past two months. For though the royal Duke was only in his mid-thirties, but a few years older than Morgan, he had the look of a man of twice the years.

It was not really a physical manifestation. There was no grey streaking the jet-black hair. Nigel did not stoop, or tremble with the palsy of the aged. It was in the eyes, Morgan decided as they strode down a long marble corridor. Nigel had always been the quieter, more studious of the two brothers, but this was something new—a haunted (or was it *hunted?*) look that Morgan had never seen there before. Nigel, too, had not taken Brion's death well.

As soon as they were out of sight and earshot of the door attendants, Nigel dropped his feigned smile and glanced at Morgan worriedly.

"We've got to hurry," he murmured, his long strides echoing on the expanse of marble tile. "Jehana's getting ready to convene the Council and prefer charges against you. And I can't remember when I've seen the Council Lords in a nastier mood. It's almost as though they believe the rumors about Brion's death."

"Oh, they believe them, all right," Morgan said. "They really think I somehow killed Brion with Deryni magic all the way from Cardosa. Even a full Deryni couldn't do that." He snorted. "And then there are the innocents who believe he died of a—'heart attack.' "

They came to a cross corridor and Nigel chose the one to the right, heading toward the palace gardens. "Well, both theories are being discussed. That's inevitable, I suppose. But Kelson has another theory—and

I tend to agree with him—that Charissa had something to do with it."

"He's probably right, too," Morgan replied, not missing a stride. "About the Council, though—do you think you can handle them?"

Nigel frowned. "Frankly, no. At least, not for long."

They passed a guard post and Nigel took the crisp salute distractedly. "You see," the Duke continued, "it would be different if Kelson were already King, of legal age. If that were the case, he could simply forbid the Council to consider any trumped-up charges against you without concrete proof. But he's not, and he can't. As long as he's still a minor, no matter how close, the Regency Council has certain viceregal powers he can't countermand. They decide what's a fit topic for discussion, and they can vote by a simple majority to condemn you. Whether or not they succeed in the end will depend largely on Kelson's personal ability to manipulate the voting."

"Can he?" Morgan asked, as the two clattered down a half-flight of stairs and into the garden.

"I don't know, Alaric," Nigel replied. "He's good—damned good—but I just don't know. Besides, you saw the key council lords. With Ralson dead and Bran Coris practically making open accusations—well, it doesn't look good."

"I could have told you that at Cardosa."

They came to a halt under a trellised summerhouse at the edge of a boxwood maze. Morgan glanced around surreptitiously for some sign of Kelson and mentally approved of the choice of meeting place.

"These latest attempts of Jehana to have me discredited, Nigel—what charges is she likely to level against me?"

Nigel put one booted foot up on a carved stone bench and looked soberly across at Morgan, one forearm resting on his upraised knee. "Treason and heresy," he said quietly. "And it's not likely. It's certain!"

"Certain!" Morgan exploded. "Damn, Nigel, it's certain to be Kelson's death if she doesn't let me help him! Doesn't she realize that?"

Nigel shrugged hopelessly. "Who can say for sure what Jehana realizes or doesn't realize? I do know that our dear Lord Rogier is going to make the formal treason charge. And there's no chance in the world that Archbishop Corrigan will refuse to support the heresy claim. Jehana's even bringing in that Archbishop from Valoret—what's his name, who keeps the Deryni persecutions going in the north?"

"Loris!" Morgan hissed, turning away in disgust.

Seething inside, he gazed out over the low railing of the summerhouse to the boxwood maze beyond. From here, the complexity of the maze was not evident, but Morgan suddenly realized it was almost symbolic of the dilemma he now faced: convoluted, enigmatic, with new and unforeseen difficulties around every turn. Except that there was a way out of the boxwood maze.

He turned back to Nigel, in complete control again. "Nigel, I'm convinced that in a fair fight, with no treachery involved, Kelson could defeat Charissa once and for all—but only if he has Brion's power. I've got to have time for that, though. Does Jehana really know what's at stake, what will happen to Kelson if he has to face Charissa without that power? You were next in line. You know what I'm talking about."

"If she knows, she won't admit it," Nigel sighed. "If you think it would help, though, I could try to talk to her again. I might gain us some time, at least."

"All right," Morgan nodded. "And if you can't reason with her, try a little coercion."

"I'll do what I can," Nigel nodded gloomily. "She'd better start acting like a grown woman with some sense, though. I'll see you later."

"I hope so," Morgan agreed, almost to himself, as the Duke disappeared around a bend in the path.

Morgan smiled wryly as he perched on the summer-house rail to wait for Kelson. Personally, he had little faith in *anyone's* ability to placate or coerce Brion's wayward Queen, least of all Nigel, who had always been an open supporter of the out-of-favor general.

On the other hand, Nigel was the Queen's brother-in-law, and that might count for something. Who knew? After all, in a world where gods rose from the dead and quasi-mortals summoned the very forces of Good and Evil at will, he supposed anything was at least theoretically possible.

He had never really understood Jehana's opposition, though. It was based, he knew, on that ancient and in-grained suspicion of Deryni magic. And this had been reinforced through the generations by the Church Militant's condemnation of all occult arts. But surely there was more to it than that.

Certainly, there had been cause for suspicion of things Deryni at one time. Morgan was first to admit it. But it had been almost three hundred years since the beginning of the Deryni Interregnum. And while the Eleven Kingdoms *had* been under heavy Deryni dictatorship for nearly three generations, those days had been past now for nearly two centuries.

Even at the height of Deryni rule, there had been only a handful of the Fellowship involved in the darker atrocities. And in the balance were the thousands of Deryni who had cherished their human ties—those same Deryni who, led by Camber of Culdi, eventually discovered that under carefully specified conditions, in certain select individuals, the full scope of Deryni power *could be acquired by humans!*

There was another coup, led by Camber, and the Deryni Interregnum was ended as quickly as it had started. The tyrant leaders were executed by their own fellows, and rule was restored to the descendants of the old human lords.

But an irate populace and a militant Church soon forgot that deliverance as well as bondage had come from the Deryni Lords. And they soon ceased to make a distinction among Deryni.

Within fifteen years of the Restoration, not even the space of a generation, the Fellowship found itself victim of one of the bloodiest persecutions ever witnessed by civilized man. The numbers of the Deryni were reduced by two-thirds in a lightning purge. And those who survived either went into hiding and denounced their heritage, or lived a fearful and uneasy life under the protection of the few human Lords who remembered how it had really been.

Over the years, the memory eased. The persecution burned itself out in all but the most hardened fanatics. A few selected Deryni families rose once again to guarded prominence. But magic, if it was used at all, was exercised with extreme care and discretion. Most Deryni, of whatever class, simply refused to use their powers, for whatever cause. Discovery without protection could mean death.

Among humans, though, the original magic of the Restoration carried on. And it became gradually accepted, if not openly acknowledged, that the rulers of Gwynedd and certain other of the Eleven Kingdoms possessed special powers, somehow mysteriously related to their divine right of rule. The Deryni origin of these powers was not spoken of, if indeed it was remembered. But it was those powers, passed by ritual from father to son for nearly two hundred years, which had enabled Brion to defeat the Marluk fifteen years ago.

Jehana's feud with Morgan had really begun even before that historic battle, however. But not at the very beginning.

When Brion first brought the auburn-haired princess home to be his Queen, Morgan had rejoiced with all of Gwynedd at the royal love match. He had been the King's squire then, and infatuated like all the young men at court with the lovely new Queen. Morgan, in the fervor of his first adolescent longing, adored her. For Jehana brought with her a new gaiety and splendor to the Court of Rhemuth. The people loved her for it.

Then came the day Brion casually let slip the fact of Morgan's half-Deryni ancestry. And Jehana's face went pale. And after that, very soon after that, the fateful war with the Marluk.

He still remembered that day vividly—that day now fifteen years past—when he and Brion, flushed with their recent victory over Marluk, had ridden back to Rhemuth at the head of the jubilant army.

He remembered how proud Brion had been of the boy-man Morgan, then but a few months past fourteen, as they romped excitedly into Jehana's chambers to boast of the victory. And the look of guarded horror and desperation which had come over Jehana's face as she realized her husband had held his throne and won his victory with the help of Deryni magic.

Immediately after that, Jehana went into seclusion for nearly two months, cloistering herself, it was said, at the Abbey of Saint Giles, near Shannis Meer. Soon she and Brion reconciled, and Jehana returned to Rhemuth with her lord. But she had avoided Morgan after that. And when Kelson was born the following year, she had made it quite clear that she wanted nothing to do with the young Deryni lord.

Her decision did not particularly alter Morgan's existence. His friendship with Brion continued to grow and mature, and at Brion's encouragement, he took an active part in Kelson's education and training.

But he and Brion both recognized the folly of a reconciliation as far as Jehana was concerned. And through the years, Brion had had to gradually accustom himself to the fact that his beloved Queen would have nothing to do with his most trusted friend.

Now Morgan never saw the Queen except when protocol or matters concerning Kelson demanded. And those few, unavoidable meetings were generally punctuated with verbal fireworks. Considering the woman, Morgan had little hope that the relationship would change.

The crunch of booted feet on gravel broke the silence of the garden, and Morgan looked up, then slipped off the rail where he had been sitting. Kelson and Kevin rounded the final bend of the main path and came to a halt just inside the summerhouse.

Kelson wore the royal crimson now. His face above the black fox collar of the velvet cloak was somber, tense. He had grown inches in the months since Morgan last saw him. And the young general's practised eye detected chain mail under the stiffly embroidered silk tunic. Black crepe banded one arm above the elbow and hung briefly from the boy's belt.

But it was the uncanny resemblance to Brion at the same age that struck Morgan most. Looking at Kelson, he saw Brion staring back at him: the wide, grey gaze beneath a velvety shock of straight black hair; the regal carriage of the proud head; the ease with which he wore the royal crimson. Clinically, he noted the apparent frailness of the slim frame, recalled the tensile steel strength it disguised, remembered the long hours of practice at arms, many of them at Morgan's side.

It was Brion of the Laughing Eyes, Brion of the Flashing Sword, of the Thoughtful Moods, teaching a young child to ride and fence; holding court in all the splendor of the monarchy, the boy spellbound at his feet. And the image of that boy wavered between light and dark, blond and raven-haired, as the memories of distant years confused themselves with those more recent.

Then it was Kelson again. And Brion, asking a friend dearer than life to swear that the boy would always have a protector, should his father die untimely. Brion, only months before his death, entrusting the key to his divine power to the man who stood now before his son.

Kelson dropped his gaze uncertainly. It appeared that Morgan was as much at a loss for words as he was.

Kelson knew what he *wanted* to do. He wanted to run to Morgan as he'd done as a child, to fling his arms around him and sob out his relief, terror, pain, all the nightmare of the past two weeks; let the calm and sometimes mysterious Deryni lord soothe away his fears and ease his troubled mind with that awesome Deryni magic. He had always felt so—*safe* with Morgan. If only he could . . .

But he did not.

He was a man, now—or supposed to be. And furthermore, he was a King!

Maybe! he interrupted himself apprehensively—*If Morgan can help me to survive long enough!*

Shyly, then, and feeling somewhat awkward in his new role, Kelson lifted his eyes once more to meet those of his father's friend, *his* friend.

"Morgan?" he nodded tentatively, trying to look more confident than he felt.

Morgan smiled a slow, reassuring smile and walked quietly to Kelson. He had been going to kneel in formal homage, but he sensed the boy's discomfort and decided to spare him the awkwardness. "My prince," was all he said.

Kevin McLain, a few paces behind the prince, could not miss the tenseness of the situation. Clearing his throat self-consciously, he looked toward Morgan.

"Duncan said to tell you he'll be at Saint Hilary's when you're ready, Alaric. I'll—ah—get back to the council meeting now. I think I can be more useful there."

Morgan nodded, but did not take his eyes from Kelson. So Kevin sketched an awkward bow and hurried back up the main path.

As the sound of Kevin's footsteps faded away, Kelson glanced down at the mosaiced floor of the summerhouse and traced a pattern in the dust with the toe of one polished boot.

"Lord Kevin told me about Colin and Lord Ralson and the others," he finally said. "I—I feel responsible for their deaths, Morgan. It was I who insisted they go to find you."

"Someone had to come, Kelson," Morgan replied. He placed a comforting hand on the boy's shoulder. "I thought you might feel that way, though. I took the liberty of having the bodies held at the Abbey of Saint Mark. Once this is over, you might want to do something for the families—a State burial, perhaps."

Kelson looked up wistfully. "Small consolation for the ones left behind—a State burial. Still, you're right, of course. Someone had to go."

"Good lad," Morgan smiled. "Come on. Let's walk."

Kevin McLain scanned the hall quickly from the doorway, then made his way across to where Derry stood alone outside the Council doors.

"Have they gone in yet?" Kevin asked, as he joined the younger man.

"No. They're waiting for some late arrivals. I hope they're *very* late—unless, of course, they're ours."

Kevin smiled. "I'm Kevin McLain, Morgan's cousin. And you can skip the formalities if you're Alaric's friend." He stuck out his hand and the younger man shook it.

"Sean Derry, Morgan's aide."

Kevin nodded and glanced around casually. "Been hearing any gossip around here? I think everyone in Rhemuth knows Morgan is back by now."

"I don't doubt it," Derry replied. "What do you think?"

"What do *I* think?" Kevin said, pointing to himself in disbelief. "My friend, I think we're all in trouble. Do you know what they're planning to charge him with?"

"I'm afraid to guess."

Kevin held up one finger. "Number one: heresy. And two?" He held up a second finger. "Treason. Care to guess what the penalty is for either offense?"

Derry sighed and let his shoulders droop dejectedly. "Death," he whispered.

CHAPTER THREE

Hell hath no fury like the woman scorned,
Or the woman mourning.

JEHANA OF GWYNEDD studied her reflection critically
in the mirror as a hairdresser coiled the long auburn
braid at the back of her head and secured it with a
pair of filigreed pins.

Brion would not have liked the hair style. Its stark
simplicity was too harsh, too severe for her delicate
features. It emphasized the high cheekbones, the
slightly squared jaw line, made the smoky green eyes
seem the only living features in the pale face.

Nor was black a good color for her. The flowing silk
and velvet of the mourning dress, unrelieved by jewel
or lace or bit of bright embroidery, only heightened the
monochrome effect of black and white, played up the
pallor, made her look far older than her thirty-two
years.

No, Brion would not have approved at all.

Not that he ever would have said anything, she
mused, as the hairdresser covered the shining tresses

50

with a delicate lace veil. Not Brion. No, he would simply have reached to her hair and removed the confining pins, let the long braid cascade loosely down her back, placed his gentle fingertips beneath her chin and tipped her mouth up to meet his . . .

Her fingers clenched tightly in unbidden remembrance, trembled in the concealment of long, close sleeves. Angrily she blinked back the familiar tears.

She must not think about Brion now. She must not believe for even an instant that he could know what she was about to do. There was good reason for her appearance thus today. For when she stood before Brion's Council this morning and told them of the fearful evil threatening Kelson, they must not think her but a young and foolish woman. She was still Queen of Gwynedd, if only until tomorrow. She must be certain the Council did not forget that fact when she asked for Morgan's life.

Her hand trembled slightly as she reached for the golden coronet on the dresser before her, but she forced herself to be calm, to place the diadem firmly atop her mourning veil. What she proposed to do today was distasteful to her. Whatever her personal feelings about this accursed Morgan and his forbidden Deryni powers, the man had still been Brion's closest friend and confidant. If Brion could know what she was about to do . . .

She stood abruptly and dismissed her maids with an impatient gesture. Brion could not know. Though it wrenched her heart to admit it, he was dead, almost two weeks in his tomb. Despite the old legends about the awesome power of the Deryni—powers so alien she could not begin to understand them—there was no way that even one favored by the Deryni could return from the grave. And if Morgan's death was necessary to insure that her only son should rule as a mortal, without the accursed powers, then it was necessary, no matter what the cost.

Resolutely, she crossed the chamber and paused in the doorway of the sun room. In one corner, a young minstrel strummed softly on a lute of pale, polished wood. Around him, a half-dozen black-clad ladies-in-waiting worked quietly at their needlepoint or listened to the mournful tune the minstrel hummed and played. Above their heads, climbing roses twined around the open beams, petals pink and red and gold against the clear autumn sky. All around, the morning sun cast hazy patterns of light and shadow on the flagstone floor and on the ladies' work. They looked up expectantly as Jehana paused in the doorway, and the minstrel stopped his playing.

Jehana signalled them to go on with their activities as she continued into the room. As the minstrel took up his gentle strumming again, Jehana wandered slowly to the opposite side of the room. Pulling a rose from a low-hanging branch, she sank wearily down on a black-draped bench under a rose arbor.

Perhaps here, among the roses and sunshine Brion had loved so well, she could find the inner peace she so desperately needed for what lay ahead. Perhaps here she could gather the strength and courage for what must be done.

A faint shudder moved across the frail shoulders, and she drew her gown more closely around her, as if against a sudden chill.

She had never had a man killed before—even a Deryni.

Nigel yanked impatiently at the brocaded bell pull outside the Queen's apartments for the fifth time, his grey eyes beginning to flash angrily. He felt a tirade coming on. And whatever good humor he had gained by his short talk with Alaric was fast dwindling away.

If someone didn't open that door in about three seconds, he was going to—

He had just raised his hand to pull the cord for the sixth and final time when he heard a soft rustling behind the door. He stepped back a pace, and a small peephole opened in the door at eye level. A brown eye peered timidly through the opening.

"Who is that?" Nigel demanded, putting his eye to the hole and looking back through.

The brown eye retreated, and then Nigel could see a young servant girl backing off from the door, her mouth frozen in a silent O.

"Young woman, if you don't open this door immediately, I'll kick it down, so help me!"

The girl's eyes widened even farther as she recognized the voice, and then she moved to obey. Nigel heard the bolt slide back and saw the heavy door begin to move. Without hesitation, he pushed it open the rest of the way and swept into the room.

"Where is the Queen?" he demanded, his practiced eye taking in every detail as he scanned the chamber. "In the garden?"

As he completed his visual circuit, he whirled abruptly and grabbed the frightened girl by the arm, shook her slightly as he glared down with those grey Haldane eyes. "Well? Speak up, child. I won't bite you."

The girl winced and tried to pull away. "P—please, Your Highness," she stammered. "You're hurting me."

Nigel loosened his grip, but did not release the girl. "I'm waiting," he said impatiently.

"She's in—in the sun room, Your Highness," the girl whispered, eyes downcast.

With a nod of approval, Nigel released her and stalked across the chamber to the arched entrance to the royal gardens. The sun room, he knew, adjoined the Queen's apartments at one end, but it was also accessible from the garden.

He strode quickly down the short, gravelled path toward the garden entrance, then stopped before a black wrought-iron gate twined with living roses. Reaching for the latch, he glanced through the thick foliage to the chamber beyond.

Inside, Queen Jehana looked up in mild surprise as the frightened servant came running through the inner entrance. As the girl whispered urgently to her mistress, Jehana lowered the single rose she had been contemplating and looked expectantly toward the gate where Nigel watched.

The air of surprise was already gone. With a decisive motion, Nigel slipped the latch and let the gate swing open. For an instant, he stood silhouetted against the doorway. Then he glided into the chamber to confront the Queen.

"Jehana," he nodded.

The Queen dropped her gaze uneasily and studied the flagstones at her feet. "I—I'd rather not talk to anyone just now, Nigel. Can't it wait?"

"I don't think so. May we be alone?"

Jehana's lips tightened as she glanced up at her brother-in-law, then at her attendants. Lowering her gaze again, she realized she was shredding the stem of the rose in her hand, and she dropped it in irritation. She carefully folded her hands in her lap before allowing herself to reply.

"I have nothing to say to you which can't be said in the presence of my ladies, Nigel. Please. You know what I have to do. Don't make it any more difficult for me than it already is."

When he did not reply, she looked up tentatively. Nigel had not moved. His grey eyes glittered dangerously beneath the shock of thick, black hair, like Brion in his darker moods. He stood resolute, threatening, thumbs hooked in his sword belt, staring at her in complete silence.

She turned away.

"Nigel, don't you understand? I don't want to discuss it. I know why you've come, and it won't do you any good. You can't change my mind."

She sensed rather than saw him moving closer, felt his cloak brush her hand as he leaned down.

"Jehana," he whispered low, so that only she could hear. "I intend to make this as difficult for you as is humanly possible. Now, if you don't send your ladies away, *I'll* have to. And that might be embarrassing for both of us. I don't think you *really* want to discuss your plans for Morgan in front of them—or how Brion died."

Her head jerked up. "You wouldn't dare!"

"Wouldn't I?"

She measured his gaze unwaveringly for several heartbeats, then turned away resignedly and gestured to her ladies.

"Leave us."

"But, Morgan, I don't understand. Why would she do a thing like that?"

Morgan and Kelson were walking along the outskirts of the boxwood maze, approaching a broad reflecting pool in the center of the main gardens. As they walked, Morgan kept a surreptitious watch for intruders, but no one seemed interested in their movements.

Morgan glanced at Kelson, then smiled. "You ask why a woman does something, my prince? If I fully understood that, I'd be powerful beyond my wildest dreams. After your mother discovered my Deryni background, she never gave me a chance to try."

"I know," Kelson sighed. "Morgan, what did you and Mother quarrel about?"

"You mean most recently?"

"I suppose so."

"As I recall, it concerned you," Morgan replied. "I reminded her that you were nearly grown, that one day you'd be King." His gaze lowered. "I never thought it would be so soon."

Kelson snorted bitterly. "She thinks I'm still her little boy. How do you convince a mother you're not a child any longer?"

Morgan considered the question as they came to a halt at the edge of the reflecting pool. "Frankly, I don't know, my prince. Mine died when I was four. And my aunt who raised me, the Lady Vera McLain, had the good sense never to belabor the issue. When my father died and I came to your father's court as a page, I was nine. And royal pages, even at that age, are no longer children."

"I wonder why royal princes are different," Kelson mused.

"Perhaps princes take longer," Morgan observed. "After all, royal princes grow up to be kings, you know."

"If they get to grow up," Kelson muttered.

Rather dejectedly, the boy sank down on a smooth rock by the reflecting pool and began pitching pebbles into the water, one by one. And as each pebble splashed, the brooding grey eyes followed the ripples until they vanished, watched as the concentric rings spread and dissipated into nothingness.

Morgan knew this mood, and knew better than to interfere. It was that air of concentration and deliberation, so hauntingly familiar in Brion, that was as much a part of the Haldane mold as grey eyes, or strength of arms, or diplomatic cunning. It had been Brion's lot; his brother Nigel had it in full measure, and would have made a formidable king had it not been for the accident of birth which made him second son instead of first. And now, the youngest of the Haldane line stood ready to claim his birthright.

Patiently, Morgan sat down to wait. And after a long, silent moment, the boy raised his head to gaze reflectively out across the water.

"Morgan," he began quietly, "you've known me since I was born. You knew my father better than any man I know," He pitched another pebble, than turned his head toward Morgan. "Do you—do you think I'll ever be able to fill his place?"

Fill his place? Morgan thought, trying not to let his pain show. *How do you fill an empty place in your heart? How do you replace someone who's been father and brother for almost as long as you can remember?*

Morgan picked up a handful of pebbles and rolled them in his hand, forcing himself once more to put aside his sorrow and concentrate on the matter at hand.

Brion was gone. Kelson was here and now. Now he must be father and brother to the son, even as the father had been to him. That was how Brion would have wanted it.

He flipped a pebble into the pool, then turned to his —son.

"I'd be lying if I said you could *replace* Brion, my prince. No man could. But you'll be a good king—perhaps even a great king, if I read the signs correctly." His voice became brisk, matter of fact.

"Brion provided well for you. From the time you could sit unaided, he had you on horseback daily. Your fencing masters were the finest to be found anywhere, your skill with the lance and bow prodigious in a child twice your age.

"You studied the annals of military history and strategy, languages, philosophy, mathematics, medicine. He even let you touch on the occult arts which would someday be such an important part of your life

—in defiance of your mother's wishes, I might add, though this was carefully concealed from all who might have objected.

"There was a more practical side to your education, though. For there was infinite wisdom in the seeming unorthodoxy of allowing a young and sometimes fidgeting Crown Prince to sit at his father's side in the Council chambers. From the beginning, though you were probably unaware of it at first, you acquired the rudiments of impeccable rhetoric and logic that were as much Brion's trademark as any feat of swordsmanship or valor.

"You learned to counsel and receive counsel wisely and unpretentiously. And through it all, you were made to understand that a wise king does not speak in anger, nor judge until all the facts are before him."

Morgan paused in his oratory and looked down at his handful of pebbles, as though surprised to realize he still held them. Gently, he tipped his hand and let them drop to the ground.

"I probably shouldn't tell you this yet, Kelson, but I think in many ways you may be even better equipped for rule than Brion was. You have a certain sensitivity, an appreciation of—life, perhaps?—that I'm not sure Brion ever really grasped. I don't suppose it made him any less a king, and he listened dutifully to the philosophers as well as the warriors. But I was never sure he really understood them. I think perhaps you do."

Kelson stared hard at the ground between his legs, blinking back tears of remembering. Then he raised his head and looked out across the pool once more.

"I know that's meant to be reassuring. But it doesn't really answer my question. Or rather, it answers the question I asked, but I didn't ask the right one. I suppose I really wanted to know about the Shadowed One's role in all of this."

Morgan raised one eyebrow warily. "What about

her?" he asked, remembering what Nigel had told him.

Kelson sighed in exasperation. "Now, Morgan, if you start evading, we'll get nowhere. I already know that Father won and held the kingdom partly through magic. You told me that yourself. And I also know why you were at Cardosa three months after the new treaty was signed. She's been behind it all the time, and I don't understand why everyone is so loath to talk about it. I'm not a child."

Morgan shifted uneasily. This was the crucial point. If the boy had truly managed to get an accurate picture of what happened, there was a reasonable chance for success even at this late date. Cautiously, he looked across at Kelson. "Did Brion tell you the Shadowed One was involved?"

"Not in so many words. But he didn't deny it, either."

"And?" Morgan urged.

"And—," Kelson began, searching for exactly the right phrasing. "Morgan, I don't think my father died of an ordinary heart attack. I think there was something else involved. In fact, I think the Shadowed One—"

"Go on."

"I think the Shadowed One somehow killed him with magic!" the boy finally blurted.

Morgan slowly smiled and nodded his head, and Kelson's face fell. "You already knew?" the boy asked, amazement and indignation written across his face.

"I suspected," Morgan amended, relaxing to a more comfortable position on his hard rock seat. "Nigel told me what you'd discussed with him, and I agree. Now, suppose you tell me exactly what happened on that hunt. I want every detail you can remember."

When all of the ladies-in-waiting had left the room, Jehana stood slowly and met Nigel's determined gaze.

"You play a dangerous game, Nigel," she said

softly. "Even if you *are* Brion's brother, I remind you that I am still your Queen."

"But Kelson is my King," Nigel answered quietly. "And what you propose to do to him, by destroying Morgan, borders dangerously close to treason."

"Treason?" Jehana asked. "I thought we had agreed to reserve that label for Morgan. I don't call protecting my only son treason."

"I made no such agreement about the label," Nigel replied evenly. "And, yes, I call it treason if it endangers Kelson. Without Brion's powers, you know he doesn't stand a chance. And Morgan is the one man in this world who can help him regain those powers."

"Brion's powers didn't save *him*."

"No, but perhaps they can save Kelson."

"I don't see it that way," Jehana said, her voice deepening. "I see that Morgan is the one man who could destroy my son in the ways that really count— that is, where his soul is concerned. And I see that it was Morgan's evil influence from the start which corrupted Brion—that unspeakably profane Deryni power which contaminated everything Morgan touched. I can't stand by and see the same thing happen to my son."

"Jehana, for the love of God—" Nigel began.

Jehana turned on him in a cold fury, her eyes blazing with a chill light Nigel had never seen there before. "Don't you dare bring God into this, Nigel! You have no right to invoke His Name for anything! If you support Morgan, you condone the Deryni heresy. And might I suggest, dear brother, that your own soul may be in danger from even your slight proximity to that man!" She turned away abruptly.

Nigel bit his lip and forced himself to control his rising anger. The discussion was going just as it always did, except that this time religious zeal had gotten the better of Jehana's common sense. He knew it was no use to continue the argument, yet he had to do it, even though he already knew the outcome. Perhaps bluntness would be a better tactic.

"I won't argue theology with you, Jehana," he said tensely. "But there are some things about Brion that you ought to know before you go off condemning his soul to that special hell reserved for consorters with heresy. For one thing, Brion's powers were his own. He didn't receive them from any outside source, Deryni or otherwise. The authority and potential Brion held have been handed down through our male line since the time of Camber and the Restoration.

"Certainly, Morgan helped Brion to realize his potential. He guided him in the use of the resulting powers. But the potential was Brion's, born in him, just as it is in every male child of the Haldane line; just as I carry it, and my sons, and Kelson."

"That's preposterous," Jehana stated flatly. "Such powers couldn't possibly be hereditary."

"I didn't say that the powers were passed on automatically—only the potential to carry them. One Haldane can hold the powers at any given time. And now, it's Kelson's turn."

"No. I won't permit it."

"Why not let Kelson decide?"

"Because Kelson is a child," Jehana said impatiently. "He doesn't know what's best for him."

"Kelson is a king, and will be crowned as such in the Cathedral of Saint George tomorrow. Would you deny him the right to continue wearing that crown after the coronation, Jehana?"

"Who would dare to take it from him?"

Nigel smiled. "Not I, Jehana, if that's what you're thinking. I'm quite content to remain the Duke of Carthmoor. Brion wanted it that way."

"And if you were not content as Duke of Carthmoor, what then? Would Brion's wishes matter?"

Nigel smiled again. "I don't think you understand. Brion was my brother as well as my king. Even had I not accepted the Duchy of Carthmoor out of my love for him—I was entitled to nothing, you know. Brion, as elder son, was heir to all—but even if my love for my brother did not bind me, I would still be bound by my oath to my liege Lord to keep the King's peace. I loved him as a sovereign as well as a brother, Jehana.'"

"I loved him, too," Jehana said defensively.

"You choose strange ways to show it."

"I can love the man, yet hate his deeds, can't I?"

"Can you?" Nigel questioned. "I think we may have rather different definitions of the word love, Jehana. To my way of thinking, it's a bit more than mere profession of some nebulous feeling for another human being. It's also accepting—accepting everything about that person, even though you don't approve of all of it.

"But you were never quite able to do that, were you? Because if you had been, you would have accepted from the start that Brion was magic in a very wonderful and special way, and that the proper way of rule for him was to use the powers he'd been given to keep peace in this land he loved so well."

He turned to face her. "If you'll think back, I think you'll have to agree that Brion never once misused those powers—or Morgan, either, for that matter. Never, in all the years they were together, did either of them use those powers for anything but good.

"When Brion slew the Marluk, for example, Jehana, I was there at his side, riding with him and Morgan. Can you possibly doubt that what they did was right? Think where we all might be today if the Marluk had won."

Jehana began twisting her fingers together uneasily as she thought back on the years. "Brion never mentioned any of this to me."

"He knew how you felt about Morgan," Nigel answered gently. "But even with that, I know he tried more than once to tell you." He turned her to face him squarely. "Don't you remember the times he mentioned his reign, his divine power of kingship? It wasn't just a convenient legend handed down by a race of kings to justify divine right rule."

"Why not?" she retorted stubbornly. "It's been the same with other royal houses. All kings claim their right of rule from God."

Nigel slammed one fist into the other palm in exasperation. "Jehana, will you listen to me? You haven't heard a word I'm saying. I'm trying to tell you that even if you *do* find Morgan's Deryni powers distasteful —and you've made no secret of that—*they* had nothing to do with Brion. Brion's powers were his own!"

There was a long silence, and then Jehana looked up, her face immobile, cold. "I don't believe you. Because if I did, I would have to believe that Brion was more than human, that he had, indeed, acquired his fearsome powers from somewhere outside the normal channels accessible to man. And that just isn't so. He may have been corrupted in life by your precious Morgan, but Brion himself was without personal taint. He was human."

"Jehana—"

"No! Brion was human, normal. And in spite of the accursed Deryni taint, he died a normal death, pursuing normal pleasures—not tempting the wrath of the Almighty by dabbling in Morgan's black arts."

"Normal death?" Nigel pounced on the phrase like an eagle after a mouse. "A normal death? Tell me about it, Jehana. What is normal about the way Brion died?"

Jehana froze, and her face went pale. "What do you mean?" she murmured apprehensively. "It was his heart. His heart stopped."

Nigel nodded slowly. "That *is* the ultimate cause of all deaths, isn't it?"

"What do you mean by that?" Jehana challenged.

Nigel folded his arms across his chest and looked down at the young Queen cautiously. Perhaps this was the very opening he'd been seeking. Evidently, Jehana had not even considered the possibility that Brion's death was not from natural causes. He mentally kicked himself for not thinking of the approach sooner. He began on a tentative note.

"Tell me, Jehana, does it seem normal for a man in Brion's peak physical condition to die of a heart attack? Remember, he was only thirty-nine, and our family has a history of longevity."

"But, his physicians said—"

"His physicians are not versed in such matters, Jehana."

She started to object, but he stayed her comment with an upraised hand.

"You didn't ask about Lord Ralson and Colin, either. Not to change the subject, but you *did* know that Kelson sent them to fetch Morgan, didn't you?"

"Against my—." She lowered her eyes. "What happened?"

"There was an ambush near Valoret. All members of the party were killed but Morgan and young Lord Derry."

Her hand flew to her mouth to mask the involuntary expression of horror.

Nigel's eyes narrowed. "Morgan thinks that the same person or persons responsible for the ambush also had a hand in Brion's murder."

"Murder!" Jehana cried. "You're trying to tell me that someone managed to assassinate Brion and make it look like a heart attack?"

"Can you think of a better way for the Shadowed One to begin her bid for power?" Nigel countered.

"She knew she couldn't stand against Brion in fair combat. But Kelson, he's just a boy. And if she could keep Morgan from reaching him and aiding him in the acquisition of Brion's powers, why, Kelson would be no problem whatsoever. After all, Kelson is entirely unschooled in such matters, thanks to you. What chance could a human boy possibly have against a full Deryni sorcorooo?"

"You're mad!" Jehana whispered, her face whiter still against the black of her mourning dress. "This is some delusion that's come over you in your grief!"

"It's no delusion, Jehana."

"Get out! Get out of here before I call a guard. If it's not a delusion, then it's an outright fabrication designed to destroy what cohesion there is left in the Council. And that borders on treason, too, my husband's brother! Now, get out!"

"Very well," Nigel said, backing off and bowing slightly. "I didn't think you'd listen, but I had to try. At least when things occur as I've said they will, you won't be able to say you weren't warned." He turned on his heel and strode toward the outer door. "I'll wait in the anteroom to escort you to the Council meeting. You won't want to keep the executioners waiting."

When he had left the room, Jehana let out a sigh of relief and tried to force her hands to stop trembling. Now that she had heard Nigel's story, she was more convinced than ever that she was doing what must be done, that Kelson must rule as a mortal. Now, if she could just get Kelson into the Council meeting and keep him from openly opposing her . . .

Resolutely, she yanked the bell pull to summon a servant. Kelson must be sent for right away. There was no time to lose.

Kelson shifted to a more comfortable position on his rock. The sun had gone behind a cloud bank, and the cool, moist air of the garden seemed to close in on him slightly.

"Then, you never got to examine the body for yourself?" Morgan asked. His face was grim with the information he had gained in the last few minutes.

Kelson shook his head. "I'm afraid not. The body only lay in state for two days, and there was a triple guard of honor around it the whole time. No one was allowed to go closer than about twenty feet—not even me. And when I asked Mother why the tight security, why the rush to bury him, she wouldn't answer. She just said it was for the best, and that one day I'd understand. At the time, I remember thinking she probably hurried so you wouldn't be able to get back in time for the interment. She knew that would hurt you."

"I can't deny that," Morgan agreed. "But I think there may have been other motives at work here. Perhaps, in spite of everything, she suspected what really happened at Candor Rhea, even though she couldn't let herself admit it. Hence, no one was allowed to go near the body. That's probably also the reason you weren't permitted to send for Duncan until it was too late. In my absence, he was probably the one person who could have told for sure if magic was used on Brion or not."

"Do you think she knows Father Duncan has been tutoring me?"

"Oh, I'm sure she knows," Morgan said. "Just as long as she doesn't know *what* he's been teaching you . . ."

Kelson grinned. "That *would* give her something to worry about, wouldn't it?"

"No doubt about it," Morgan agreed. "There's something else you ought to consider, though, Kelson. It's only a possibility, and I didn't even want to mention it, but is there any chance that your mother was somehow involved in what happened?"

"Mother!" Kelson sat up straight. "Morgan, you don't think—"

"I don't *know* at this point. But right now, there are only three people I trust. Two of them are sitting here right now, and the third one isn't Jehana. If she is involved, even without her own knowledge, it could make this whole situation even more difficult than we'd anticipated."

"I—I really don't know what to say," Kelson stammered. "She *has* been rather—"

"Kelson, don't move!"

Morgan had frozen in his place, and now stared fixedly at a point about a foot behind Kelson, where the boy's arm supported him.

"What—?"

"Not a word, not a move . . ." Morgan murmured softly, his hand going slowly to his sword. "There is a very large, very poisonous multi-legged creature not two inches from your right hand. If you move, it will kill you."

As the sword whispered silently from its scabbard, Morgan eased himself to one knee and stealthily raised the blade. Kelson sat immobile, trusting, only his eyes betraying his apprehension as they darted from Morgan's face to the sword to his own side, trying vainly to see behind himself without moving his head.

With the flash of gleaming steel, the blade descended. And in that same instant, a woman's scream shattered the silence.

As the blade struck, Kelson rolled clear and leaped to his feet, his wrist-stiletto flicking into his hand as he regained his balance. But as he glimpsed the writhing horror there on the ground, he stopped to watch spellbound as Morgan's blade bit again and again into the creature.

He had a fleeting impression of a bulbous orange

body about the size of a man's head, spotted with blue, of many brittle legs which waved frantically as it tried to scuttle away from Morgan's sword, of two angrily gnashing pincers or stingers—he couldn't be sure which.

Then the thing was but a twitching ruin of red and orange flesh, it's identity lost in the carnage. Morgan poked it a final time with the tip of his blade, and Kelson was at last aware of the woman screaming— the sound which had continued full volume throughout the episode.

As Kelson shook the immobility from his limbs and eyes, he was surprised to see more than a dozen armed men, their weapons drawn, racing across the garden toward him, a dark-clothed woman right behind them. Morgan lowered his sword, still breathing heavily, as the men surrounded him and the prince.

"Drop your weapon, sir!" the guard captain called out, as he deployed his men. The woman whose screams had summoned them half-shielded herself behind the captain, her eyes wide with terror.

"I saw him, I saw him!" she cried hysterically, pointing at Morgan. "He was trying to kill Prince Kelson! He put a spell on him, and was about to slay him when I screamed!"

"I said drop it, you!" the captain repeated menacingly, gesturing with his sword. "Sire, please! Move away from him slowly. We'll take care of him."

Morgan made no move to drop his weapon, and Kelson stepped deliberately in front of Morgan, his back to the tall general.

"It's all right, Captain," he said calmly, making a placating gesture with one hand as the guards stiffened to see him put himself before Morgan's sword. "It's not what you think. Lady Elvira, there's been a misunderstanding."

"A misunderstanding?" the lady shrieked indignantly. "Your Highness, you must be still under his spell! He nearly murdered you where you sat. Only my screams caused him to miss the mark and—"

"Madame—" Morgan's voice was cold, controlled, and it cut through the confusion like a knife. "What I aim for, I hit. And no silly woman's hysterical screaming has yet made me miss the mark!" With a defiant gesture, he plunged the tip of his sword into the soft ground, and it stood there quivering, as though punctuating his statement.

The disgruntled guards had lowered their weapons during this exchange, and now, at a hand signal from their leader, they resheathed their blades.

"Sire, forgive me, but it did look like—"

"I know what it looked like," Kelson said impatiently. "No apology is necessary. You and your men were merely trying to protect me. As you can see, however," he stepped aside to view the remains of his would-be killer, "General Morgan was merely killing a —what the devil *is* it, Morgan?"

Morgan retrieved his weapon and sheathed it, then moved closer to the mutilated plot of grass. The guards, too, eased in for a closer look, though they kept their distance from the man in black. They had all caught Kelson's casual mention of the infamous Morgan, and they were not eager to test out the rumors which had been circulating about him.

"It's a Stenrect crawler, my prince," Morgan replied matter-of-factly, prodding the carcass with the toe of his boot. "And if my first blow *had* missed," he glanced at the woman, "and the creature had bitten you, my second blow would have severed your wrist. There is no antidote for the sting of a Stenrect."

There was an uneasy stirring among the soldiers, and several crossed themselves furtively. The Stenrect was supposedly a mythical creature of supernatural origin, spawned, it was said, of fire and acid-hatred be-

fore the world was born. Of all creatures, real or imag-
ined, there was none deadlier. And though none there
had ever seen a Stenrect before—indeed, if asked before, they would have said no such creature existed—
all knew the legends. None cared to consider how close
their young lord had been to a painful and lingering
death.

The guard captain had by now recovered from the
shock of seeing a Stenrect in the flesh, and at last he
realized the significance of the man who had slain it.
For Morgan, too, was a creature of legend. And the
man suddenly realized he might inadvertently have in-
sulted the powerful Deryni Lord. That could be even
more dangerous than a Stenrect, if the rumors were
correct.

Bowing nervously, he addressed Morgan. "My apologies, Your Grace. Had I realized My Liege to be
under the protection of your sword, I would not have
been so quick with mine. Your reputation goes before
you." He signalled his men to disperse.

Morgan returned the bow, concealing a smile. "I'm
sure it does, Captain. I understand your position."

The captain cleared his throat uncomfortably and
turned to Kelson. "My apologies again, Sire. Shall I escort the Lady Elvira back to her quarters?"

"By all means, Captain," Kelson said, glancing aside
at the lady in question. "Unless, of course, the lady
wishes to stay and look at the Stenrect a while longer."

The lady turned pale and backed off a few steps,
shaking her head. "Oh, no, Your Highness! Please, I
meant no harm. I didn't know it was His Grace, and
from across the garden, I—" She stammered to a stop.

"Your concern is appreciated, Lady Elvira," Kelson
said easily, waving dismissal.

The lady bobbed a quick curtsey as she took the
captain's arm. Then the two of them fled across the
grass, the lady casting one last furtive glance over her

shoulder as they went through an arched doorway. It was not difficult to imagine what their next topic of discussion would be.

As the two disappeared from sight, Morgan chuckled. "Your ladies and your guards seem to be keeping quite an eye out for you, my prince."

Kelson snorted. "The Lady Elvira has an overactive imagination. She's been warned about that before. And as for my guards, they're so edgy, they'd try to arrest anything that moved. It's a good thing they didn't recognize you at first, though. The rumors about you haven't helped their morale any."

"I'm getting rather used to that reaction," Morgan replied with a wry grin. "It's that Stenrect that worries me."

Kelson nodded. "Is that really what it is? I always thought Stenrects were just myths, fairy tales to scare children with."

"No, they're quite real, as you saw. I'm wondering how one got into your garden, though. Stenrects are creatures of the night. It takes a great deal of power to call one out in broad daylight. Charissa is capable, of course, but if she means to challenge you tomorrow, I hardly see the point."

"Then, you don't think I was meant to be killed anyway?"

"Intended to frighten, not kill, I think," Morgan said. He glanced around, then took Kelson's arm and propelled him along the path toward the far gate. "I hardly think this is the place to belabor the point, however. After that little adventure, I think I prefer the relative safety of four walls and a roof. Now that there's been an attempt on your life, serious or no . . ."

"You don't have to convince *me*," Kelson replied, opening the gate and leading Morgan through. "Where are we going now?"

"To Duncan," Morgan said, heading them down a long foyer toward the outer courtyard. "The good father has some things in safekeeping for you."

"Then, you *do* have the key to Father's power!" Kelson exclaimed. "Why didn't you say so before? When you didn't mention it, I was afraid to ask."

"I had to see how much you'd deduced for yourself," Morgan grinned. "As it is—"

"Ooooh, Your Highness!" squealed a young, female voice. "There you are!"

Morgan stopped in his tracks and winced, and Kelson turned to breathe an unbelieving, "Oh, no!"

"Kelson," Morgan muttered through clenched teeth, "if you tell me that's the imaginative Lady Elvira again, I'll . . ."

"Sorry to disappoint you," Kelson murmured, trying hard to keep a straight face, "but it's the flighty and overexcitable Lady Esther this time." He folded his arms patiently. "What is it, Lady Esther?"

Morgan turned just as a plump and very out-of-breath young lady-in-waiting came to an undignified stop in front of them and curtsied.

"Oh, Your Highness," she fluttered, "your Lady Mother sent me to find you. She's been looking *everywhere* for you, and you *know* she doesn't like for you to wander off alone. It's very *dangerous!*"

"Do you hear that, Morgan?" Kelson said, glancing sidelong at his friend. "It's very dangerous."

' "Indeed," Morgan said, raising one eyebrow. "I hadn't noticed."

As the Lady Esther tried in vain to follow this exchange, Kelson turned back to her. "My dear Lady Esther, would you be so good as to inform my Lady Mother that I'm quite safe with my Lord General Morgan."

Lady Esther's eyes grew round as she finally realized the identity of Kelson's companion, and a plump hand flew to her lips to mask the scarcely breathed, "Oh!"

She curtsied again and whispered, "I did not recognize Your Grace."

Morgan frowned and half-turned to Kelson. "Blast it, Kelson, do I look that different? This is about the twentieth person today who hasn't recognized me. What good is notoriety if no one knows who you are?"

"Perhaps it's because you're not wearing your horns and cloven hooves," Kelson remarked dryly.

"Hmmm, no doubt. Tell me, Lady Esther. Did you also not recognize your King?"

"I beg your pardon, Your Grace?"

Morgan sighed and folded his arms across his chest. "Lady Esther," he continued patiently, "I'm sure you've been at court long enough to learn how one addresses one's King. Your entrance was not, by any stretch of the imagination, a model of decorum. You would do well to show more respect in the future. Is that clear?"

"Yes, Your Grace," she whispered, swallowing visibly.

Kelson glanced at Morgan, as though to ask if he was quite finished, and Morgan nodded slightly. Kelson turned back to the nervous Lady Esther.

"Very well, then. Other than the predictable report that my mother has been worried about me, is there any other message?"

Lady Esther curtsied again. "She commands me to tell you that the Council is convening right away, Your High—Your Majesty. She requests your immediate presence."

"Morgan?" Kelson glanced at the general.

"Later, my prince. We have urgent business elsewhere first. Lady Esther, you may inform the Queen that His Majesty will be delayed."

"And that I'm quite safe," Kelson added emphatically. "You may go."

As the lady bowed and hurried off, Kelson sighed. "You see what I have to put up with? It's not just a matter of convincing Mother that I'm not a child any more. I've got to retrain the whole blasted staff of servants!" He grinned. "I *will* be safe with you, won't I, Morgan?"

Morgan smiled. "From assassins and Stenrects—always, my prince. Just don't ask me to contend with any more of the Queen's ladies today. I don't think I'm up to it."

Kelson laughed with glee. "So! There *are* things you're afraid of, Morgan! I never thought I'd hear you admit it."

"If you tell anyone, I'll deny every word!" Morgan retorted. "Come on. Let's find Duncan."

In the Council chamber, all conversation stopped as Jehana entered on Nigel's arm. The men seated around the long, polished table came to their feet as one, as Nigel escorted the Queen to her seat and continued to his own place at the opposite end. They noticed that the two did not look at each other, but that was to be expected. All in the room knew that the Queen and the Royal Duke did not agree on the matter at hand today. It would be a unique Council meeting, for neither was likely to give in without a struggle. It *was* unusual that Kelson had not shown up yet, though.

Jehana glanced around the room nervously as she took her place beside Brion's empty throne, recalling other, happier times when she and Brion had entered this room together, and the faces around the table had all been friendly.

Then, she had not felt so alone, so threatened. Then, the dark-stained walls had not seemed so confining, the high-ceilinged vault with its dark-stained beams so dismal. It was not the fault of the room. There were windows along the entire right side that let in the daylight, to be sure. And what light they did not provide was amply augmented by the banks of ornate candelabra flanking the long table on either side. Still, the big room seemed dank and depressing. Perhaps it did not like being filled with so many people in the dark colors of mourning.

Jehana watched the slight movement of a rivulet of yellow wax oozing along the rim of one of the fat candles on the bul down. And her fingers automatically sought out the long gash on the table top between her place and Brion's—the scarred spot where Brion had once impaled a writ with his dagger, nailed it to the table until he was able to persuade a balky Council that it was not a wise legislation. She forced herself to look down the table, then, to study the pale, questioning faces who stared back at her as they took their seats.

Other than those of Brion and Kelson, and the dead Lord Ralson, all the seats at table were filled today. Someone, she noted with annoyance, was even sitting in Morgan's chair, there between Kelson's and Ralson's. She was not certain, but she guessed the young man with the unruly brown hair must be Lord Derry, Morgan's military aide. No doubt Nigel had given him permission to sit in today.

No matter, she thought to herself, as she continued to scan the table. If the young Marcher lord thought he was going to vote in Morgan's absence, she would straighten him out about that soon enough. She was not going to allow Nigel or Morgan's minions to ruin *this* Council meeting.

She swept her gaze coolly back up the table to the right, then—past Nigel, who would not look at her, past Bran Coris, and Lord Ian, who looked his usual dapper self, past Lord Rogier and Bishop Arilan, past

Ewan. She nodded greeting to Archbishop Corrigan on her left, then let her glance take in Duke Jared and his son Kevin.

She did not greet the last two, though. Next to Nigel, the two McLains were perhaps the staunchest of Morgan's supporters in Council. She wished she didn't have to face them today.

She turned back to Ewan. "Lord Ewan," she said, her voice clear and firm, "would you call the Council to order? We have important matters to take care of this afternoon, and I think we dare not wait any longer."

Before Ewan could stand, Nigel jumped to his feet and waved him back. "A moment's indulgence, Your Majesty, but His Royal Highness has been unavoidably detained, and asked that I delay the start of this meeting. He wished to be present when certain charges are brought before the Council."

Jehana did not acknowledge his request, but turned again to Ewan. "My Lord Ewan, if you please."

"I'd like an answer, Jehana," Nigel demanded.

"Lord Ewan, you will continue!"

Ewan stood uncertainly and glanced at Nigel, at Kelson's empty chair beside him, then cleared his throat uneasily. "Your Majesty, if you command it, I shall, of course, convene the Council without Prince Kelson. But if His Royal Highness wishes to be present, common courtesy dictates—"

"Common courtesy seems to have no place in this Council today as far as my esteemed son is concerned, my Lord of Claibourne," Jehana interrupted evenly. "Prince Kelson was summoned more than half an hour ago. He has deemed it unimportant to appear. It seems he has other business which he considers more important that his duty to his Council Lords. I can only apologize for his inconsiderate and immature behavior and hope that he will improve with age and wiser counselling. As for today, this *is* a Regency Council, and therefore his presence is not mandatory. Are there any questions?"

There was a low murmur of discussion around the table, and Nigel sat down wearily, knowing that he had done all he could. Jehana had really lashed out about Kelson's absence. It was not starting out to be a good meeting at all.

Ewan looked helplessly around the table, then coughed nervously and bowed toward his Queen.

"There are no questions, Your Majesty," he said impassively. "If things are, indeed, as you say, I see no reason to delay any longer. As Hereditary Lord Marshal of the Royal Council of Gwynedd, I call this session of the Regency Council to order. Let Justice, tempered by Mercy, prevail in all our judgements."

As he took his seat, grumbling under his breath, another murmur drifted around the table, to cease as Jehana rose at her place.

"My Lords," she began, her face terrible and pale against her widow's weeds, "it distresses me to come before you like this today. It distresses me because I dislike admitting that my late husband and lord was not infallible as I had always believed him to be.

"For my Lord Brion made a dreadful mistake in his appointment of one of his Council Lords. The man he appointed was and is a traitor and a blasphemer, and even now conspires against Brion's legitimate heir. That is why Prince Kelson is not with us today."

Her gaze swept the stunned faces before her, and her eyes took on a smoky darkness in the green.

"The man is well known to you, my Lords. He is, of course, the Duke of Corwyn, Lord General Alaric Anthony Morgan—the Deryni!"

CHAPTER FOUR

And I will give him the morning star.
                          Revelation 2:28

As HE WATCHED water bubble into the marble stoup he was filling, Monsignor Duncan McLain let his thoughts wander, sent his mind forth at full receptivity, searching.

Time was growing short. Alaric should have been here hours ago. And it worried him that he'd had no communication from his kinsman in so many months. Perhaps he wasn't coming. Possibly, he'd never even gotten word of Brion's death, though the news had reached every corner of the Eleven Kingdoms by now, as far as Duncan knew.

As the water neared the top of the stoup, Duncan froze for the merest fraction of a second, then straightened quickly and set his water bottle on the floor.

Alaric was coming, and the young prince with him. And urgency was unmistakable in the growing rapport which intruded more and more now on Duncan's senses.

78

He moved toward the open doorway of the west portal, smoothing his rumpled cassock with a quick, automatic motion of slim-fingered hands, then stepped into the sunlight and shaded his eyes against the midday glare.

There, against the grey of the far wall, just past the courtyard gate, he caught the flash of Kelson's royal crimson, its golden embroidered crest glittering in the sunlight. And at his side stalked a dark shadow topped by sleek golden hair, its long legs eating up the distance between them.

As the two mounted the steps to the west porch, Duncan felt the reassuring aura which almost always accompanied his illustrious cousin. He gave a sigh of relief as he stepped out to greet them.

"By Saint George and Saint Camber, it's about time you got here," Duncan stated, pulling Morgan and the prince back into the shadow of the doorway. "What took you so long? I was worried."

"I'll explain later," Morgan said, peering anxiously down the clerestory aisle and into the nave. "Are you being watched?"

Duncan nodded. "I'm afraid so. There've been Queen's guardsmen in the basilica every day since Brion's burial. I don't think they suspect me, though. I *am* Kelson's confessor, and they may just have guessed you'd come here first."

Morgan turned back to Duncan and Kelson and sighed. "Well, I hope you're right. Because if they do have any inkling you're functioning in any other than your official capacity, we're all dead."

"Then, let's keep up the facade," Duncan said, scooping up his empty bottle and motioning them to follow him down the side aisle. "If anyone stops us, you've come to make confession and receive the Sacrament before your trial. I don't think they'd interfere with that."

"Right."

As they walked slowly down the aisle, Morgan tried to scan the worshippers without appearing too obtrusive. Duncan had definitely been right about the Queen's guardsmen. There were at least three or four among the faithful. And judging from the way they looked at him, it was not an excess of piety or devotion which had brought them to Saint Hilary's so regularly for the last week.

The three paused at the end of the aisle to bow respectfully before the high altar, and Morgan tried hard to keep the proper look of contrition on his face for the benefit of his observers. Evidently he was sufficiently convincing, for no one made an effort to stop them as they slipped out through a side door.

When they reached the privacy of Duncan's study, Morgan slid the bolt home with a decisive clink of metal against metal. And as Duncan crossed the room to get rid of his bottle, Morgan allowed himself to once again take in the familiar surroundings.

It was a small room, no larger than twelve feet by fifteen, and it was lined on the two longer walls with waist-high bookcases and rich tapestries depicting scenes of hunting and court life. Across the far end, opposite the door, a wide window was curtained from floor to ceiling in rich burgundy velvet. A huge grey stone fireplace dominated the fourth wall with the door, its wide mantle unadorned except for a pair of simple pewter candlesticks with fat yellow candles and a small icon of Saint Hilary, the patron of the basilica.

To the right of the window, an intricately carved prie-dieu faced the corner, the kneeler and armrest covered with the same burgundy velvet as the drapes. An ivory crucifix stood on a small stand in the corner itself, flanked on either side by twinkling votive lights in ruby glass holders. To the left and in front of the window was a small desk of dark polished wood, its surface covered with books and documents.

In the center of the room, back perhaps four paces from the fireplace, a heavy round table of burnished oak dominated the rest of the room, claw-footed legs resting solidly on the polished marble floor. Two matching chairs with high backs faced each other across the table, and several more of a similar design sat closer to the fireplace, facing toward the flames. A heavy tapestry rug covered the floor between table and fireplace, muffling the cold and hollowness which might otherwise have pervaded the room.

Morgan pulled out one of the chairs at table for Kelson, then dragged a third chair from in front of the fireplace. As he did, Duncan deposited his empty bottle beside the desk and began opening the heavy drapes.

"Do you think that's wise?" Morgan asked, his attention turned momentarily from the task he was engaged in.

Duncan glanced briefly at his cousin, then turned to peer through the amber leaded glass. "I think it's safe enough," he finally said. "No one can see in in the daytime, and the glass distorts anyway." He crossed to the table and took his seat. "Besides, now we'll be able to see if anyone approaches from outside. That will be very important in about half an hour, if I've judged correctly."

"That soon?" Morgan replied matter-of-factly, reaching into his tunic to remove a small black suede pouch. "We haven't much time, then, have we?"

He glanced casually around the room as he placed the pouch on the table and began untying the leather thongs which bound it. "I'll need some more light here, Duncan, if you don't mind. And by the way, since when do you have to refill the holy water yourself? I thought the monsignori were above such things."

Duncan snorted in derision as he brought a tall candelabrum from his desk and placed it on the table. "Very amusing, Cousin. You know very well that all my assistants are at the cathedral preparing for Kelson's coronation tomorrow." He smiled at the boy and sat down again. "And I hardly think I need remind you where our esteemed Archbishop is at this moment. I had to get special permission to stay here today in case Kelson needed me—which I surmise he does, though not in precisely the way our Archbishop thinks."

He and Morgan exchanged knowing grins, and Kelson nudged Morgan's elbow impatiently, craning his neck to see what was in the bag Morgan still had not opened. Morgan smiled reassuringly at the boy, then finished untying the bag. Reaching gloved fingers inside, he carefully extracted a bit of gold and crimson fire and laid it in the palm of his hand.

At Kelson's gasp of recognition, Morgan wistfully extended his hand toward the boy. "You know the ring, my prince?—don't touch it. You're not properly shielded."

Kelson exhaled softly and withdrew his hand, his eyes wide with awe. "It's the Ring of Fire, my father's seal of power. Where did you get it?"

"Brion gave it to me for safekeeping before I left for Cardosa," Morgan replied, turning his hand slightly so that the stones sparkled.

"May I?" Duncan asked, pulling a silk handkerchief from his sleeve and reaching for the ring.

Morgan nodded and extended his hand.

Gathering the folds of silk around his fingers, Duncan gingerly picked up the ring and held it closer to the candlelight. As he turned it, the scarlet stones cast tiny, bright reflections on the three observers and on the tapestried walls.

Duncan examined the ring minutely, then placed it

in the center of the table, still nestled in its shroud of white silk.

"It's genuine," he said with a slight note of relief. "I can still feel residual power in it. Do you have the seal?"

Morgan nodded and began stripping off his gloves. "I'm afraid you're going to have to make the retrieval, though, Duncan. I don't dare approach the altar area with Jehana's spies out there." He slipped off an ornate signet ring and held it up between thumb and forefinger. "Are you willing?"

Kelson leaped forward eagerly to inspect the ring. "*Sable, a gryphon segreant vert*—those are the old Corwyn arms, aren't they, Morgan?"

"Correct," Morgan agreed. "Brion had the ring made long ago. And since the arms are those of my Deryni mother, he thought them eminently suitable for carrying the key to your powers." He shifted his attention to Duncan. "I'll have to attune it to you. Are you ready?"

"What about—" Duncan inclined his head toward Kelson.

Morgan looked at the boy, then back at his cousin, a faint smile on his face again. "I think it's all right. If he hasn't already suspected, he's sure to find out by tomorrow anyway. I think our secret will be safe."

"Good," Duncan nodded, then turned to smile reassuringly at Kelson. "It's nothing all that mysterious, Kelson. The gryphon seal, when properly activated, will open a secret chamber in the high altar. Long ago, it was attuned to Alaric by your father, so that when the time came, he would be able to retrieve the things which have been put aside for you.

"You can see that the embedded inlay of the gryphon has a slight glow to it as Alaric holds it. This lets us know that it's still activated to him. If anyone unattuned were to try to use it, like myself right now, or you, it wouldn't work."

He turned back to Morgan, though he still spoke for Kelson's benefit. "I might add that only certain people can be attuned to such a device. I am—like Alaric."

Before the impact of that statement could sink in with Kelson, Morgan held up the gryphon seal between himself and Duncan and raised an eyebrow. "Ready?"

Duncan nodded, and the two began to concentrate on the gryphon device in the center of the seal.

Kelson watched, spellbound, as the two stared at the ring, then closed their eyes. There was a long period of silence, when Kelson was certain the only sound in the room was that of his own harsh breathing, and then Duncan's hand moved slowly toward the ring, his eyes still closed.

Just before he touched it, a faint spark arced across the short intervening space, and then Duncan held the ring also. At that, both men opened their eyes, and Morgan relinquished his hold on the ring. The gryphon still glowed faintly.

"It worked," Kelson whispered, his words half statement, half question.

"Certainly," Duncan replied. "Hold out your hand and see for yourself."

Kelson extended his hand gingerly, flinched slightly as the ring dropped into his palm. It felt cold to the touch, even though it should have been warmed to body temperature. And when he looked at the gryphon seal in the center, he put the ring down quickly.

"It's not glowing! What did I do to it?"

Duncan snapped his fingers and smiled. "I forgot. You're not attuned." He picked up the ring and held it in front of Kelson, and the gryphon resumed its pale glowing. Kelson grinned sheepishly.

Duncan got to his feet, tossed the ring lightly into the air and caught it again. "I'll be back shortly."

Kelson watched with awe until the priest had disappeared through the study door, then turned back to Morgan.

"Morgan, did I hear right—Duncan is Deryni? You must be related on your mothers' sides, then—not your fathers'."

"Both, actually," Morgan amended. "We *are* fifth cousins through the paternal line. But Duncan's mother and mine were actually sisters. Of course, that's been a well-kept secret. Deryni blood could definitely be embarrassing, if not fatal, to one in Duncan's position. There are few among us who don't remember the Deryni inquisitions and persecutions a little more than a century ago. The bad feeling is far from gone, even today. You know that."

"But, *you* aren't afraid to let people know you're Deryni, Morgan," Kelson replied.

"But I'm an exception, as you well know, my prince," Morgan countered. "For most, there's little future in being a kept Deryni. As a result, most of us conceal our Deryni heritage, even if inclined to use our powers for good." He cocked his head wistfully. "There's a basic conflict which arises from that decision, of course: wanting to use your native abilities on the one hand, yet bound by guilt, by the condemnation of Church and State, if you do."

"And yet, you made that decision," Kelson persisted.

"Yes. I chose to use my powers more openly from the start, and damn the consequences. And I was extremely fortunate to have your father's protection and patronage until I could take care of myself." He glanced down at his hands. "Being only half Deryni helps."

"And Duncan?" Kelson asked quietly.

Morgan smiled. "Duncan chose yet another solution —the priesthood."

Duncan paused at the sacristy peephole to scan the nave, mentally thanking whichever of Saint Hilary's builders had shown the foresight to install the spying device. No doubt, this was not precisely what the architects had had in mind—the peephole was intended as an aid in timing services and the like—but Duncan didn't think they would object.

He could see the entire nave from where he stood, from the very first row to the doors at the rear, from one clerestory aisle to the other. And what he saw but reinforced his belief that this would not be as easy a task as he had hoped.

The Queen's guardsmen he'd mentioned to Alaric were still there, including the two he thought had been watching him in particular for the past week. He knew that they were members of the Queen's personal regiment, and he wondered in passing if they did, indeed, suspect him. He didn't think he'd done anything to warrant their special attention—other than being Kelson's confessor, and Alaric's cousin—but one could never tell with men like these.

He took a brocaded stole from a cabinet to his right and touched it to his lips, settled it around his shoulders. With his royal watchdogs out there, it was obvious he could not simply walk out, open the altar chamber, and retrieve the contents. They would be suspicious the minute he entered the sanctuary. He would have to have a diversion.

He checked the peephole again, then formulated a plan.

Very well. Let them be suspicious. If the Queen's guards insisted on complicating the matter, it was all the same to him. He was not above using a bit of sacerdotal sleight-of-hand to mask his real intent. And if that failed, there was always the traditional might and authority of the monsignori to fall back on. When dealing with men such as these, intimidation was generally not too difficult, especially when one had the threat of anathema to work with.

Breathing deeply once to compose himself, Duncan opened the side door and entered the chancel. And as he suspected, one of the guards immediately left his seat and hurried down the center aisle.

All right, Duncan thought, making a deep genuflection to give the man time to get closer *He's alone, and he hasn't drawn steel. Let's see what he'll do.*

As Duncan rose, he listened to the hollow echo of the man's footsteps approaching and let his hand go casually to his waist to remove the tabernacle key from his sash. Then, as his senses told him the man had nearly reached the altar rail, he let the key slip from his fingers. A carefully blundered attempt at interrupting its fall sent the key skittering down the marble steps to land at the feet of the surprised guard.

Duncan turned innocent blue eyes on the man, a slight look of embarrassment on his face, then hurried down the steps with a show of concern. His manner so disarmed the guard, that by the time Duncan reached him, he had bent and picked up the key almost without realizing what he did. With an embarrassed half-grin, he dropped the key gingerly into Duncan's out-stretched hand.

"Thank you, my son," Duncan murmured in his best paternal tone.

The man nodded nervously, but made no move to leave.

"Did you wish something?" Duncan asked.

The man squirmed uncomfortably. "Monsignor, I have to ask you this—is General Morgan with you?"

"You mean, in my study?" Duncan asked patiently, his innocence still at peak efficiency.

The man gave a slight nod.

"General Morgan has come to me as a penitent son," Duncan said softly. "He wishes to receive the Sacraments before his trial, as does Prince Kelson. Can there be any harm in that?"

Duncan's explanation took the man by surprise. Evidently, the idea of Morgan being anything but a heathen and infidel had never occurred to him before. It was obviously not what he'd expected to hear. And who was he to interfere with a man's salvation—especially one in so great a need as Alaric Morgan?

Convinced he'd interrupted something very normal and very holy, the guard shook his head sheepishly and backed away from Duncan, bowing from the waist. As Duncan turned toward the altar, the man hurriedly glided back up the center aisle to the pew where his colleagues knelt, to join them and cross himself superstitiously.

Duncan ascended the altar with relief. He knew the man was still watching, and he was certain he was telling his henchmen what had just happened—though all of them appeared to be immersed in prayer. But he doubted they would make any move to interfere again, providing he made no glaring departures from routine. Of course, someone would go to tell Jehana of Kelson and Alaric's whereabouts as soon as he left, but that couldn't be helped.

Duncan bowed slightly before the tabernacle, then carefully retracted the green silken curtains from in front of its golden doors. As his right hand unlocked the doors, his left shifted its grip on the gryphon seal. And then, as he withdrew a covered chalice with one hand, it was a simple matter to touch the seal to the altar stone with the other.

At the touch, a six-inch-square section of the altar directly in front of Duncan indented slightly, then withdrew to disclose a flat black box. Working quickly, Duncan brought out two more chalices and made a show of consolidating the contents of three into two. Then, instead of simply covering the empty chalice with its jewelled cover and veil, he slipped the black box between chalice and cover and veiled both with green silk.

This done, he replaced the other two chalices and closed the doors with a flourish, locked the doors again while his other hand closed the opening in the altar stone. Then he picked up the remaining chalice with its added burden, bowed once more, and swept out of the sanctuary. The entire operation had taken less than two minutes.

Back in the sacristy, Duncan whisked off his stole and glanced through the peephole again. As he had suspected, one of the guards was on his way out of the basilica—to tell the Queen, no doubt. But apparently he had aroused no further suspicion. For no one else seemed interested in the least where Duncan had gone. The other guards had not moved from their places.

Duncan tucked the flat black box into his sash and placed the empty chalice with several others, then returned to the study and locked the door behind him.

"Any difficulty?" Morgan asked, as the priest withdrew the box and placed it on the table.

"None at all," Duncan replied. He dropped the gryphon seal into Morgan's hand and sat down. "There will be a messenger on his way to tell Jehana where you are, though."

Morgan shrugged. "That was to be expected. Let's see what we've got here." He picked up the box.

"Does the gryphon seal open this, too?" Kelson asked eagerly, edging his chair closer to Morgan and the box. "Look, there's a gryphon imprinted on the cover."

Morgan touched his seal to the indicated area and the lid snapped open with a musical chime. Inside were a piece of parchment, much folded, and a slightly smaller box, this one covered with red velvet and stamped with a golden lion. As Duncan plucked out the parchment, Morgan removed the second box and inspected it briefly.

"This one takes a different seal, Duncan," he said, putting the box down on the table beside the silk-shrouded Ring of Fire. "Are those our instructions?"

"It looks like it," Duncan replied, smoothing the rumpled parchment and holding it closer to the light. "Let's see:

When shall the Son deflect the running tide?
A Spokesman of the Infinite must guide
The Dark Protector's hand to shed the blood
Which lights the Eye of Rom at Eventide.

Same blood must swiftly feed the Ring of Fire.
But, careful, lest ye rouse the Demon's Ire:
If soon thy hand despoil the virgin band,
Just retribution damns what ye desire.

Now that the Eye of Rom can see the light,
Release the Crimson Lion in the night.
With sinister hand unflinching, Lion's Tooth
Must pierce the flesh and make the Power right.

Thus Eye and Fire and Lion drink their fill.
Ye have assuaged the warring might of Ill.
New morn, ring hand. Defender's Sign shall seal
Thy Force. No Power Below shall thwart thy will!"

Morgan sat back in his chair with a low whistle. "Did Brion write that?"

"It's in his hand," Duncan replied, dropping the parchment to the table and tapping it with a well-manicured forefinger. "See for yourself."

Morgan leaned forward and gave the verse a cursory inspection, committing the lines to memory, then leaned back again with a sigh. "And we thought *Brion's* power ritual was obscure . . . If he'd given it a little thought, I think he could have made it *difficult*."

Kelson, who had been following the exchange with

wide-eyed awe, could no longer contain himself. "You mean, this isn't the same ritual?"

Duncan shook his head. "The ritual is changed with each inheritance, Kelson. It's a safeguard to keep the power from falling into the wrong hands. Otherwise, someone could theoretically learn the technique, gather the elements of the ritual, and assume the power for himself. Strictly speaking, the power is only supposed to pass to the legitimate heir, but there are always ways to get around such technicalities."

"Oh," Kelson said, his voice small and uncertain. "Then, where does one start with something like this?" He picked up the parchment as though it were a small, not-quite-dead creature that might bite, regarded it suspiciously, then dropped it to the table again.

"Alaric?" Duncan queried.

"You go ahead. You know more about these things than I do."

Clearing his throat nervously, Duncan moved the parchment in front of him again and glanced at it, then looked across at Kelson. "All right. With a verse like this, the first thing to do is to break it down into its component parts: the basic elements of the ritual. In this case, we have two trios and a quarto. Three people: the Son, the Spokesman of the Infinite, and the Dark Protector—you, myself, and Alaric. These are named in the first stanza, and they comprise our human element."

"Well, not *quite,* Cousin," Morgan murmured, placing his fingertips together and gazing across at Duncan with a sly grin.

Duncan raised one eyebrow meaningfully.

"Three people," Kelson said, nudging Duncan impatiently. "Go on, Father Duncan."

Duncan nodded. "We also have three objects: the Eye of Rom, the Ring of Fire, and the Crimson Lion. These are our—"

"Wait," Morgan said, sitting up abruptly. "I am just reminded of a horrible possibility. Kelson, where is the Eye of Rom?"

Kelson looked blank. "I don't know, Morgan. Tell me what it is, and maybe I can tell you where it is."

Duncan glanced at Morgan. "It's a dark, cabochon-cut ruby, about the size of my little fingernail. Brion always wore it in his right earlobe. You must have seen it before."

Kelson's eyes widened in sudden realization, and a look of apprehension came over his face. "Oh, no. Father, if that's what I think it is, it was buried with him. I didn't know it was important."

Morgan pursed his lips in concentration as he traced the golden lion on the box lid with a fingernail. Then he looked up resignedly at Duncan. "Open the crypt?"

"We have no choice."

"Open the crypt?" Kelson echoed. "But, you can't! Morgan, you just can't!"

"I'm afraid it's necessary," Duncan replied quietly. "We have to have the Eye of Rom, or the ritual is no good." He lowered his eyes. "It's—a good idea anyway. If Charissa really did have a hand in Brion's death—and there's every indication that she did—then, there's a—well, a possibility that he's not entirely free."

Kelson's eyes widened even farther, and the remaining color drained from his face. "You mean, his soul is—"

"Where is he buried?" Morgan asked sharply, cutting Kelson off and changing the direction of conversation before the boy's horror could get entirely out of hand. "We're going to have to have a plan of action if we're to get anywhere."

"He's in the royal crypt below the cathedral," Duncan replied. "As far as I've been able to tell, there are at least four guards on duty at all times. They have orders not to let anyone inside the gate. And you can't even see the tomb from outside."

Morgan's eyes narrowed as he toyed with his ring. "Four guards, eh? There're probably fewer at night, don't you think? Once the cathedral doors are closed after Compline, there'd be no need for that strong a force. We can handle them, I think."

Kelson stared at Morgan in disbelief, the color gradually returning to his face. "Morgan, are we really going to open the casket?" he breathed.

Morgan's answer was cut off by the sound of many horses arriving in the courtyard outside. Duncan jumped to his feet and dashed to the window, then began hastily drawing the drapes.

Morgan was instantly at his side, peering through a crack in the curtains. "Who is it? Can you tell?"

"Archbishop Loris," Duncan said. "From the size of his entourage, though, it's difficult to tell if he's only just arriving in the city, or if he's come to get you."

"He's after me. Look at the way he's deployed his men. He knows we're in here. We'll be surrounded in a matter of seconds."

Kelson joined them at the window, a look of consternation on his face. "What are we going to do now?"

"I'll just have to give myself up," Morgan said mildly.

"Give yourself—Morgan, no!" Kelson cried.

"Morgan, *yes!*" Duncan contradicted, guiding the boy firmly back to the table. "If Alaric flees the just summons of the Council, *your* Council, he flouts the very laws he swore to uphold as a Council Lord." He sat the boy down. "And if you neglect your duty as head of that Council, you do the same thing."

"It's not my Council right now, though," Kelson argued. "It's Mother's Council. She's trying to kill Morgan."

Duncan picked up the Ring of Fire, the parchment, and the red velvet box and carried them to the prie-dieu. "No, it's still your Council, Kelson. But you're going to have to remind them of that." He touched a hidden stud in the prie-dieu and a small compartment opened in the wall beside it.

"Besides, there's little more we can do until tonight anyway. And the longer you can stall in Council, the less chance there is for other treachery afoot. I suspect that some of your most formidable enemies are sitting on that Council right now, but at least you'll know where they are and what they're doing if everyone's in Council." He put the ritual items in the compartment and closed it. "These will be safe here until tonight."

Kelson was not impressed. "Suppose they find him guilty, though, Father. Suppose they already have. I can't stand by and condone his death sentence."

"If it comes to that, you must," Morgan said, squeezing the boy's shoulder reassuringly. "But remember, I'm not convicted yet. And even unarmed, a Deryni still has some formidable defenses to fall back on."

"But, Morgan—"

"No arguments, my prince," Morgan admonished, guiding the boy to the door. "You must trust that I know what I'm doing."

Kelson hung his head. "I suppose so."

Duncan slipped the bolt and eased the door open. "Here, after Compline, Alaric?"

Morgan nodded. "I'll send you word of the outcome."

"I'll know anyway," Duncan smiled. "Godspeed, Cousin."

Morgan nodded thanks and herded the reluctant Kelson through the door. As they walked through the short passage to the outer court, he heard the study door close behind him and felt the reassuring blessing which Duncan murmured. It was comforting to know that he could always count on Duncan.

Morgan and Kelson stepped into the outer sunlight and were immediately surrounded by soldiers, their weapons drawn. Kelson glared at the men, and they turned their swords away from him when they saw his identity. But Morgan was careful to keep his hands in full view, well away from his own weapons. An ill-timed sword thrust by some well-meaning but nervous guard could end Kelson's chances for survival once and for all—not to mention Morgan's own life. He noticed that Kelson stuck very close to his side, pale but determined, as Archbishop Loris strode toward them.

The Archbishop of Valoret was still in his riding clothes, his black travel cloak stained and rumpled from his long ride. But even after such a journey, and in such garb, he was not a man to be taken lightly. Though Morgan was well aware what the man had done to some of his Deryni colleagues in the north, he had to admit that Loris was one of those rare individuals who seemed to radiate that traditional aura of power and dignity which was supposed to go hand in hand with high ecclesiastical office.

The bright blue eyes glittered with the fire of the religious fanatic, the fine grey hair a wispy halo behind the proud head. His left hand clutched a roll of milky parchment affixed with several pendant seals of red and green wax. And on his right hand gleamed the amethyst signet of an ecclesiastical lord.

He bowed slightly as he approached Kelson, and made a move as though to extend his ring. But the prince pointedly ignored it. Loris withdrew his hand vexedly and glanced at Morgan, but he made no effort to extend the ring to him.

"Your Royal Highness," he said, still watching the general, "I trust you are well."

"I was quite well until you arrived, Archbishop," Kelson said tersely. "What is it you want?"

Loris bowed again and returned his full attention to Kelson. "If you had been at the Council meeting as your duty demands, you would not have to ask that question, Your Highness," Loris replied pointedly. "However, there is little to be gained by talking around the issue. I have here a warrant for the arrest of His Grace, Lord General Alaric Anthony Morgan, the Duke of Corwyn. I believe that is he in your company."

Morgan smiled lazily and folded his arms across his chest. "I believe that is more than obvious, M'lord Archbishop. If you have some business with me, I suggest you tell it to me. Don't pretend I'm not really here just because you wish I weren't."

Loris turned back to Morgan, and his eyes flashed angrily. "General Morgan, I have here a warrant from the Queen and her Lords in Council commanding you to present yourself immediately and answer to certain charges."

"I see," Morgan said quietly. "And what might those charges be, M'lord Archbishop?"

"Heresy and high treason against the King," Loris replied emphatically. "Do you contest them?"

"I do, indeed," Morgan replied. He reached for the parchment, then froze as a dozen swords were leveled at his throat. He smiled patronizingly. "May I see the warrant, M'lord?"

Loris gave a curt signal, and the soldiers lowered their weapons. Morgan took the warrant Loris extended, and glanced over it briefly, holding it so that Kelson could read over his shoulder. Then he rolled it up and returned it to Loris.

"I find your warrant in order as far as format and letter of the law," Morgan said calmly. "However, there is some dispute as to the facts as they have been set out. I shall, of course, contest the charges." He reached to his belt and removed his sword. "As the summons to appear *is* valid, however, I do lawfully comply, surrendering myself voluntarily to the jurisdiction of the Council."

He handed his sword to the surprised Archbishop, then extended his wrists. "Do you wish to bind me, too, M'lord Archbishop? Or will my word be sufficient?"

Loris drew back suspiciously, half-afraid, and his left hand clutched the pectoral cross on his chest. "Morgan, if this is some Deryni trick," he hissed, crossing himself. "I warn you . . ."

"No tricks, M'lord," Morgan stated mildly, holding his hands palm up. "I'll even surrender my back-up weapon as further evidence of my good faith."

His left wrist twitched, and there was suddenly a stiletto in his hand. Before Loris or his guards could react, he offered it to Kelson across his forearm, hilt first. "My prince?"

Without a word, Kelson took the slim dagger and thrust it grimly through his belt. Loris finally reacted.

"Now, see here, Morgan! This is not a joke, or a game. If you think you can——"

"Archbishop," Kelson interrupted, "I will not hear threats, either from you or from him. General Morgan has demonstrated his good faith, and I think it's about time you started demonstrating yours. Might I remind you that this dagger could just as easily have found its way into your chest as it did to my hand."

Loris drew himself up to full height. "He wouldn't have dared!"

Kelson shrugged. "If you say so, Archbishop. Now let's get on with this farce. I have more important things to do."

"Such as consorting with this disciple of Evil, Your Highness?" Loris hissed.

"Your definition of terms leaves much to be desired, Archbishop," Kelson retorted.

Loris forced himself to regain control, taking a deep breath. "Legal procedures have been followed to the letter, Your Highness. I do not think there is much chance of him escaping his just punishment this time."

"Words, Archbishop," Morgan said.

Loris clenched and unclenched his fists several times, then gestured to a pair of his guards. "Bind him." As the two moved to obey, pinning Morgan's arms behind him, Loris returned his attention to Kelson.

"Your Highness, I realize that you have been under considerable stress during these past weeks, and I am willing to forget the words that passed between us earlier. And if you should wish to return to your quarters and rest now, I am certain that the Council would understand under the circumstances."

Kelson fumed. "Under what circumstances, Archbishop? Do you really think I'd abandon Morgan to your mercy—or my *mother's?* And regardless of my personal feelings in the matter, I think it's rather important that the next King of Gwynedd be present at any session this important. Don't you agree, Archbishop?"

Loris' eyes flashed, but he had finally realized the folly of continuing his argument. The fact had finally sunk home that this boy before him was, indeed, the next King of Gwynedd, however unorthodox his ideas might be at present.

Loris bowed low, but there was challenge and defiance in his eyes.

"As you wish, Your Highness," was all he could be heard to murmur.

CHAPTER FIVE

O God, with your judgement endow the King,
And with your justice, the King's son.
Psalms 72:1

THE COUNCIL was in turmoil when Kelson and Morgan finally arrived.

There were several dozen men besides the Council Lords in the chamber now, for Jehana had given permission for certain other of Brion's retainers and advisors to join the Council for this final confrontation with Morgan. Extra chairs, mostly unoccupied at present, had been set up behind the regular seats on either side of the Council table. But their would-be occupants milled about in seeming confusion, arguing and discussing at the top of their voices. Though unable to vote, the newcomers had nonetheless explicit ideas on what should be done with the powerful Deryni Lord who was the topic of their conversation. Whatever feelings Lord Alaric Morgan inspired in humans, total apathy was not one of them.

At the head of the table, Jehana sat very quietly, trying to appear more composed than she felt. From time to time, she glanced down at the pale hands folded in her lap and fingered a wide, ornate gold band on her left hand.

Mostly, though, she was trying to ignore the entreaties of Bishop Arilan, to her right. She knew, from long experience, that the young prelate could be extremely persuasive, especially when he had a favorite cause to espouse. And he had made it pointedly clear where his loyalties lay during the voting earlier. Indeed, there had been few Morgan supporters more enthusiastic or vehement.

As Kelson entered the room, followed by Loris and his guards, all discussion in the room came to an abrupt halt. Those who were not already on their feet rose respectfully and bowed as Kelson passed, and all others hurriedly found their places. Kelson took his place at the foot of the table beside his Uncle Nigel, while Loris crossed slowly toward Jehana.

But neither Kelson nor Loris was to receive the major share of the attention today. For as Morgan entered, flanked by four of Loris' guardsmen, all eyes shifted immediately to follow his progress across the chamber. There were whispers and low-voiced discussions as they realized he was bound, and they exchanged suspicious glances as Morgan was placed to the right and slightly behind Kelson's chair. Kelson's face was grim as he sat down.

As the assembly took their seats, Loris bowed before Jehana, then placed the Queen's writ on the table before her. Its pendant seals tapped hollowly against the tabletop—the only sound in the still room.

"I have served the Council's writ and procured the prisoner as you commanded, Your Majesty," Loris said. He turned to an aide and took Morgan's sword. "I now present the prisoner's sword, as proof of his surrender to the just summons of the—"

"Archbishop!" Kelson's voice rang out in the hushed chamber.

Loris froze, then turned slowly toward Kelson, and all eyes followed. Kelson had risen to his feet.

"Your Highness?" Loris replied warily.

"You will bring the sword to *me*, Archbishop," Kelson said steadily. "Morgan is *my* prisoner."

Kelson's voice had taken on that crack of command which had been so much Brion's trademark, and for just an instant, Loris started to obey. Then he recovered, and cleared his throat nervously.

"Your Majesty?" he questioned, turning to Jehana for support.

Jehana looked sharply at her son. "Kelson, if you think—"

"His Excellency will bring the sword to *me*, Mother," Kelson interrupted. "By law and custom, that is my right. I am still head of this Council, if only in name."

"Very well," Jehana said, her eyes flashing angrily, "but that won't save him, you know."

"We shall see," Kelson answered enigmatically, taking his seat.

Loris took the sword to Kelson and placed it on the table with a curt bow. As he returned to his chair beside Jehana and Archbishop Corrigan, Kelson glanced aside at Morgan.

Morgan had said nothing since entering the chamber, but he had watched the exchange with approval. He kept his features impassive as the councillors settled back to await Kelson's next move, for the men sitting here in judgement would not be easy to sway. There would be no quick victory by lawful means, and right now those were the only means they dared use.

He gave a mental shrug as he eased the leather thong binding his wrists behind him. It would be interesting to see if Kelson could salvage anything from the situation.

Kelson looked around the room with only half-concealed disgust, making a steeple of his fingers the way Brion had done when he was particularly vexed. His eyes swept each face searchingly, then returned to that of his mother at the opposite end of the table.

"Nigel," he said, not taking his eyes from those of his mother, "I believe you were given strict instructions to delay the Council meeting until I could arrive. Perhaps you can explain?"

Nigel, too, stared down the table at Jehana. He was certain Kelson knew he had tried. What he said now would be solely for the benefit of the men seated around this Council table.

"Indeed, I can, Your Majesty," Nigel replied coolly. "I did try to inform the Council that you had asked for a postponement, but there were certain others who ignored that request. Her Majesty, the Queen, informed us that you were engaged in more important matters. She insisted we begin without you."

Jehana lowered her eyes as Kelson frowned.

"Is this true, Mother?"

"Of course, it's true!" Jehana snapped, jumping to her feet. "There were things to be done, Kelson—things that should have been done a long time ago. At least your Council shows some common sense. Your precious traitor Morgan was convicted by a vote of five to four!"

Kelson started to reply hotly, then thought better of it and rechose his next words. Beside him, he was aware of Morgan shifting his weight from one foot to the other, felt the edge of the general's cloak brush against his knee. He forced himself to relax and scan the tense Council again.

"Very well, my lords," Kelson said evenly. "I see that nothing I can say will change your minds at this point." Out of the corner of his eye, he was aware of Jehana taking her seat triumphantly as he continued. "I would ask one indulgence before I pass judgement in this case, however. I shall require each of you to re-cast your vote as you did before." His eyes continued to sweep the Council, slightly challenging. "As I understand it, you are questioning General Morgan's fidelity to Crown and Church. I should like to know who believes this patent lie."

Lord Rogier stood uneasily and turned to Kelson. "Are you challenging the findings of your lawful Council, Your Highness?"

"Not at all," Kelson answered promptly. "I merely wish to reassure myself that your verdict was, indeed, secured through lawful means. Come, gentlemen, we waste precious time. How say you? Is Morgan, indeed, traitor and heretic? Nigel?"

Nigel stood. "Lord Alaric is innocent of the charges, Your Majesty."

"Thank you, Uncle," Kelson nodded as Nigel took his seat. "And you, my Lord Bran?"

"Guilty, Your Highness."

"Lord Ian?"

"Guilty, Your Highness."

"And Rogier?"

"Guilty, M'lord."

Kelson frowned. "My Lord Bishop Arilan, how say you?"

"He is innocent, Your Majesty," Arilan replied confidently. He ignored the glares coming across the table from Corrigan and Loris.

"Thank you, Excellency," Kelson nodded. "And you, Ewan?"

Ewan could not look at his prince. He had never particularly disliked Morgan, but he had seen Brion die. If the rumors were true . . .

"Well, Ewan?"

"He is guilty, Your Majesty," Ewan whispered.

Kelson nodded sympathetically and then skipped over his mother to confront Archbishop Corrigan with the fatal question. There was no doubt in his mind how this prelate would react, though.

"My Lord Archbishop?"

Corrigan met Kelson's gaze levelly. "Guilty, Your Majesty. We have not yet even *begun* to list the sins of the Deryni!"

"A simple 'guilty' is sufficient, Archbishop," Kelson snapped. "The entire race is not on trial here. One man is. A man, I might add, who has done much for Gwynedd."

"Who has done much *to* Gwynedd!" Corrigan interjected.

"Enough, Archbishop!" Kelson retorted. He fixed the prelate with an icy stare, then moved on to the McLains, grateful for a few friendly faces. "Duke Jared?"

"Not guilty, Sire," the old Duke replied.

"And Lord Kevin?"

"Innocent, Your Majesty."

Kelson nodded, mentally tallying the votes. "I know that Lord Derry also voted for acquittal, so that makes —five to five." He looked down the table at his mother. "I hardly think that constitutes a conviction, Mother."

Jehana flushed. "Lord Derry was not permitted to vote, Kelson. He is not a member of this Council."

Kelson's eyes narrowed dangerously, and several of the Council Lords mentally cringed. It was the old Haldane glare they had learned to fear and respect in the boy's father. Was it possible that the boy would be able to continue in his father's footsteps? That look had meant trouble in the old days.

Kelson nodded slowly. "Very well. I had intended Derry to vote in Morgan's place in his absence, but since Morgan is here now, he can vote for himself. I think there will be no question how his vote goes."

"Morgan cannot vote!" Jehana said. "He's on trial."

"But he is still a member of the Council until convicted, Mother. Until and unless his powers and prerogatives are stripped away by lawful action, you cannot deny him his vote—especially since he was not even allowed to speak in his own behalf."

Jehana leaped to her feet, her face red with fury. "And if you cannot deny him *his* right to vote, neither can you deny me mine! Since you decided to join us and assume leadership of the Council, I am no longer so bound. And I say Morgan is guilty as charged, which brings your vote to six to five against him. Your precious Morgan is doomed, Kelson! What do you say to that?"

Stunned, Kelson sank back in his chair, his face going white as the import of his mother's words overwhelmed him. He could not look at the tall figure standing so statuelike to his right. He could not force himself to meet those grey eyes and admit defeat. Dejectedly, he let his gaze sweep the Council once more. And as his glance flicked from Derry to the empty seat beside him—Lord Ralson's empty seat—a ghost of a plan began to take shape in his mind.

He forced himself to continue his visual circuit of the room, forbidding any indication of growing hope to show on his features. He must not let them guess that he now had a plan. He had not heard the bells toll three yet, and until they did, he must stall for time whatever way he could.

He sat up and folded his hands wearily, allowing an expression of resignation to shape his features.

"My Lords," he began, letting a trace of real weariness tinge his speech, "it seems that we have lost." He gestured vaguely to include Morgan and Nigel in his "we." "I—I would beg your indulgence in one more

matter before I pronounce sentence, however. I would
request that the full charges against General Morgan
be read out first. Are there any objections?"

Jehana controlled a victorious smile and sat down
again. "Of course not, Kelson," she said, picking up
the writ and handing it across to Ewan. "Lord Ewan,
would you read the charges in their entirety?"

Ewan swallowed and nodded, then stood and
cleared his throat apologetically. "To His Grace, Lord
Alaric Anthony Morgan, Duke of Corwyn, and Lord
General of the Royal Armies. From the Queen and the
Lords in Regency Council in session this twelfth day of
the reign of Kelson Cinhil Rhys Anthony Haldane,
King of Gwynedd, Prince of Meara, and Lord of the
Purple March.

"Your Grace: You have been summoned before the
Royal Council of Gwynedd to answer to certain
charges pertinent to your behavior toward the Crown.
Namely, you . . ."

As Ewan began reading the charges, Kelson at last
risked a glance at Morgan. He had wondered all
through the proceedings why Morgan had not even at-
tempted to clear himself, but he saw now that any defense, no matter how clever or true, would have been
useless with the mood of the Council as it was today.
In all the world, there was nothing a Deryni could
have done or said to convince them of his innocence.

Now, the golden head was bowed, the grey eyes
shrouded by the thick, long lashes. And Kelson could
see at a glance that the general recognized his plight.
Even now, he was probably formulating some fantastic
escape tactic, marshalling that awesome Deryni power
to regain his freedom—that freedom which must be
maintained at all costs if he was to be of any help to
his young king. Of course, he could not know that Kelson had a plan.

Kelson realized he now had a double deadline to

work against. For if Morgan made his move before Kelson could make his—and Kelson could not until the bells tolled out the hour—then all hope for a lawful settlement of the matter was lost.

Gingerly, Kelson eased his booted toe to the side, managed to bring it to within inches of Morgan's near foot. Then, as Ewan began the closing of the writ, Kelson shifted in his chair, at the same time nudging Morgan's boot with his.

Morgan glanced at the boy, saw an almost imperceptible shake of the head, and nodded. The boy had a plan. He would let him try.

". . . set before me this day, *Jehana Regina et Domini Consilium.*" Ewan's voice rumbled to a halt and he sat down expectantly. But even as he sat, basilica and cathedral bells began tolling out the hour.

One. Two. Three. Four.

Kelson listened as the bells tolled, and mentally kicked himself when he heard the fourth hour struck. Four in the afternoon. He had been waiting for three, and it was already long past. He could have been acting long ago.

Silently, he stood at his place, still allowing no inkling of what he was about to do to show on his face.

"My Lords, Your Majesty," he began formally, bowing slightly toward his mother, "we have heard the charges against our general." He saw Jehana's sudden suspicious expression as she caught the royal "we."

He gestured toward Morgan with his right hand as he continued. "We have also heard the wishes—indeed, the demands—of the Council in this matter. However, it pleases us to consider one further item of business before pronouncing judgement on him."

There was a murmur of question which rippled through the assembly, and Kelson caught his mother's ill-masked look of surprise and fearful anticipation.

"It has occurred to us," Kelson continued in the

same conversational tone, "that our ranks have recently been saddened by the loss of our good and loyal servant, Lord Ralson of Evering." He gestured toward Ralson's empty chair, then crossed himself piously. The rest of the assembly followed suit, wondering curiously what he was about.

"Therefore," Kelson continued, "we have decided to appoint a new Council Lord to fill his place."

"You can't do that!" Jehana shouted, jumping to her feet.

"We are aware, of course," Kelson went on, his voice cutting through Jehana's opposition, "that Lord Derry can never replace Lord Ralson, but we are certain he will bring his own measure of devotion to that honored post. Sean Lord Derry."

As the Council erupted with dissention, Kelson signalled Derry to rise. The young man glanced aside at Morgan for reassurance, but even Morgan looked a bit startled.

Kelson held up his hands for silence, then pounded the table with the hilt of Morgan's sword as the din continued. Jehana stood defiantly at the other end of the table, trying to make herself heard above the discord.

"Kelson, you can't do this!" she shouted, finally able to top the volume of the dying discussion around her. "You have no right! You *know* you can't appoint a new Councillor without the approval of the Regents. You're not of age!"

Kelson's eyes went cold and steely grey as he glared down the table, and the room was suddenly hushed.

"Lords of the Council, my esteemed mother has apparently forgotten that it was precisely fourteen years and one hour ago, in another room of this very palace, that she brought into this world a son: Kelson Cinhil Rhys Anthony Haldane; that as her labor ended, the royal physicians placed me in her arms—and the bells tolled three in the afternoon!"

Jehana's face went ashen and she sank back in her chair, nodding slowly to herself, her eyes glazed, stunned.

"And you, my Lords: the reason for our Coronation tomorrow instead of today has apparently slipped your minds, also. As you are well aware, royal writ decrees that no King of Gwynedd shall be crowned in his own right until he has fully reached legal age. Since I was not due to reach that legal age until three this afternoon—too late for a Coronation, you must admit—the ceremony was scheduled for tomorrow. But I rule today!"

No one moved or spoke as Kelson finished his speech. They simply watched, dumbstruck, as Kelson motioned Derry to approach him. As Derry reached his side, Kelson picked up Morgan's sword and held it in front of Derry, hilt uppermost.

"Sean Lord Derry, do you swear by this cross that you will render true and loyal service in this Royal Council?"

Derry dropped to one knee and placed his hand on the hilt of the sword. "I do solemnly swear it, my Liege."

Kelson lowered the sword, and Derry got to his feet.

"And how say you in the matter now at hand, my Lord Derry?" Kelson asked. "Is Morgan guilty, or no?"

Derry glanced triumphantly at Morgan, then faced Kelson. His voice was clear and steady. "Lord Alaric is innocent, Your Majesty!"

"Innocent," Kelson repeated, savoring the word. "Which brings us to a vote of six to six—another tie vote." He looked at his mother, who still had not moved from her huddled position in her chair. "I hereby declare Lord Alaric Anthony Morgan, Duke of

Corwyn and Lord General of the Royal Armies, innocent of the charges which have been set out against him. If after tomorrow anyone wishes to reopen proceedings, and can produce definite proof, I will entertain such action. In the meantime, this Council stands adjourned."

With that, he whipped Morgan's dagger from his belt and cut the general's bonds. Then, after returning Morgan's sword, he bowed curtly to the stunned Council and swept out of the chamber, Morgan and Derry at his heels.

Silence persisted only until the doors had closed behind Kelson and his colleagues. Then the room erupted into loud discussion and argument. There was no doubt that what Kelson had done was legal, but it had been a totally unexpected coup. To the assembled Council Lords and other noblemen, it had been a feat worthy of Brion at his very best and most cunning. There were mixed emotions as to whether that was a good thing or not, for there had been many who had chafed under Brion's rule.

There was no ambivalence in Jehana, though. For her, what had started out as a certain victory against the impetuous Deryni had become a shambles, a resounding defeat of everything she had hoped for Kelson.

Her nails punched little half-moon depressions in the palms of her hands as she clenched and unclenched her fists in dismay.

Morgan was free.

And worse, Kelson had stood before the Council and defied her—not with childish threats and impotent taunts, but with decisive, adult action. It was a development Jehana had not been prepared for, and it bothered her even more, perhaps, than Morgan's freedom. If only Kelson had shown some indecision, some sign of doubt in the proud Deryni he defended so avidly, there might have been a chance she could still get through to him. But now that Kelson was King in fact as well as in name—a development she hadn't even considered before—how could she possibly lure him away from Morgan's evil influence?

From across the room, Ian watched the confusion with interest. It was difficult to form any concrete conclusions in the chaos following Kelson's stormy exit, but Ian had the distinct impression that the boy had scored points with more than one of the Lords who had opposed him earlier. Even Rogier and Bran Coris' outraged comments were tinged with a healthy portion of respect. And that would never do. Though Ian had been forced to concede this particular encounter to Kelson and the proud Deryni half-breed, he had no intention of losing the entire war.

In truth, Ian had never really expected to win this round. He had suspected when Morgan entered the chamber in custody that the man had some plan in mind. Morgan would never have allowed himself to be taken if there had been the slightest doubt that he could escape where and when he chose.

But he didn't think the encounter had gone precisely the way the general had expected. He was almost certain that Kelson's coup had been a spur of the moment affair. For surely, even this precocious boy-king could not have seriously expected to find so pat an escape clause, to have Morgan legally walk out a free man.

Yes, there was no doubt about it. Kelson had not acted according to prediction, and that bore closer watching. It would never do to underestimate Brion's son at this late date. And in the meantime, there was much to be done. With Morgan once again a free agent, it would not hurt to continue blackening the already infamous name—a pursuit Ian frankly relished. And Charissa must be informed of the afternoon's momentous turn of events.

Taking leave of Bran Coris and Rogier, Ian slipped out of the noisy Council chamber and proceeded toward the barracks area of the palace compound. He had a pretty piece of work ahead of him this afternoon, and there was no sense in delaying.

Morgan clapped his hands together with glee as he, Kelson, and Derry hurried across the inner courtyard toward the royal apartments.

"Kelson, you were magnificent!" he said, throwing an affectionate arm around the boy's shoulders. "Your performance in there was worthy of Brion at his very best. I think you even took *me* by surprise."

"Did I really?" Kelson asked delightedly. He was grinning from ear to ear as he glanced behind to see if they were being followed, and then he had to skip a few steps to catch up again. Several guards *had* been watching them rather curiously, but as far as he could tell, there was no one headed in their direction.

"I don't know about you," the boy continued, "but I was terrified the entire time. I nearly had heart failure when the bells tolled four instead of three."

Morgan snorted. "Be glad it wasn't the other way around. Think how foolish you would have looked if the bells had tolled only *two*."

Kelson rolled his eyes. "I thought of that."

"And another thing," Morgan continued. "Not to belittle Derry's new appointment, but once you declared yourself of age, you didn't have to go through all that hocus-pocus of appointing a new Council Lord and retallying the vote. You could simply have overruled them."

"I know," Kelson replied. "But it's a bit of a facesaver for them, don't you think? I mean, at least they can't say I dictated an arbitrary decision in this case. We stayed within regular legislative channels."

"A prudent move," Morgan agreed. "And all in all,

I'd say there was enough excitement to suit even my tastes. Living dangerously is a very good thing, but—"

"If you ask me," Derry interrupted, "I could've done with a lot less excitement, M'lord. I would've been perfectly happy to know in advance that everything was going to turn out all right."

Kelson laughed as they started up the stairs to his apartments. "I'm afraid I have to agree with Derry. I wasn't exactly the most confident I've ever been." He glanced aside at Morgan. "By the way, don't you think we ought to get word to Father Duncan? You did promise to let him know what happened."

"So I did," Morgan nodded. "Derry, would you mind going to Saint Hilary's and telling Duncan what's happened? Tell him we're all right, but that we're going to try to get some sleep the rest of the afternoon."

"Aye, M'lord," Derry said. "Shall I come back here when I'm finished?"

Morgan nodded. "But get some rest, too. I'll want you to command the guard outside Kelson's apartments through the night, if you don't mind. I know I can trust you."

"I hear and obey, M'lord," Derry replied with a grin. "And do try to stay alive until I can get back to guard you."

Morgan could only smile and shake his head as Derry disappeared from view.

Ian had nearly reached his destination deep in the heart of the palace. Down several flights of stairs, through a wide subterranean vault used as a training area for swordplay, through the corridor skirting the armory and beyond to the storage area he sped, his catlike tread smooth and silent on the cold stone flooring. His eyes glittered dark and dangerous as he passed guard post after guard post, always unchallenged. Ian was known here.

He finally came to a halt just before the intersection of another minor corridor and rested his hand on the hilt of his sword to silence it, then inched his way forward until he could peek around the corner.

Good. The guard was there, just as Ian had hoped he would be.

Smiling grimly to himself, he slipped around the corner and glided up to the guard. The man did not see him until he was already alongside, no more than two feet away, and he started.

"M'lord! Is anything wrong?"

"No, of course not," Ian replied, raising one slim eyebrow in feigned innocence. "Should there be?"

The guard relaxed slightly, then grinned. "No, M'lord," he replied rather sheepishly. "It's just that you startled me. People don't generally come down this far unless there *is* something wrong."

Ian smiled. "No, I don't suppose they do," he said, raising his right hand and extending a forefinger in front of the man's eyes. "What's your name, guard?"

The man's eyes moved involuntarily to the finger, and he stammered slightly. "Michael DeForest, M'lord."

"Michael DeForest," Ian nodded, slowly moving his finger toward the man's face. "Do you see my finger, Michael?"

"A—aye, M'lord," Michael stammered. His eyes followed the finger as it approached, unable to break their stare. "M'lord, I—what are you doing?"

"Just follow my finger, Michael," Ian murmured, his voice low and slightly menacing in the stillness, "and you will go—to—sleep."

As he spoke the last word "sleep," his forefinger touched the man's forehead lightly between the eyes, and the eyes fluttered closed. A low muttered phrase deepened the trance, and then Ian reached out calmly and removed the man's spear from his hand, resting it against the wall.

After glancing around to be sure no one had approached in the meantime, he backed the man a few paces so that he, too, stood against the wall. Then he placed his fingertips on the man's temples and closed his eyes.

Presently, a pale blue aura began to crackle around Ian, gradually extending itself from his head, down his body and legs, along his arms and into his hands. Nor did it stop there, but continued to engulf the head of the guard. As the sparkling net of light touched the man's head, he shuddered, as though to make one last effort to break away from the unholy bond which was being formed, then relaxed as the aura extended itself over the rest of his body. When both men were engulfed in the pale fire, Ian spoke.

"Charissa?"

There was no sound but the breathing of the two men for a moment: Ian's light and controlled; the guard's quick, shallow, labored. Then the man's lips began to tremble.

"Charissa, do you hear me?"

The man's voice whispered, "I hear."

Ian smiled slightly and he spoke again in a low, conversational tone, his eyes still closed. "Good. I'm afraid I have some disappointing news, my love. Our Council ploy failed, as expected. Kelson declared himself of age, appointed a new Council Lord to fill Ralson's place, then broke the ensuing tie by royal prerogative. There was nothing I could do. And I'm sure you know the Stenrect attempt was unsuccessful."

"I heard it die," the man's voice replied. "What of Morgan now?"

Ian pursed his lips wistfully. "I'm not sure. He and Kelson have gone off to Kelson's apartments for the night. Our young princeling appears to be taking no chances of anything else happening to his champion. But just so they don't get into any mischief, I've a few diversionary tactics planned which should occupy some of their valuable time and energy between now and tomorrow morning. Agreed?"

"Very well," the man's voice whispered.

"Aren't you even going to ask what I have in mind?" Ian persisted.

For the first time, there was a trace of emotion in the man's voice as Charissa answered. "You'd like that, wouldn't you?" There was an edge of sarcasm to the question. "Another chance to boast of your cleverness, no doubt." There was a pause. "No matter. If you have things to do, you'd best end this communication before you tire yourself and drain your subject beyond recovery. He can't keep this up forever, you know."

Ian smiled once more. "As you wish, my pet," he said calmly, "though I don't really think your concern will help our medium, here. I have special plans for him. Good hunting, Charissa."

"And you," the voice replied.

With that, the light surrounding Ian and the guard died, and Ian dropped his hands to his sides, shook his head slightly as he opened his eyes. His subject slumped slightly against the wall as he was released, but still could not seem to force his eyes to stay open. Ian still maintained control.

Ian glanced around again, then took the man's arm and guided him back to his post.

"M'lord, I—," the man mumbled, shaking his head to try to clear it. "What's happened? What are you . . . ?"

"Never mind, Michael," Ian replied, reaching down to his boot top and withdrawing a slim dagger. "You'll hardly feel a thing."

As the man saw the flash of steel, he mustered his last remaining strength, struggled weakly to pull away from Ian's grip. But it was no use. His resistance was gone. Dumbly, he stood where Ian placed him, watched helplessly as the gleaming blade approached.

With clinical detachment, Ian opened the front of the man's mail-lined leather jerkin and placed the point of his dagger against the man's chest, just left of center. Then he slipped the blade home with a lightning thrust, sliding the blade deftly between two ribs to pierce the heart.

As Ian withdrew the weapon, the man's eyes glazed and he sank to the floor with a stifled moan. Blood gushed crimson from the wound, running down his side to form an ever widening pool beside him. But still the heart continued to beat, the tortured lungs pumped air to prolong the agony.

Ian frowned as he crouched down beside the dying man. It had not been a clean kill—a mistake Morgan would never have made. And worse, now he would have to finish the man on the ground.

He chewed his lip thoughtfully as he studied the man, then quickly reinserted his dagger in the original wound and gave it a precise twist. This time when he withdrew the blade, the heart stopped. The lungs ceased their heaving. The man was dead.

With a grunt of satisfaction, Ian wiped his dagger clean on the edge of the man's cloak, then turned the body slightly on its side, being careful not to disturb the widening pool of blood. Then, taking the man's hand in his, he dipped the dead fingers in the blood and smeared a rough outline on the clean stone by the man's head—the outline of a gryphon.

He stood to survey his work and nodded approvingly, slipping his dagger back into its boot sheath as he checked his clothing for any telltale signs of the deed he had just done. Then he placed the dead guard's spear alongside the body, surveyed the scene a final time, and turned to make his way away from there.

Now, if some of Morgan's vassals should just happen to stumble onto the murder later that night, there was little doubt in Ian's mind what they would think. A cold-blooded murder, on top of all the other accusations against the Deryni general, should be all that was necessary to trigger the men to rebel against their liege lord. And Ian would be sure that the men found the corpse.

And if Kelson should also fall in the ensuing scuffle? Ian shrugged contentedly. Ah, how very unfortunate.

CHAPTER SIX

And a voice shall speak from legend.

As THE VESPER chimes finished their pealing in the distance, Morgan awoke with a start, simultaneously aware of the place, the time—much later than he had planned—and the fact that he was cold. The fire before him had burned down to nothing but embers, and a glance to the left confirmed his suspicion both that the balcony doors were still open and that a storm was brewing. No wonder the room was freezing.

With a low grunt, he heaved himself out of the overstuffed chair which had been his bed for the past three hours and half-staggered to the balcony doors. It was very quiet outside, and quite dark for so early in the evening, the air heavy, oppressive, charged with the energy of the coming storm. It would undoubtedly rain, and possibly snow, before midnight—which was just about what one might expect of a night in which he obviously had so much to do.

Wearily, Morgan closed the glass-paned doors,

paused for a moment with his hands on the latch, his forehead against the doors, eyes closed.

He was so tired—God! how tired he was! The bone-weariness of a week's hard ride, the afternoon's tension, had hardly been dented by the few hours' sleep he'd had. And there was still so much to be done, so little time. Even now, he should be downstairs in Brion's library, searching for some clue which might make tonight's task a little more bearable.

It wasn't really that he expected to find anything. Brion had been much too cautious to leave anything of major import lying around where just anyone might stumble onto it. But there might be some small telltale sign. He had to look. And before he could do anything, he must see to Kelson's safety while he was gone.

Straightening with an effort, he stared for a moment at the closed doors before him, as though gathering his strength, then rubbed his left hand lightly across his eyes, willing the weariness to vanish. The ploy worked, as usual, though Morgan realized he couldn't keep it up indefinitely. Sooner or later, he would have to get some sleep, or he'd be no good to anyone. Perhaps tonight, after they were finished.

He pulled heavy blue satin drapes across the double doors, then crossed briskly back to the fireplace and added wood to the fire. After a few minutes, when it was blazing strongly again, he scanned the room in the dim firelight, finally spotting what he searched for.

Over against the wall by the door, he saw his black saddlebags, brought up by Derry after the Council meeting. He dragged the saddlebags over by the fire and hastily unbuckled the clasp of the lighter side, felt the smooth whorls of intricately tooled leather beneath his finger as he opened the pouch.

Now, if Derry had just put them back where he'd found them—he simply couldn't convince the young

Marcher lord that the cubes were not just a strange dice game.

Aha!

A brief forage in the bottom of the pouch produced the familiar shape of the red leather case, the reassuring rattle of contents still in place.

Without a second glance, Morgan dropped the case on the chair, then crossed to Kelson's wardrobe closet and began searching for something that would fit him. He was still cold. And if he was going to go galavanting about the palace in this weather, he was determined not to do it in misery.

Finally, he found a blue wool robe with fur-lined collar and cuffs that looked as though it would fit, and he shrugged it on as he returned to the fireplace. The sleeves ended at mid-forearm, and the robe reached only to his knees, but he decided that it would suffice for his purposes.

From the mantle, he took a candlestick with a fat yellow candle in it, lit it from the fire, then scooped up the red leather case and crossed to Kelson's bed.

Kelson still slept soundly, sprawled diagonally across the wide bed on his stomach, his face nestled in the crook of his left arm. There were extra blankets at the foot of the bed, and Morgan gently eased one from beneath the boy's stockinged feet. Putting the candlestick and red leather case on the floor beside the bed, he shook out the blanket and draped it across the sleeping form. Then he knelt down beside the bed and opened the red leather case, shaking out the contents on the spread.

There were eight cubes in all—"wards" in the terminology of the professional wielder of magic—four white and four black, each no larger than the end of his little finger. Deftly, he arranged the cubes in the proper pattern: four white in a square at the center, one black at each of the four corners, but not touching. Then, beginning with the white cube in the upper left-hand corner, he began touching each one, at the same time softly speaking its defensive position in the master ward he was building.

"*Prime.*" The first white cube glowed softly.

"*Seconde.*" He touched the upper right cube, and it, too, winked to milky brilliance.

"*Tierce. Quarte.*" The remaining white cubes lit, forming a single white square which glowed with a ghostly white light.

Next, the black: "*Quinte. Sixte. Septime. Octave.*" The black cubes glowed faintly with a green-black fire deep within.

Now came the real effort: the joining of black and white cubes to complete the master ward; the ward which, once set in place around the sleeping Kelson, would protect the boy from any possibility of harm.

Morgan wiped the palms of his hands against the spread to either side of the black and white pattern he had set up, then picked up prime. Gingerly, he touched it to quinte, its black component.

"*Primus!*"

There was a muffled click, and then the two cubes merged into a single oblong unit which glowed silvery-grey in the candlelight.

Morgan ran his tongue nervously across his lips and picked up Seconde, mated it to Sixte.

"*Secundus!*"

Again, the click, the silver glow.

He inhaled and exhaled slowly, gathering his strength for the next sequence. The procedure was draining much of his already depleted power reserve, but he had no choice but to continue if he wished to search the library. He couldn't leave Kelson unprotected. He picked up Tierce and touched it to Septime.

"*Tertius!*"

As the coupling glowed, Kelson stirred, then opened his eyes with a start.

"What the—Morgan, what are you doing?" He raised up on both elbows and leaned toward the cubes, then looked up at Morgan.

Morgan raised one eyebrow in surprise, then rested his chin against one hand in resignation. "I thought you were asleep," he said accusingly.

Kelson blinked at him in amazement for an instant, still not quite fully awake. Tentatively, he reached his left hand toward the remaining cubes.

"Don't touch!" Morgan commanded, blocking Kelson's touch with an outstretched hand. "Just watch."

With a deep breath, he brought the remaining two cubes gently together.

"Quartus!"

Then he placed the resulting unit with the other three and sighed.

"Now," he said, looking across at Kelson once more, "why are you awake?"

Kelson rolled over and sat up. "I heard you mumbling Latin in my ear. What are these things, anyway?" He eyed the four glowing oblongs suspiciously.

"They're components of a Ward Major," Morgan said, climbing to his feet. "I have to go out for a while, and I didn't want to leave you unprotected. Once the wards are set, only I can break them. You'll be perfectly safe."

He reached down and picked up the units, stretched across the bed to place one at each of the far corners, the remaining two on the near corners.

"Wait a minute," Kelson said, beginning to inch toward the edge of the bed. "Where are you going? I'll come with you."

"You'll do nothing of the kind," Morgan said, pushing the boy back on the pillow. "You're going back to sleep, and I'm going down to your father's library to hunt for clues. Believe me, if there were any way, I'd still be asleep, too. You're going to need all the rest you can get before this night is over."

"But, I could help you," Kelson protested weakly, as though surprised to find himself lying down again. "Besides, I couldn't possibly get back to sleep now."

"Oh, I think that can be arranged," Morgan smiled, placing his hand lightly on the boy's forehead. "Just relax now, Kelson. Relax and dream. Forget about the dangers. Forget about the fears. Relax. Sleep. Dream of better times. Sleep deep, my prince. Sleep safe."

As he spoke, Kelson's eyelids fluttered briefly, then closed, and his breathing slowed to that of profound slumber. Morgan smiled and smoothed the tousled black hair, then straightened and pointed in succession to the wards.

"Primus, secundus, tertius, et quartus, fiat lux!"

Instantly, the wards blazed with a new life, then flared around the sleeping Kelson with a cocoon of misty luminescence. Morgan nodded to himself, then made his way toward the door.

Now, for some useful information. . . .

Half an hour later in the library, Morgan had not met with any success. He had gone through virtually every book in Brion's private collection, and most of the general references in the section, but all had been fruitless.

If only he could find some clue: a significant marked passage, some notes from when Brion concocted the ritual verse, some hint as to how the problem should be approached. It was, of course, possible that they would be able to figure it out without help. But he hated to be less than one hundred percent certain on something this important.

Because the ritual verse *had* to work. If it didn't, Kelson was doomed, and Morgan and Duncan with him. Nor was it possible for Morgan or Duncan to do

Kelson's fighting for him. Occult practice simply would not permit it.

If only he could remember more about Brion's reading habits, that might give him some idea of where to look. He knew that there had to be a link somewhere, that Brion must have left something, if only as a reassurance for the friend he had known would come looking for such a thing. Perhaps the clue was in the verse itself.

Wearily, he sat down at Brion's reading desk and propped himself up on his elbows. Somewhere he would find the clue—he knew it must exist.

As his eyes scanned the room once more, the gryphon seal on his left forefinger caught his attention. He had read once of a Deryni Lord who had used a similar ring as a point of focus for deep concentration— the Thuryn technique, named for Rhys Thuryn, who had first made it a part of the Deryni arsenal. Morgan had used the technique several times before, though never for something like this. But it had worked well then. Perhaps it would work again.

Focusing all his attention on the ring, Morgan began to concentrate, willing his mind to put aside all outside worries and relax, to shut out superfluous sounds, sights, sensations. As his eyes drifted closed, his breathing slowed, became more shallow. His tense fingers relaxed.

As he concentrated on keeping his mind clear, he permitted an image of Brion's face to form in his thoughts, tried to put himself into that image, to fathom what had been there concerning what he now sought.

Suddenly, the image of Brion winked out of existence, to be replaced by a swirling blackness, dizziness. There was a fleeting impression of a man's face surrounded by a black cowl, strange, yet hauntingly familiar, a feeling both of urgency and reassurance—and

then the moment was past. Then, there was nothing
but a stunned young man sitting rather foolishly at a
desk in a library with his eyes closed.

Morgan opened his eyes abruptly and glanced
around, but there was no one else in the room.

Khadasa! the picture had been real while it lasted.
He'd never achieved an effect like that before from
using the Thuryn technique. And he couldn't for the
life of him recall ever having seen the strange face before. So much for the Thuryn technique for today.

Absently, he went back to the shelf containing
Brion's personal collection of favorite books and
pulled one out at random.

"Talbot's *Lives of the Saints*," he read, half out loud.

He flipped idly through its worn pages until it suddenly fell open to a place marked by a slip of parchment. There was writing on the parchment, in Brion's
hand, too, but that fact was completely overshadowed
by the impact of the open pages it marked. For on the
left, in full color, was a portrait of the face Morgan
had seen in his vision.

Apprehensively, he bent closer to read the name beneath the portrait, squinted as he held the book toward
the candlelight and read: "Saint Camber of Culdi, Patron of Deryni Magic."

Morgan glanced nervously behind him as he lowered
the book. It was impossible, and yet—this was the face
he'd seen while in the Thuryn trance. There was no
doubt about that.

Preposterous. He didn't believe in saints—or at
least, he didn't think he did. After all, Camber had
been dead for nearly two hundred years, and his sainthood recalled, to boot.

But what had made him think of Camber at precisely that moment? Had Brion once said something
about the renegade saint which somehow stuck in his
mind, remaining there, dormant, all these years until

the time it should be recalled by just such a chain of events as this? Question: What did he really know about Saint Camber of Culdi? Answer: Not very much. It simply hadn't been useful knowledge until now.

Irritatedly, because he realized he should remember more, Morgan picked up the volume and moved himself closer to the candlelight, absently pocketing the scrap of parchment. He read:

Saint Camber of Culdi, 846-905(?). Legendary Earl of Culdi, a full Deryni Lord, who lived during the Deryni Interregnum. Toward the end of the Interregnum, Camber discovered that under certain controlled conditions, in select individuals, the full scope of Deryni power could be acquired by humans. He it was who assisted the heirs of the old human rulers to acquire this power, and later led the revolt which crushed the Deryni Interregnum for good.

Morgan turned the page impatiently. He knew all of this already. It was common knowledge from general history. Now he needed facts concerning Camber's sainthood, or something which might explain what had happened to him a few minutes ago. He read on:

Now, in those days, there was more tolerance for the occult arts. And in gratitude for what the Culdi had done for humankind, the Council of Bishops proclaimed him a saint. But it was not to last. About fifteen years later, there was a bloody persecution of things and persons Deryni. And shortly, the name of Camber of Culdi was stricken from the rolls of the blessed. At the Council of Ramos, a number of the previous Council's edicts were reversed. And with them went the Culdi's sainthood.

Camber had been revered as the patron of occult arts, the defender of humankind. But when the Council of Ramos repudiated Camber, they declared all occult practice anathema. Camber's name became a symbol of evil personified. Every atrocity ever committed by the Lords of the Interregnum was ascribed to the former Deryni saint, and the people ceased to mention his name except to curse him.

Some controversy over Camber's reputation has died out over the years. It is difficult to maintain a lie for two hundred years. But rumors persist to feed the fire: that Camber's alleged death in 905 never occurred, that he went into hiding, to wait for a chance to reappear and again work his deeds of magic. The truth of this allegation is not known, nor is it likely to be discovered in the near future. It is known that a handful of high Deryni Lords do remain, and that magic, however outlawed, is still practiced among them. But it is highly improbable that Camber is still among them— even a Deryni could hardly be functioning after more than two hundred years. Yet the rumors persist. And the few Deryni alive who might know the truth about Camber of Culdi do not comment.

As Morgan finished the passage, he turned the page back to look again at the portrait. Camber of Culdi. Amazing. Now he was certain he'd never seen this portrait before. Nor had he read this particular account of Saint Camber. He was sure he would have remembered, for nothing he had read previously had gone into such detail.

But what had he actually learned from the passage? And how did it apply to his present dilemma? And why did that face on the page there still seem so hauntingly familiar, even though he was certain he'd never seen it before?

As he closed the volume, he heard the sound of the library door opening softly behind him. He turned carefully, catching a glimpse of someone in grey gliding into the room from the outside corridor.

It was a woman. And as she turned toward the door

to close it gently behind her, he could see that it was
—Charissa!

He smiled complacently and settled back in his chair
to see how long it would take her to discover his presence, watching her glance around the room and see the
faint glow of his candle streaming around the corner.

"Good evening, Charissa," he said softly, not moving from where he sat. "Are you looking for someone,
or something?"

Charissa started, covered her surprise, and walked
cautiously around the corner of the aisle to confront
Morgan. Morgan nodded greeting as she stepped into
the candlelight, but Charissa was not amused.

"What are you doing here?" she asked, her voice
low, strained in the hush.

Morgan stood up casually, made an elaborate show
of stretching and restraining a yawn. "I was just looking for something to read, if you really must know. In
spite of the fact that I should be tired from the trials
you've given me during the past few days, I found I
couldn't sleep. Isn't that strange?"

"Decidedly so," she answered carefully, her moment
of uncertainty past now. "But what makes you think I
have anything to do with your insomnia?"

Morgan held up a protesting hand. "Oh, not my insomnia, my dear. My fatigue. I have a rather good
idea what you've been up to: telling nasty stories about
me, turning the Council Lords against me, having my
escort ambushed on the way here. I suspect you even
had a hand in Brion's death. Of course, I can't prove
anything yet," he gestured depreciatingly.

Charissa's eyes narrowed as she studied him, trying
to ascertain the proper proportion of bluff and boast.

"I think you'll have a difficult time gathering evidence
to support such allegations, my dear Morgan. And I
think that if you ask, you'll find that all these things
you've accused me of have been ascribed to you."

Morgan shrugged noncommittally.

"And as for the charge that I had anything to do with Brion's death," Charissa continued, "why, that's preposterous. Everyone knows he died of a heart attack."

"I don't know that," Morgan replied tersely. "I know nothing of the kind. I do know that one of his entourage was given a flask of wine that morning of the hunt. Very strange, but he described the donor as a beautiful lady with pale hair. And only Brion and Colin drank from that flask."

"So?" Charissa retorted. "Are you accusing me of poisoning Brion? Come, now. You can do better than that."

"I intend to," Morgan answered. "I also happen to know that you developed the *merasha* mind-muddling drug a few years ago, and that the drug affects only those of Deryni blood or Deryni powers, like Brion."

"Really, Morgan, you're fishing."

"Am I? You knew Brion was vulnerable in this way, that being mortal, he wouldn't be able to detect the drug in his system until it was too late." He stood straighter, loomed tall and menacing as he glared down at her. "Why didn't you call him out in honorable combat, Charissa? You might have won. He was mortal, after all."

"And risk my reputation, my powers, against a mere mortal, in an unnecessary duel with a human?"

"You're planning to duel with a 'mere human' tomorrow, aren't you?"

She smiled a slow, lazy smile. "Yes, but that's different. I cannot lose with Kelson. He's but a boy, unskilled in his father's trade. And you won't be able to help him as you did his father fifteen years ago."

"Don't be too certain," Morgan retorted. "There is much of his father in him. And unlike his father, I am here this time to see that you don't resort to treachery."

"Why, Morgan, what a thing to say. Do you really think I'd bother? Of course, I did peek in on your precious princeling a little earlier this evening. . . ."

Morgan came to full attention. "He's safe from you this time. Tonight, all the powers in the universe couldn't have broken my defenses."

"That is probably true," she conceded. "You set your wards most effectively. In fact, even I was impressed with your skill. I had thought a half-breed Deryni incapable of such highly developed expertise."

Morgan forced himself to control his rising anger. "Having a goal helps immensely, Charissa. I'm determined you won't succeed with *this* Haldane."

"Why, that sounds almost like a challenge, my little Morgan," Charissa murmured archly. "That's heartening, at least." She glanced at her nails. "Well, you can depend on an energetic battle tomorrow—maybe even tonight. And I warn you in advance: there will be no quarter, no mercy." Her eyes narrowed. "I intend to make you pay for what you did to my father. And I'll do it by destroying the ones you love best, one at a time, slowly. And there is nothing, dear Morgan, nothing at all that you can do about it."

Morgan was silent for a long moment as he glared at the incredibly beautiful and evil woman in grey. "We'll see," he finally whispered. "We'll see."

As he headed slowly for the door, watching her every flicker of an eyelash, every rustle of her gown, she smiled languidly. "Take me at my word, Morgan. No quarter. And that being the case, I suggest you look to your prince. He may need you very shortly."

Morgan slowly opened the door and went through, never taking his eyes from the terrible woman in grey. When the door had finally closed behind him, Charissa walked slowly over to where Morgan had been sitting, then picked up the book he had been reading.

Casually, she flipped through the pages.

Lives of the Saints.

Now, what possible interest could Morgan have had in a book like this?

Nothing came to her, and she frowned. Morgan had been looking at this book for a reason. Of that, she was certain. But why?

The book didn't fit the pattern. It wasn't within the elements she'd predicted for Morgan's actions, and that bothered her.

Charissa did not like it when things did not go exactly her way.

CHAPTER SEVEN

"A Spokesman of the Infinite must guide. . . ."

As MORGAN APPROACHED Kelson's quarters, he felt a twinge of dread. What if Charissa had been bluffing, had somehow found a way to get at Kelson through the wards? Suppose she had killed him?

Derry was commanding the guard tonight, and he glided up beside Morgan as the general reached Kelson's door.

"Anything wrong, M'lord?"

"I don't know yet," Morgan said in a low voice, signalling the two regular guards to stand aside. "Did you see anyone while I was gone?"

"No, sir. I have this entire wing sealed off." He watched as Morgan put his hand on the door latch. "Do you want me to come with you, M'lord?"

Morgan shook his head. "It isn't necessary."

Stealthily, he eased the door open just enough to slip through, then closed it gently behind him. He stood with his back to the door while he slipped the bolt into place, trying at the same time to peer across the darkened room and see if Kelson was safe.

He need not have worried. For his wards were, as he had boasted, impervious to almost any power in the universe tonight. As he approached the royal bed, he was able to discern the faint protective aura still glowing around his young lord. And he could sense the boy's undisturbed sleep patterns on the very surface of his awareness if he concentrated.

But he did not. It was enough that the boy was safe. Wearily, he sank into the deep chair before the fireplace and shifted some of the logs with an ornate poker. When the blaze had been stabilized once more, he rose catlike and stretched.

The bells would be ringing Compline soon, and he and Kelson still had a short journey ahead of them. He didn't want to have to hurry. Haste led to carelessness, and that was a luxury they could ill afford tonight.

He shrugged out of his woolen robe and draped it over the chair, then slung his own heavy cloak around his shoulders once more. The clasp snicked shut with a satisfying clink of metal against metal as he crossed to kneel at Kelson's bedside. The fat yellow candle he had left on the floor there still flickered its pale light over the sleeping form.

Morgan allowed himself a feeling of satisfaction as he glanced over his Ward Major, for it had served him well tonight. He would not be able to use it again for some weeks, as the cubes must be recharged, but that was no matter. He had had the use of its protection when he needed it most. And he didn't intend to leave Kelson alone for even a minute until after the coronation tomorrow.

Standing up, he spread his hands over the sleeping prince, palms up, and began murmuring a counterspell, slowly turning his hands palms down as he finished the verse. As he did, the glow of the wards slowly diminished to nothing and the cubes died. Then there were but eight tiny cubes, four white and four black, cast like strange dice, a pair at each corner of the bed.

As Morgan reached across to retrieve the cubes, Kelson opened his eyes and looked around.

"I must have fallen asleep," he said, raising to one elbow. "Is it time?"

Morgan smiled and put the remaining cubes into their red leather case. "Almost," he replied, picking up the candlestick and returning to the fireplace. "Did you sleep well?"

Kelson sat up and rubbed his eyes, then rose and padded over to join Morgan by the fire. "I suppose so. I certainly would like to know how you did that, though."

"Did what, my prince?" Morgan queried absently as he sank back down in his chair by the fire.

"Made me go to sleep, of course," the boy answered. He plopped down on the fur rug in front of the fire and began pulling on his boots. "I really wanted to come with you. But when you touched my forehead, I just couldn't keep my eyes open any longer."

Morgan smiled and ran an idle hand through his burnished hair. "You were very tired, my prince," he said enigmatically.

Kelson had finished with his boots, and now he stood and began rummaging through his closet for a warmer cloak. The weather was definitely colder now, and Morgan could hear an icy wind whistling outside the balcony doors.

Kelson found a fur-lined crimson cloak with a hood and pulled it over his head. Then he took the sword Morgan offered and belted it around his slim waist. Morgan stood and slipped his own sword into its scabbard at his belt.

"Are you ready, my prince?"

Kelson nodded and started to head for the door.

"Not that way," Morgan said, motioning the boy to come back to the fireplace.

Kelson looked suitably puzzled, but he went where he was bidden, watched as Morgan paced off a precise distance from the wall to the left of the fireplace and traced an intricate design in the air with his forefinger. With a sigh, a portion of the wall recessed to reveal a dark stairwell descending into the cold night air. Kelson gaped incredulously.

"How did that get there?"

"I rather imagine someone built it, my prince," Morgan said, taking the candle from the mantle and indicating that Kelson should enter. "Didn't you really know this was here?"

He extended his hand as the boy shook his head and followed him into the dark passage. Behind them, the wall closed softly, and their muffled footsteps echoed hollowly on the damp stone treads.

Kelson stuck very close to Morgan as they descended the stairs, peering apprehensively into the darkness ahead. Here in this cold, wet unknown, the tiny circle of light from their one candle seemed small comfort indeed. He dared not speak until they reached a flat landing, and even then his voice was hushed.

"Are there many of these secret passages, Morgan?" he asked, as they rounded a turn and came to a blank wall. They stopped, and Morgan handed the candle to Kelson.

"There are enough so that you can get to almost anyplace in the palace without anyone knowing—if you know where you're going. Get ready to douse that light, now. We've reached the end. This will take us out just across the square from the basilica."

Morgan pressed the recessed latch, and a small square quietly opened at eye level. Morgan put his eye to the hole for a long moment, then put his hand on the latch again.

"All right, douse the light and set it down at your right."

Kelson obeyed, and the chamber was plunged into darkness. There was a soft sigh, and Kelson felt a cold, damp draft blowing into his face. Then he was aware of a lighter rectangle of darkness directly in front of him. Morgan took his arm and led him through, and the opening closed silently behind them. A fine, icy mist was drifting in the night air, and its chill quickly penetrated even the heavy clothes the two wore. Kelson pulled his hood over his head and huddled back farther in the shadows as he and Morgan waited.

The courtyard was almost deserted, now, and the massive presence of the basilica loomed dark against the night sky. Far in the distance, they could hear the cathedral bells striking Compline, last of the canonical hours. And the last stragglers were filing from the lighter square of the basilica door across the way. Here and there, soldiers crossed the square in twos and threes, sometimes holding sputtering torches aloft in the fine drizzle, but more often just hurrying along, eager to get where they were going, in out of the cold and wet.

The two waited perhaps five minutes there in the shadows, until the courtyard was nearly deserted. Then Morgan took Kelson's arm and guided him around the perimeter of the square to the portico. They waited there for what seemed to Kelson like an interminable time, then slipped unobtrusively through one of the side doors and into the narthex.

The silent church was deserted now, as they had hoped it would be. The darkness was broken only by the low, pale wash of votive candles, splashing their ruby and sapphire glows over the stone floors and dark stained glass.

In the sanctuary, a single crimson vigil lamp burned steadily in its place of honor, casting a rosy glow over the entire chancel area. As the two moved quietly down the side aisle, a lone, black-clad figure detached itself from the shadows in the chancel, bowed once before the high altar, and came to meet them in the transept.

"Any trouble?" Duncan whispered, as he led them to the study and closed the door.

"None worth mentioning," Morgan replied. He crossed to the curtained window and peered outside intently for a long moment, then came back and sat down at the table in the center of the room. Kelson, too, took a seat and regarded his elders apprehensively. Duncan did not sit, but instead took a heavy wool cloak from the chair at his desk and flung it around his shoulders.

"You might as well make yourselves comfortable for a few minutes. We're going to use an old Deryni Transfer Portal to get to the cathedral from here—left over from the days when being Deryni was a respectable occupation." He struggled with the clasp of the cloak for a moment, then mastered it. "I want to check out the other end before the three of us go through. With our phenomenal luck, someone would be in the sacristy just as we winked into existence. And the result then is not a happy thought."

He crossed to the prie-dieu in the corner and touched a series of hidden studs along its surface, and a new section of the wall opened, no more than four feet wide and two feet deep, as high as a man.

With a reassuring wave of his hand, Duncan stepped into the cubicle—and disappeared.

Kelson was amazed.

"How did he do that, Morgan? I swear, I didn't take my eyes off him. And what is a Transfer Portal?"

Morgan smiled and leaned back in his chair. "Kelson, you have just seen a practical demonstration of an almost lost art—that of portal transfer. You'll notice, as you learn more about him, that our Duncan is a man of many talents. He's made a fantastic reconciliation of that basic conflict we talked about earlier. He approaches his powers as a God-given gift, to be used for the good of all men."

"And that's why he became a priest?"

Morgan shrugged. "In his own way, Duncan is a very religious man. Things being what they are, what better place for one who is half Deryni?"

As Duncan appeared in the sacristy of the Cathedral of Saint George, he scanned the room. Other than the tiny vigil light burning in the far corner, there was no other light in the chamber. And as far as Duncan could tell, there was no one about, either.

He was just about to breathe a sigh of relief and transfer back to bring Morgan and Kelson when he heard a movement in the shadows near the door. A voice said, "Who's there?"

Duncan turned slowly toward the source of the sound, uncertain just what he'd blundered into. Now, as his eyes adjusted to the dim light, he was able to make out the stooped figure of a man in dark clothing standing there.

"I thought everyone had left for the night," the voice continued. The stranger struck a light and lit a slim white candle, then held it aloft. "Oh, 'tis you, Monsignor McLain. I'm Brother Jerome, the sacristan. Do ye remember me?"

Duncan relaxed with an almost audible sigh. Thank God, it *was* Brother Jerome! The elderly monk was almost half-blind, and beginning to grow a bit senile. If he *had* seen anything in the dim light, no one would believe him anyway. Duncan crossed to Brother Jerome with a genuine smile on his face.

"Brother Jerome, you startled me," he chided

mildly. "What are you doing sneaking around like this in the middle of the night?"

The old man chuckled. "Aye, I suppose I did startle ye at that, me boyo. Why, when I first called out to ye, ye nearly jumped out o' yer skin!" He chuckled again, almost to himself, and Duncan wondered if he had seen more than he was telling, or if it was just his senility flaring up tonight.

Duncan said, "You surprised me, Brother. I thought I was the only one here. I came back to make one last check of all the coronation regalia for tomorrow. I was rather busy today, you know. His Highness had me on call all afternoon."

Brother Jerome shuffled over to the cabinet where the special vestments were stored and patted the counter top reassuringly. "Ah, ye needn't have worried, laddie. I've kept everything in order, as I have for forty-five years. 'Tis no second rate King ye'll be makin' tomorrow if I have anything to say about it. Our young lord will be a bonnie King if he lives through the night."

Duncan stiffened slightly, and he felt a chilly finger raise the hackles on his neck. "What do you mean, 'if he lives through the night'?"

"Why, laddie, do ye not harken to the rumors? 'Tis said that monstrous evil powers stalk the streets of Rhemuth this night, an' their target is young Prince Kelson, God bless him." Jerome crossed himself piously. " 'Tis said that Deryni magic guides them to his chamber."

"Deryni magic?" Duncan repeated. "Who told you that, Brother Jerome? The Deryni lords of this time have always been friends of the Haldane line."

"Not *all* the Deryni, M'lord," the old monk contradicted. "Some say 'tis the spirit of that dead Deryni sorcerer that the lad's father, God rest his soul, killed in that terrible duel many years ago, that he's returned to take his revenge. An' some say 'tis the sorcerer's daughter, Charissa, the Shadowed Lady of the North, what means to kill our prince an' set herself upon the throne of Gwynedd.

"Still others say 'tis a coalition of all the evil powers in the world, come to destroy our prince and despoil his kingdom, because we do nae pay homage to the Dark Ones any more.

"But I think, an' there be those who agree wi' me, that it's all the fault o' that Morgan fellow, his Deryni blond finally gettin' the better o' him. Mind ye, *he's* the one to watch out for!"

Duncan forced a laugh, though he was extremely troubled by what he had just heard. For even if the old man's ramblings had been liberally laced with superstitious embellishment and legend, there was a hard core of truth to much of what he said. Charissa *was* involved, and her father's spirit, too, if one believed that parents lived on in their children. And he had no doubt that the forces of darkness were massing even now, ready to move in on the entire world once mighty Gwynedd fell.

As for the stories about Alaric, he'd heard them. And that part of the rumors was utter nonsense. At least he could attempt to correct Brother Jerome on that point.

Duncan moved closer to Jerome and leaned against the cabinet there. "Brother Jerome, you don't really believe all that about Morgan, do you?"

"Ah, now, laddie, it's all gospel truth."

Duncan shook his head disapprovingly. "No, I'm afraid you've been misinformed. For example, I can tell you for certain that Lord Alaric is not what you claim him to be. I saw him just this afternoon, and believe me, he has only Prince Kelson's best interests at heart."

Jerome's eyes narrowed. "Can ye prove that, laddie?"

"Not without violating my priestly vows," Duncan replied calmly.

Sudden insight appeared on Jerome's face. "Oh, I see. Ye're his confessor, then." He paused, obviously in deep thought. "But, can ye be sure he's telling ye the truth?"

Duncan smiled. "I think I can tell. I've known him a very long time, brother."

Jerome shrugged, then began shuffling slowly toward the door. "Weel, ye should know, if any man does, laddie. But there must be *sommat* to the rumors. Anyway, we'll not solve the dispute here, tonight. If ye don't mind, I'll be gettin' on. The guards will let ye out when ye're ready to leave."

Duncan picked up the candle Brother Jerome had lit and followed him to the door. "That's fine, Brother Jerome. There's just one other thing."

"Aye?" The old monk paused at the door, his hand on the latch.

Duncan took the lighted candle and put it in Jerome's other hand, put his hand on Jerome's.

"Do you see this candle, Brother Jerome?"

Jerome's eyes darted to the candle and were held there.

"Aye," he whispered.

Duncan's voice became lower, softer, and his eyes glittered from within. "You'd better take this candle with you, Jerome. Because it's dark out there. There's been no one here but yourself, so you don't want to leave a lighted candle here like this. Why, it might burn down the whole cathedral. And that would be terrible, wouldn't it?"

Jerome whispered, "Aye."

"And you didn't see anyone here, either, did you, Jerome? There was no one else in the sacristy tonight besides yourself. You talked to no one. Do you understand?"

The old monk nodded, and Duncan dropped his hand.

"You'd better go, then, Jerome. Everything is as it should be. You've done your duty. And you didn't see me here tonight. Go, now."

Without a word, Jerome turned and opened the door, slipped out quietly, closed the door behind him. There was no chance now that he would ever speak of what had happened here tonight.

Duncan nodded to himself and returned to the spot where he'd first materialized. He paused only long enough to collect his thoughts—and appeared back in his study.

As Duncan appeared in the niche in his study, Kelson jerked his head around in amazement, then bounded from his chair to meet the young priest.

"Is everything all right, Father Duncan? You were gone so long, we were certain something terrible had happened."

Morgan, too, joined Duncan by the Transfer Portal. "Kelson is exaggerating a little, Duncan, but you *were* gone quite a while. Anything wrong?"

"Not now," Duncan said, shaking his head and smiling. "I just ran into an old acquaintance. Brother Jerome was in the sacristy checking up on things. I don't think he saw me appear, though. And he's too old and senile to figure out that I didn't enter through any of the normal channels. He had some rather interesting views on the current situation. Remind me to tell you about them sometime."

Duncan stepped back into the transfer cubicle, then motioned Morgan and Kelson to join him. The compartment was small, but they managed to squeeze into the space provided. Morgan and Duncan both put their hands on Kelson's shoulders.

"Ready?" Duncan asked.

Morgan nodded. "Kelson, I want you to just relax and let your mind go blank. You aren't able to operate one of these portals on your own, yet, so we're just going to carry you through between us like so many potatoes in a sack."

"Very well," Kelson replied.

The priest glanced at the boy sharply, made suddenly aware that, all unconsciously, the youth had spoken as a king giving consent—where no consent had even been asked. He wondered if Alaric had noticed.

Kelson closed his eyes, trying to think of nothing at all. He tried visualizing total blackness, letting his mind detach itself from its awareness. He was dimly aware of Morgan's hand tightening on his shoulder. Then there was a sickening wrench in the pit of his stomach, a fleeting impression of falling, a slight dizzy sensation.

He opened his eyes to darkness. They were no longer in the study.

Duncan glanced around carefully. The sacristry was just as he'd left it—dim, deserted. Signalling Morgan and Kelson to follow, he glided across the room to ease the door open and peer through. Outside, in the nave, the cathedral was likewise deserted.

Morgan peered over his shoulder, then pointed toward the perimeter of the nave. "Circle around?" he whispered almost inaudibly.

Duncan nodded and pointed toward the rear of the nave, where the doorway leading to the royal crypt made a lighter patch against the dimness of the deserted cathedral.

"I'll take the right; you take the left."

Morgan nodded agreement, and the three began to circle toward the doorway. When they had almost reached their destination, Duncan slipped off to the right and melted into the shadows. Kelson took up a station in the darkness just outside the entrance to the crypt and positioned himself so he could watch Morgan approach one of the just-visible guards.

Morgan glided ahead like a spectre, darting from shadow to shadow, back and forth, each step bringing him that much nearer to his quarry. At length, he was within a few yards of the unwitting guard.

Carefully, so that he would make no noise to warn the unsuspecting man, Morgan inched his way closer, reaching gingerly toward the back of the man's neck. Then, gently, his fingers lightly touched the man.

At Morgan's touch, the guard stiffened, then relaxed, his eyes slightly glazed, staring straight ahead—unaware, helpless, unremembering. Morgan studied the entranced guard carefully for several seconds. Then, satisfied that his control was complete, he motioned Kelson to join him. As Duncan also joined them, Kelson looked at both men admiringly.

"All right?" Morgan queried in a low voice.

Duncan nodded. "He won't remember a thing."

"Let's go," Morgan replied, moving toward the gate to the crypt.

The gate was massive, designed both to keep intruders out and to form a decorative barrier between the world of the living and the dead. A full eight feet high, it was formed of hundreds of sturdy but delicately wrought bars of brass, gilded over with a thin wash of gold, for this was a Kings' crypt it guarded.

Morgan ran his hands fleetingly over the grillwork, peering at the same time through the bars to the crypt beyond. At the end of the short corridor, a simple altar faced the gate, intended, perhaps, to comfort those royal mourners who came here to lay their dead to rest. To the left, the corridor made a sharp turn into the crypt itself, and from around that bend, a bank of candles was casting its glow along the polished marble floor and over the altar. Also around that bend lay the royal sepulchers, the objects of tonight's expedition.

Morgan ran his fingers briefly over the locking mechanism, then knelt to inspect the lock in earnest. As Duncan slipped off to check once more on the guards, Kelson crowded closer to Morgan to peer fascinatedly over his shoulder.

"Can you open it?" the boy whispered, glancing around nervously.

Morgan held a finger to his lips for silence, then let his sensitive fingertips hover over the intricate lock, his face taut with concentration as he visualized each part of the locking mechanism. As Kelson held his breath, there was a soft, metallic click, then another. Morgan's half-closed eyes opened and he pushed gently at the gate. It opened easily.

Morgan stood and opened the gate the rest of the way in a single, continuous motion. As he turned to see if Duncan had returned, he froze, then placed a warning hand on Kelson's shoulder.

"Good evening, Rogier," he said quietly, his fingers tightening on Kelson's shoulder as the boy spun in alarm.

Rogier stood menacingly just within the outer entrance to the vault area, a look of outrage and disbelief on his face. His dark green velvet glowed around him like a malevolent aura, casting eerie highlights on his face and hair. Torchlight from the fiery brands in their wall sockets only added to the ghostly effect. And Rogier's indignation and disgust were almost a living thing.

"You!" Rogier spat, his voice low and deadly in the chill silence. "What the Devil are you doing here?"

Morgan shrugged casually. "I couldn't sleep, Rogier. Neither could Kelson. So we thought we'd come and visit Brion. You know, I haven't seen him in over three months. I thought I might even say a prayer or two. Will you join us?"

Rogier's eyes narrowed and his hand moved toward his sword. "How dare you!" he murmured, each word clipped between thin, tight lips. "How dare you! After the mockery of justice in Council today, after spreading your cursed Deryni lies over all the realm, you have the gall to bring His Highness here, of all places, for what purpose only the Devil knows—why, I could . . ."

As Rogier began to unsheath his weapon, Morgan's eyes flicked behind to where a flash of movement had caught his eye. He stepped back a pace to keep the timing right. And as Rogier's sword cleared its scabbard, Duncan's fingertips touched Rogier's neck lightly on either side.

At that touch, Rogier froze for just an instant, then relaxed and started to slump to the floor. As he crumpled, Morgan reached out to catch the sword before it could clatter onto the flagstones, and Duncan eased the unconscious man to a half-sitting position against the wall.

Duncan dusted his hands together ceremoniously as he straightened.

"What was he doing here?" Kelson breathed, eying the unconscious Rogier with suspicion and growing distaste. "Do you think *she* sent him?"

Morgan stepped through the gate to the royal crypt and motioned the other two to follow him. "Do you mean Charissa or your mother?" Morgan asked, pulling the gate closed behind them. "I would say that Rogier just happened to be in charge of the guard detail tonight. There won't be any trouble. He won't remember a thing, and neither will the guards. Come on."

A few steps carried them to the rear of the approach, past the family altar. Then they were among the tombs of the Haldanes.

The vault was enormous, higher than the height of two men, its insides hewn from the solid rock of the cathedral's foundations. All along the walls, carved out of the living rock, were coffin-sized niches, each holding the bones of one of Kelson's distant ancestors, each bedecked in rotting garments of fine materials, the empty eye sockets staring unseeing at the rock above. In the rest of the chamber, the tombs of the kings and queens of Gwynedd for the last four hundred years were placed in ordered rows, each one more magnificently carved than the next, each inscribed with the name and reign of the royal son or daughter who lay within.

Over to the left, a newer sepulcher was lighted by the fire of many candles, ranged in banks of twinkling red and blue on either side. Kelson paused and looked in that direction for a long moment, then led Morgan and Duncan toward the place where his father lay.

When they had nearly reached the tomb, Morgan put out a restraining arm across Duncan's chest, then continued alone as Duncan and Kelson looked on in silence.

Morgan stood silently by the sepulcher for several heartbeats, then reached out and placed a gentle hand on the cover of the sarcophagus. That the good and gentle Brion should end this way was not fitting. Life had been too short; the good done well, but not enough done, for lack of time. Why? Why had it been necessary for him to end this way?

You were father and brother to me, Morgan thought dully. *If only I had been at your side that day, I might have spared you this indignity, this useless gasping out of your life's breath! Now, with you gone . . .*

He took himself in hand, removed his hand from the sarcophagus, gestured for Duncan and Kelson to join him. Once, there had been joy, comradeship, and, yes, love. Perhaps there would be again. But now, he must only get on with the task at hand.

Carefully, he and Duncan lifted the cover of the sarcophagus, rocking it gently to break the seal, then slid it toward the foot until perhaps a square yard of interior was visible. Inside, the ghostly, shrouded body lay cold and still.

Morgan waited until Kelson had moved a candelabrum closer, then reached down with steady fingers to withdraw the silken shroud that covered the face.

What he saw was enough to shake his universe, to clench an icy hand round his heart, to send a frigid chill over his entire body. As he stared into the coffin in shocked disbelief, Kelson leaned closer and finally got a good look. The boy swallowed with difficulty and murmured, "Oh, my God!" and the stunned Duncan finally regained enough power of movement to cross himself with a shudder.

For the body in the sarcophagus was not Brion!

CHAPTER EIGHT

Things are not what they seem.

UNBELIEVINGLY, Morgan leaned down to inspect the face of the corpse more closely. But even without closer scrutinization, it was obvious that the body was not Brion's. The face he had uncovered was that of a very old man, bearded and grey. Some long-dead king or relative, perhaps, but not Brion.

Considerably shaken, Morgan straightened and pulled the silk back into place, then leaned both hands against the edge of the sepulcher and shook his head uncomprehendingly. He still could not believe what he had seen.

"Well," he finally said in a flat, dull tone, "what we've just seen is impossible, but there it is. Kelson, are you certain this is where your father was interred?"

Kelson nodded slowly. "I watched them seal the body into this sepulcher. It is the right one."

Duncan folded his arms across his chest in concentration and brought one hand up to rub his forehead wearily. "Well, it looks as if we're going to have to accept the fact that we now have the wrong body. Does anyone recognize this man?"

His companions both shook their heads.

"All right, then," he continued, half thinking out loud. "Let's try to approach this from a slightly different angle. Given: Kelson saw Brion's body being sealed into *this* sepulcher, but now that body is not Brion's. Given: guards have been posted outside the crypt around the clock since before the interment. Hypothesis: it would be very difficult, given those circumstances, to have taken the body out of the crypt without someone noticing. Does that suggest anything to you?"

Morgan nodded. "I see what you're driving at. Possible conclusion: Brion's body is quite conceivably still within the crypt somewhere, but hidden—in another sepulcher, one of the wall niches, perhaps. We just have to find it."

Kelson had been following the exchange with rapt attention, but now he shifted uneasily. "I don't mean to be pessimistic, but suppose someone did take him out. I mean, if *we* got in and no one will know we were here, maybe someone else has already done it."

"He's right, you know," Duncan sighed, leaning dejectedly against the next sarcophagus. "If Charissa's responsible, for example, she *could* have done it. And if she did, you know where that leaves us."

Morgan pursed his lips in concentration, then shook his head. "No, I don't think Charissa had anything to do with it. She'd have no reason to suspect the body was important to us. *We* didn't even know until this afternoon. But, Jehana—now, there's another story altogether. She's so worried over my alleged hold on Brion, she might have had the body moved just on the chance I might try to influence him after death. I must say, she overestimates my powers considerably."

"Then you think the body *is* still here, in the crypt somewhere?" Duncan asked.

"I think we'll have to operate on that premise," Morgan replied. "Other than that, we haven't got any alternatives. So I suggest we get to work."

At Duncan's nod of agreement, Morgan took a lighted taper from the candelabrum Kelson had brought and handed it to the boy. Duncan took another and headed across the chamber to begin searching other sepulchers, and Kelson made his way to the wall niches to inspect their occupants. Morgan glanced again at the silk shrouded form in Brion's sarcophagus, then took a light with him to search the sepulchers on his side of the crypt.

It was not a pleasant task. As Morgan slid back the covers of casket after casket, only to find mouldering bones and rotted cloth, he was aware of Duncan's progress in a similar manner. And around the periphery of the chamber, at the edge of the candlelight, he knew Kelson was finding his own search distasteful as well.

A glance at the boy confirmed his belief. For Kelson, though he inspected each open niche conscientiously, was moving nervously, clutching his candle tightly in his moist hand, his eyes darting apprehensively around him with each flickering movement of candle-sprung shadow.

Morgan slid back another cover. He felt badly that the boy was having to do the most grisly task—that of peering into the open niches. But there had been no other choice. Kelson simply lacked the physical strength to master the heavy sarcophagus covers. Indeed, it was all Morgan could do to budge some of them.

A glance inside his latest possibility was enough to assure him that it was not Brion who lay within, and he eased the cover closed once more. They had opened nearly a third of the sarcophagi now, all without result.

And indications were that the other two-thirds would prove no more fruitful than the first.

Could it be that someone had, indeed, managed to spirit the body away in the past weeks? Where else in this den of decay could one hide a body, if not in the obvious places? Perhaps Charissa had, in fact, been here. Yet, how could she have known of the importance of finding the body? Mere harrassment, perhaps? And if so, perhaps the answer was more obvious than he'd thought. Indeed, what if Brion's body had never been moved at all?

Suspicion dawning, he raced back to the original sepulcher and pulled back the silken shroud. "Duncan! Kelson!" he called urgently, peering shrewdly at the face of the stranger in the coffin. "Come here. I think I know where Brion is!"

Duncan and the boy joined him immediately.

"What are you talking about?" Duncan queried.

"I think he's been under our noses all the time," Morgan said, never taking his eyes from the body before him. "No one moved him. I think he's right here."

"But, that's not—" Kelson started to protest.

"Hush, Kelson," Duncan interrupted, skepticism draining away. "You think there's been a shape-changing, an illusion, Alaric?"

Morgan nodded. "See for yourself. I think this is Brion."

Duncan frowned as he replaced his candle in the candelabrum, then wiped his palms on his thighs. Holding his hands, palms down, a scant half inch over the body, he proceeded to inspect the strange corpse, his eyes half-closed. After a moment, he removed his hands, opened his eyes, sighed deeply.

"Well?" Morgan questioned. "What do you think?"

Duncan nodded. "You're right about the illusion. It *is* Brion. The shape-changing was done by a master. There's a weird aura about it: a definite impression of evil." He shook his head lightly. "I'm fairly certain it's not insurmountable. Do you want to break the spell, or shall I?"

Morgan glanced at the body again, then shook his head. "You do it. I think this one is better suited to priestly hands."

Duncan took a deep breath, exhaled slowly, then gingerly placed his hands on the forehead of the corpse. After a few seconds, his eyes closed and his breathing became more shallow, strangely harsh in the gloom.

Kelson, who had listened to the exchange of the two Deryni Lords with awe and only partial comprehension, cast a sidelong look at Morgan, then shuddered as he returned his attention to the priest. He wasn't sure he liked what was happening here, and he would be glad when it was over.

Duncan's breathing was even faster now, and droplets of cold sweat dotted his brow and the backs of his hands, even in the icy cold of the crypt. As the boy and Morgan watched, the features of the body beneath Duncan's hands began to waver, flicker, blur before their eyes. Duncan finally gasped and stiffened slightly, and in the same instant, the features of the corpse stabilized into Brion's familiar face. Abruptly, Duncan removed his hands and staggered back from the casket, his face drawn and pale.

"Are you all right?" Morgan asked, reaching across the coffin to steady his kinsman.

Duncan nodded weakly and forced his breathing to regularize. "It was—bad, Alaric," the priest murmured. "He—wasn't entirely free, and the bond was powerful. As I released him, I felt him die. It was—unspeakable."

A shudder rippled through Duncan's form, and Morgan gave his shoulder a reassuring squeeze, dropped his hand and blinked rapidly as his own vision blurred.

Between them, the body of Brion slept peacefully now, the gentle grey eyes closed forever, the lips relaxed, the lines of tension which had been part of Brion's appearance for as long as Morgan could remember erased now in death.

Gently, Morgan reached down and removed the Eye of Rom which glittered balefully in Brion's right earlobe. He gazed into the depths of the stone for a long moment, then placed it securely away in his belt pouch.

The movement roused the stunned Kelson, who had watched dumbstruck, awed, horrified, throughout the shape changing. The boy reached down and touched his sire's hand one last time, and a muffled sob escaped his lips. But then he swallowed hard and looked up at Duncan beseechingly.

"Is he truly free now, Father Duncan?" he whispered, searching for some reassurance. "She won't be able to harm him any more, will she?"

Duncan shook his head. "He's free, my prince. You have my word on that. And no one can ever harm him again."

Kelson glanced down at his father again, then continued in a small voice. "Somehow, it doesn't seem right to take the Eye of Rom and leave nothing in return. Could we . . . ?" His voice trailed off uncertainly, and Duncan nodded.

"How about this?" he asked, reaching deep into the pocket of his cassock and producing a small gilded crucifix.

Kelson smiled wanly and took the crucifix, placed it gently in his father's hands. "Thank you," he whispered, his eyes filling with unbidden tears. "I think he would have liked that."

As the boy turned away, shoulders convulsing silently, Morgan looked across at his cousin and raised one eyebrow in question. Duncan nodded, then sketched the sign of the cross over the body. Then he and Morgan eased the cover of the sarcophagus back into place. Duncan snuffed out the additional candles they had lit and returned the candelabrum to its proper place. Then he and Morgan guided Kelson back out of the crypt and through the gate.

As the gate clicked shut behind them, Duncan stepped carefully over to where Rogier still slumped against the wall, and touched his forehead. Immediately, Rogier stood up, still under control, and Duncan replaced the man's sword in its sheath. Another light touch sent the man on his way, and Duncan rejoined his comrades. It was time to return to the study.

Duncan opened the compartment where he had hidden the Ring of Fire and other elements of the power ritual and transferred them to the table in the center of the study. As he took his seat beside Kelson, Morgan went to Duncan's desk and rummaged in several shallow drawers until he found what he was looking for—a small surgical kit in a leather case. Returning to the table, he opened the kit and spread its contents on the tabletop, then dug in his belt pouch until he found the Eye of Rom.

Kelson eyed Morgan apprehensively, then gestured toward the surgical instruments with his chin. "What're you going to do with those?"

"Why, I'm going to pierce your ear," Morgan replied good-naturedly. He opened a small bottle of pale greenish liquid and dampened a scrap of cotton wool. Then he took the Eye of Rom and wiped it carefully on all surfaces, especially careful to cleanse the gold wire which would go through Kelson's earlobe.

"Duncan, would you read me the first two stanzas of the ritual verse? I want to be sure I'm doing this right." He took a silver needle from the kit and began wiping it as Duncan read.

"When shall the Son deflect the running tide?
A Spokesman of the Infinite must guide
The Dark Protector's hand to shed the blood
Which lights the Eye of Rom at Eventide.

Same blood must swiftly feed the Ring of Fire.
But, careful, lest ye rouse the Demon's Ire.
If soon thy hand despoil the virgin band,
Just retribution damns what ye desire."

Morgan nodded and put the needle down on the
table, wrapped in a piece of protective cotton. "Good.
With you looking on, I pierce Kelson's ear and let the
blood touch the Eye of Rom, which activates that.
Then we touch the same blood to the Ring of Fire,
being careful not to touch the Ring with our bare
hands. That should be simple enough."

Duncan got up and stood beside Kelson's chair.
"All right. What do you want me to do besides
watch?"

Morgan moved his chair closer to Kelson's and
picked up another piece of cotton wool, again moisten-
ing it with the greenish liquid. "Just hold his head so it
doesn't move," he said, smiling reassuringly at Kelson.
"We don't want a lopsided hole in his ear."

Kelson smiled weakly, but he said nothing as he took
the Ring of Fire in his hands, being careful not to let his
skin come into contact with the bare metal or stones.
The deep garnet-red gems glittered darkly from their
nest of white silk, mirroring the dark glitter from the
Eye of Rom on the table before him.

As Duncan's cool hands steadied his head on either
side, Kelson felt a cold sensation on his right earlobe
as Morgan swabbed the area with the greenish liquid.
There was a pause as he sensed Morgan positioning
the needle; then the slight popping sound of the skin
being pierced, once going in, once coming out the
other side. There was no pain.

Morgan exhaled softly and bent to look more closely at his handiwork. The thrust had been sure; the needle was positioned in precisely the right place. With a deft movement, he removed the needle and wiped the earlobe a second time, then watched a small drop of blood well out at entry and exit. He picked up the Eye of Rom in its insulating lint and touched the stone to the front droplet of blood, then held it down where Kelson could see it.

As all three watched, the dark stone in the earring took on a new appearance. Where the smooth ruby had glowed with a cold and smoky fire before, now it warmed, cleared, glowed with an inner light of its own, the way Morgan remembered it when Brion had worn it.

As soon as the Eye of Rom had made this strange transformation, Morgan motioned Kelson to hold out the Ring of Fire. He touched it with the bloody Eye of Rom, and true to its name, the Ring of Fire began likewise to glow with a deep garnet radiance which permeated each of the brilliant cut stones.

Morgan breathed a sigh, then wiped Kelson's earlobe again and inserted the Eye of Rom. With the touch to the Ring of Fire, the huge ruby had given up all its blood. Now it glowed darkly in Kelson's ear, tangible sign of the power to come, first fulfillment of the ritual verse.

Duncan took the glowing Ring of Fire from Kelson's hands and wrapped it securely in its silken shroud. It would not be used again until tomorrow at the coronation, so Duncan took it quickly to his security vault and locked it up. Returning to the table, he found Kelson fingering the velvet-covered box which housed the Crimson Lion.

Morgan spread the ritual verse out on the table once more and scanned the third stanza.

"How do we get this open, Morgan?" the boy asked,

shaking the box gently and listening for some telltale rattle which might give them a clue.

As the box neared his ear, it began emitting a low, musical hum, which ceased when Kelson lowered it in surprise.

Duncan leaned closer, then spoke. "Do that again, Kelson."

"Do what?"

"Shake the box gently."

Kelson shook the box as he was bidden, this time a bit more gingerly. But he did not hold it as near his head as the previous time. Morgan noticed the fact.

"Bring it closer to the Eye of Rom, Kelson," he suggested.

Kelson did, and the hum resumed.

"Now touch the box to the earring," Morgan ordered.

Kelson complied, and there was a soft, musical click as the lid of the box sprang open a crack. Lowering the box, he raised the lid the remainder of the way; and there was the Crimson Lion. All three looked at the open box in awe.

The Crimson Lion was not really crimson. That was a misnomer coined many years ago by some long-forgotten cataloguer of royal gems. The man had gotten his terminology twisted, and the name had stuck.

In reality, though, the Crimson Lion was the Haldane arms: a golden lion rampant guardant on a crimson enamel background, a massive brooch the size of a man's fist, secured with a heavy clasp at the back. Gold-etched scrollwork traced the deeply carved edges of the piece—the work, again, of the fine craftsmen of the Concaradine.

As Kelson carefully lifted the brooch from its bed of black velvet, Duncan sat down again and pulled the parchment of the ritual verse before him.

> "Now that the Eye of Rom can see the light,
> Release the Crimson Lion in the night.
> With sinister hand unflinching, Lion's Tooth
> Must pierce the flesh and make the Power right."

Kelson turned the brooch over and over, then held out his left hand. " 'With sinister hand unflinching . . .', I understand that part, but . . ." He placed the brooch on the table. "Look, Morgan. The Gwynedd Lion is rampant guardant. It faces toward us."

Morgan looked puzzled. "So?"

"Don't you understand?" Kelson continued. "Rampant guardant is the one heraldic configuration where the lion faces outward, toward the viewer. And that means the Gwynedd Lion *has* no tooth!"

Morgan frowned and picked up the brooch. "No tooth? But that's impossible. If there's no tooth, there's no ritual. And if there's no ritual. . . ."

Kelson gingerly touched the brooch, then looked unseeing at the polished tabletop. There was no need for Morgan to complete his sentence, for Kelson already knew the answer. And the enunciation of that answer chilled him worse than anything he had ever known. For there was only one way to complete the sentence: if there was no ritual, he would die.

CHAPTER NINE

*In the unknown lies terror,
and in the night, deceit.*

No TOOTH on the Lion of Gwynedd! No tooth on the Crimson Lion!

Duncan reached for the brooch, took it in his two hands, turned it over and over in his fingers as he mulled over the seeming inconsistency.

Somewhere—he did not remember where; perhaps it had been one of those obscure and highly technical treatises on the ancient magic that he had read many years ago—somewhere, he seemed to recall something about verses of this sort, some detail about double meanings, figures of speech, standard requisites for—*yes!*

Turning the brooch over, he lightly fingered the clasp of the ornament, his eyes not focused on it as he murmured, "Yes, of course. There is always the obstacle, the barrier, the need for bravery."

Morgan stood slowly, his face dark with suspicion, as he, too, realized the meaning of the verse.

"The *clasp* is the Lion's tooth?" he whispered chillingly.

Duncan's gaze flickered back to the present.

"Yes."

Kelson stood and reached across the table to run his fingertip along the three inches of chill, gleaming gold. He swallowed.

"And it is *this* which must pierce my hand?"

Duncan nodded impassively. "It seems this is the true key, Kelson. Everything before was but preparation for this event, and all else is postscript. Also, it must be done by you alone. We can prepare the way for you, we can stand by you, guard you afterwards. But this you must do yourself. Do you understand?"

Kelson was silent for a long moment. Then he nodded slowly. "I understand," he said very quietly. "I'll do whatever is necessary." His voice caught. "I—I'd like to think about it for a bit though—if there's time. . . ."

He looked up at Duncan with a frightened, beseeching look in his wide grey eyes, a boy again, and Duncan nodded.

"Of course, my prince," he replied gently, rising and catching Morgan's eye as he moved toward the door. "Take as long as you need. Alaric will help me to vest for the ceremony."

As soon as he and Morgan had left the room, Duncan closed the door securely and motioned for Morgan to follow him down the short corridor. When they reached the darkened sacristy, Duncan glanced briefly through the peephole to satisfy himself that there was no one there, then struck a light and leaned both hands against a storage cabinet, his back to Morgan.

"There's no real preparation on our part, Alaric," he finally said. "The boy needed a few minutes to collect his wits. I hope we're doing the right thing."

Morgan began pacing the floor energetically, his hands clasping and unclasping with nervous energy.

"So do I. Frankly, I'm getting more uneasy as the night progresses. I didn't tell you what happened just before we came here, did I?"

Duncan looked up sharply.

"Before I tell you," Morgan continued before Duncan could speak, "let me ask you a question. Where are you planning to finish tonight's business—the Lion brooch? In the study?"

"I was planning to use the secret chapel behind it," Duncan replied cautiously. "Why do you ask?"

Morgan pursed his lips. "That chapel was once sacred to Saint Camber, wasn't it?"

"Among others," Duncan nodded warily. "Saint Camber was the patron of Deryni magic; you know that. What does that have to do with what happened? Get to the point."

"All right, I will," Morgan said. He took a deep breath, as though reluctant to finish what he had started. "Duncan, would you believe me if I told you I had a vision?"

"Go on," Duncan replied, listening carefully.

Morgan sighed. "Before we came here, I left Kelson asleep under Ward protection so I could go down to Drion's library to look through his books and papers. I thought I might find some clue to help us unravel the ritual verse—perhaps even some of the notes he used in preparing it.

"Well, for a long while, I didn't find anything, so I used the Thuryn technique, hoping I might be able to pick up enough residual energy to give me an idea where to look next. I was using my gryphon seal as a point of focus."

He held up his left hand, let it fall to his side again as he searched for the right words. "I remember, I had my eyes closed, and suddenly I seemed to see the face of a tall, cowled man, surrounded by darkness. At the same time, there was a distinct impression of reassurance—and urgency. I opened my eyes, but the instant of vision was past. There was no one else in the room."

"Anything else?" Duncan asked, his eyes narrowed in concentration.

Morgan glanced at the floor. "I decided to flip through the books once more, just on the chance that I'd overlooked something important. The first volume I picked up was Talbot's *Lives of the Saints,* an old copy, and it fell open in my hands to—oh, my God! I'd forgotten all about it!"

Duncan watched mystified as Morgan began searching furiously through all of his pockets.

"There was a piece of parchment marking this place in the book," Morgan continued excitedly. "I was so surprised at what was in the book, I didn't even bother to read it—just stuffed it in my—here it is!"

He found the parchment in an inner pocket of his tunic and pulled it out triumphantly. In his eagerness to get the paper unfolded, his fingers trembled. More calmly, Duncan reached across and took the folded scrap of parchment, moved closer to the candle.

"What was in the book that was more important than this, Alaric?" the priest asked, smoothing the rumpled parchment and holding it up to the light.

"It was a picture of the man I saw in the vision," Morgan answered absently, peering anxiously over Duncan's shoulder and trying to see. "And what was most startling was that the section was about Saint Camber."

"Saint Camber?" Duncan questioned, looking up startledly. "You think you saw Saint Camber?"

Morgan nodded and gestured impatiently toward the paper. "Yes, yes. What does it say?"

Duncan returned his attention to the scrap of parchment in his hand as Morgan crowded closer to see. On one side, in Brion's hand, he could make out Brion's full name, inked in the familiar, rounded uncials of Brion's script. As Morgan peered over his shoulder, he turned the paper over. His hand began to tremble as he read the other side.

" *'Saint Camber of Culdi, defend us from evil!'* " Morgan whispered, echoing Duncan's unspoken words. "My God, Duncan, do you think I really *did* have a vision?"

Duncan shook his head solemnly and gave the parchment back to Morgan. "I don't know," he whispered, unconsciously wiping his palms against his cassock. "Alaric, I—this puts a slightly different light on what we're doing. Let me think about it for a minute or two."

Turning away from his companion, Duncan covered his face with his hands for a moment to regain his composure, then forced himself to consider this new information.

He was frankly uncertain, now. For as priest as well as Deryni, he was well aware how slender was the balance between Good and Evil. As Deryni, there was no doubt in his mind that Camber of Culdi had, indeed, been the savior of his people in the dark times following the Deryni coup. Why, it was Camber himself who had discovered that the Deryni powers could sometimes be shared with humans. That was what had ended the Deryni Interregnum of Terror almost two hundred years ago, what had made it possible for men like Brion Haldane to stand against the forces of Evil and defeat the awesome powers of the Marluk.

But, Camber of Culdi—the very name chilled the part of him that was priest. For though the Deryni Lord had, indeed, earned sainthood following his death (or disappearance, at any rate), that sainthood had been recalled long ago by a fearful Church—that same Church which had declared all Deryni powers to be forbidden, inherently evil.

He resisted a sudden impulse to cross himself in defense against the infamous name, then mentally shook himself back to sanity.

Saint or demon, Camber of Culdi had evidently been well revered by Brion Haldane. And if Brion, who had done so much good for his people, had invoked the name of Camber—no, *Saint* Camber, by God!—then it was unthinkable to suspect there could be evil attached to that name.

As for Alaric's vision, he would have to reserve judgement on that question until later. Quite candidly, he was not much more inclined to believe in visions than Alaric was. And yet, stranger things than that had surely happened. . . .

He turned back to Morgan with a sheepish expression on his face.

"Well?" Morgan ventured tentatively. He did not pretend to fathom what had just occurred in his kinsman's mind.

Duncan shrugged apologetically. "I'm all right. It was the priest warring with the Deryni in me again." He smiled faintly and sent the compressed images of his reverie towards his cousin in the same instant.

Morgan gave a wry grin. "I see," he nodded. "I just wish we had a little better idea what we were doing. I feel as though I'm walking in the dark."

"So do I," Duncan agreed. "But we really don't have any choice but to continue. If Kelson has to face Charissa without Brion's powers, whatever their origin, he'll die. That fact is inescapable. On the other hand, the power transfer itself could kill him. If we've made a mistake—or if we should make one in the next minutes—he'll be just as dead as if we'd handed him to Charissa and said, 'Here you are, M'lady. Take him with our blessings. We wanted you to rule Gwynedd all along.'"

He turned and took a heavily brocaded stole from

the storage cabinet and touched it to his lips, settled it around his shoulders.

"Of course," he added, turning back to Morgan, "we'll never know until we try, will we?" He stepped to the candle and cupped his hand behind the flame. "Are you ready?"

Morgan shrugged resignedly.

"Let's get on with it, then," Duncan said, blowing out the candle and ushering Morgan through the sacristy door. "You know, this is really ludicrous. Here I am, priest and Deryni sorcerer—heresy to begin with —about to help a Deryni warrior-lord give forbidden powers to a mortal King of Gwynedd. I must be out of my mind!"

Kelson sat in the study with his hands folded, his grey eyes focused dreamily through the candle flame flickering before him. Beside the candle, the Crimson Lion winked palely from its cushion of black velvet, throwing dancing flecks of pale fire on the boy's face and hands.

But the candle and the Lion were not Kelson's chief concern just now. For he was well aware that a cusp had been reached, that all his future, indeed, his very survival through the night, depended upon his conduct in the next half-hour.

The thought was not a comforting one, but he was loath to let it slip past and vanish in the night stillness. Fear was a thing that must be faced. Brion had drummed that into his head from the first time he could remember. He dared not shrink from what would be required of him.

He unfolded his hands, then twined his fingers together as he allowed the image of Morgan to take shape in the candle flame.

Morgan would not be afraid, were he in this situation. No matter what the danger, Kelson was certain that the wise and powerful Deryni Lord had never allowed even a trace of fear to show. Those of the Deryni born were not subject to the hopes and fears of mortal men.

And Father Duncan—he would not be afraid, either. For besides being Deryni, he was also a man of God, a priest of the cloth. With the power of the Deryni and the might of the Lord behind him, what evil would dare to rear its head in his presence? Indeed, under the protection of two such men, how could he possibly come to harm? Only if he allowed his fear to overpower him . . .

He lowered his head to rest his chin on his folded hands and study the Lion brooch more closely. There was nothing so difficult about what he had to do, really. He reached out and flipped the brooch over on its back so that he could see the clasp, then rested his chin on his hands again.

No, what he had to do would not really be so painful, either. He had had training injuries, hunting accidents, much more painful than the wound of three slim inches of gold was likely to be.

Of course, he wasn't sure just what to expect once he'd accomplished the deed. According to what he'd read, almost anything could happen. But if his father had devised the ritual, had wanted him to have the powers, he was certain he could come to no harm. Brion had cared about him—no, *loved* him—there was no doubt in his mind about that.

He was mentally congratulating himself for having reached so logical a conclusion when the study door opened softly and Duncan and Morgan reentered. Both men wore confident expressions, for his benefit, he was sure, but he could detect the tension beneath their calm exteriors even as they sought to reassure him. They knew he'd been nervous.

He straightened up and smiled slightly, to show them he wasn't afraid any more.

Duncan took the candlestick from the table, smiled and brushed Kelson's shoulder reassuringly as he continued across the room. Morgan watched as Duncan knelt at the prie-dieu, then picked up the Lion brooch and the vial of pale green liquid. He looked down at Kelson.

"Duncan is preparing a place, my prince," he said quietly. "Are you ready?"

Kelson nodded and got calmly to his feet. "I'm ready."

At the prie-dieu, Duncan reached carefully under the armrest and pressed a series of hidden indentations. As he did, a portion of wall behind the adjacent tapestry suddenly withdrew, sucking the tapestry briefly against the opening. Then the pressure released and the hanging was still once more. Duncan rose and pulled it aside, motioning Kelson and Morgan to enter.

The chapel was very small, perhaps half the size of the room they had just left. As the opening closed behind them and Duncan moved to the other end with the light, they were able to see that the side walls and ceiling were painted with frescoes depicting the lives of various saints. Gold paint had been used to highlight the paintings, and it caught and reflected what little light there was, making the scenes stand out as though illuminated from within.

Behind the tiny altar, the wall had been painted a dark blue, sprinkled with small gilded stars. An ornate ebony crucifix hung from the ceiling above the altar, suspended from fine wires so that it seemed to float against the starry sky. As Duncan lit the candles on the altar, the added illumination was reflected from the highly polished surfaces. And a single vigil light hung from a long chain to the left of the altar, casting crimson highlights on the ebony cross.

There were two small prie-dieus in the center of the room, and Kelson and Morgan took their places there as Duncan inclined his head toward the altar, then bowed his head in silent meditation.

Morgan put the Lion brooch and vial on the floor between them, then unbuckled his sword and laid it quietly on the floor, motioning Kelson to do the same. Morgan doubted that the action was really necessary, but there was no sense taking unnecessary chances. The tradition of coming into the House of God unarmed was an old and strong one. Somewhere, sometime, there had been a good reason.

As Kelson laid his sword on the stone floor, Duncan finished his meditation and joined them.

"I think we're ready to begin," he said in a low voice, dropping to one knee in front of Morgan and the boy. "Alaric, if you'll prepare the brooch . . ." he gestured toward the vial.

"Now, then, Kelson. I'll start by reciting a short series of prayers, with you and Alaric giving the proper responses. Then I'll come back here and give you a special blessing. After that, I'll return to the altar and say, 'Lord, let it be done according to Thy will.' That will be your signal."

Morgan wiped the clasp of the brooch with liquid and covered it with a piece of protective linen. "What about me?" he asked, taking Kelson's left hand and wiping it, front and back. "Is there anything I'm supposed to do besides watch?"

Duncan shook his head. "No. And whatever happens, you mustn't touch him or attempt to aid him in any way until the reaction has run its course. We're dealing with fantastic amounts of power here, and if you interfere, it could kill him."

"I understand," Morgan replied.

"Good. Any questions, Kelson?"

"No, Father."

"All right."

Duncan rose and looked down at Kelson for an instant, then smiled and made obeisance. Then he turned away and mounted the three short steps to the altar.

Kelson watched wide-eyed as Duncan genuflected, kissed the altar stone, then extended his arms to either side with the practised ease of much experience.

"Dominus vobiscum."

"Et cum spiritu tuo."

"Oremus."

As Duncan's lips moved in prayer, Morgan stole a glance at Kelson to his left. The boy seemed calm as he knelt there, and terribly young and vulnerable. Morgan was not afraid for himself. He and Duncan could protect themselves, he was sure, from any evil which might be summoned up by what they were about to do. But Kelson, a human boy, with no defenses as yet . . .

Of course, it was possible that there was no need for alarm, even possible that the Eye of Rom glittering there in the boy's right earlobe might offer some protection if there was need, but still—Kelson was so young, so trusting. Morgan was glad the boy didn't know of the doubts he and Duncan had raised in the past hour. What the boy must do now required the utmost of confidence and trust. There could be no room for doubt.

Morgan returned his attention to the altar and found that Duncan was just finishing the prayers prerequisite to what must follow. The priest bowed once more before the altar, then turned to face them.

"Per omnia saecula saeculorum," he intoned.

Morgan and Kelson responded with a solemn "Amen."

At that, Duncan stepped back down the three steps and stood before the kneeling Kelson. Then, placing both hands lightly on the boy's head, he spoke again, his voice low but strong in the stillness.

"Kelson Cinhil Rhys Anthony Haldane. Though the cords of the nether world enmesh thee, though the snares of death surge about thee, thou shalt fear no evil. With His pinions the Lord will cover thee, and under His wings thou shalt take refuge." He made the sign of the cross over the boy's head. *"In Nomine Patris et Fils et Spiritus Sancti, Amen."*

As the boy lifted his head, Duncan reached down and took the Lion brooch from Morgan, removed the protective linen covering the clasp, placed the brooch in Kelson's right hand.

"Courage, my prince," he whispered; then turned back toward the altar and spread his arms once again.

"Domine fiat voluntas tua!"

It was time.

Kelson's hands trembled slightly as he poised the golden clasp over his left palm, rested the point of the slender shaft against the skin. He hesitated for just an instant, mentally steeling himself for the pain he knew must follow.

Then he plunged the clasp into his hand.

Pain! Searing fire! Anguish!

Suddenly, the tortured hand was like a thing alive and apart, transmitting its anguish to explode in his brain like sparks from a fiery forge, like the searing white light of sunlight on unprotected eyes. He felt pain lance through the hand like the thrust of a blade, hot, cold, was aware of the shaft taking what seemed an interminable time to pass through fascia, tendons, muscles—felt it glide between the small bones of his hand, saw the tip of the shaft, darker now, emerge at last on the other side.

An involuntary gasp escaped his lips as the brooch itself came to rest against the palm of his hand, seemed to sear into his flesh. He doubled over, moaning softly, as the hand began to throb with a rhythm of its own, closed his eyes tightly as lights began to explode inside his head, in his eyeballs.

It was all Morgan could do to keep from reaching out to steady his young lord. Anguish was etched across the boy's face, pain screamingly obvious in every taut line of the small body. Never had he seemed so helpless.

But Duncan, too, had turned to watch. And his sharp glance reminded Morgan that he dared not try to assist.

As Kelson sank back on his heels, cradling the wounded hand against his chest, he began to glow with a pale, ghostly golden light. The glow increased, and then the boy suddenly froze and ceased moaning. As his companions watched breathlessly, the young King's eyes flickered open, glassy, staring, following things only he could see.

Brightness . . . pain . . . swirling colors . . . pain throbbing . . . a cool shiver of—what? . . . Pain subsiding . . . better now . . . a cool weight in the hand . . . Look! . . . Colors . . . swirling . . . faces: . . . light, dark . . . light fading . . . faces . . . growing darker . . . spinning . . . darkness . . . Father! . . . the darkness! . . . Father . . . darkness . . .

"Father, the darkness . . ."

Suddenly, the slender body crumpled softly to the floor. The light around him died.

"Kelson!" Morgan cried, frantically turning the boy's face to the light and feeling for a carotid pulse. "Kelson, are you all right?"

As Duncan, too, knelt beside the still form, Morgan's fingers found what they sought; and even as he relaxed the pulse grew stronger. He lifted one of the boy's eyelids, saw the pupil react to light. The pulse became stronger.

" 'The right hand of the Lord has struck him with

power,'" Duncan whispered, crossing himself. "'He shall not die, but live.'"

He reached for the boy's left hand and gently removed the Lion brooch, then wrapped the hand in a handkerchief of white silk.

"Do you think it worked?" Morgan asked, raising the boy's head and shoulders and wrapping the crimson cloak more closely around him.

Duncan nodded as he stood and removed his stole. "I think so. It's too soon to tell for sure, but he's showing all the proper signs." He touched the stole to his lips, then tossed it easily to the altar as he headed for the secret door. "One thing is fairly evident, though. More happened to him than just a hole in his hand. We'll have to ask *him* when he comes to."

As Duncan activated the door, Morgan picked up the unconscious Kelson in his arms, again pulling the crimson cloak more closely around his young charge. Duncan picked up the swords from the floor, scanning the chapel once more, then held aside the tapestry to reenter the study.

Soon, he and Morgan were making their way back through the secret passage toward Kelson's apartments.

"I still dinnae see how they could've got past wi'out us seein' 'em!"

The speaker struck a light and touched it to the candelabrum beside Kelson's bed, then turned to his two companions. "I thought ye were watching, Lawrence."

Lawrence sheathed his sword with a gesture of finality, then threw the dark cloak back off his shoulders, let his hood fall back.

"I cannae explain it, M'lord. I did nae see any man come in or out since late this afternoon when the prince and His Grace entered." He paced to the fireplace and stirred the embers with the toe of his boot, then pulled several logs into the dying fire.

"Well, if ye ask me," the third man said, also lowering his sword, "I'm glad they're not here. I'm not sure it's a good idea to strike at Lord Alaric. After all, he *is* our sworn Lord." He sat gingerly on the edge of the royal bed and tested it with a slight bounce, then hastily stood again at the sharp glance of Lawrence.

"Do ye think there could be another way out o' this place?" Lawrence said, looking suspiciously around the room from his vantage point by the fire. "Methinks I've heard rumors o' secret passages an' the like. Do ye think they could ha' gotten out that way?"

Edgar, the first speaker, frowned and considered the idea. Though he was of the nobility, and one of Morgan's vassals, he was not known for his mental agility. He functioned adequately in his role as border lord, and was widely touted as a fine fighter, but it took him longer to function when matters requiring thought were involved. At length, he cocked his head and nodded, drawing his sword.

"Aye, 'tis possible. And if 'tis true, they might come back any minute."

As he began roaming suspiciously around the room, poking into corners with his blade, the third man moved cautiously to the fireplace.

"Do ye really think Lord Alaric has enslaved the young master like they say? 'Tis bad enough he must murder the King's own men, but when he threatens the life of the King himself, that's another matter entirely."

"Both deeds are from the same wickedness!" Edgar retorted, striding darkly around the room like a caged animal. "He cannae——"

"Hsst!" Lawrence suddenly said, holding up his left hand for silence. "I think I hear somethin'."

"Harold, over there," Edgar ordered, motioning the third man to the left of the fireplace by the wall.

From the wall beside the fireplace, the three men could hear faint scraping sounds, as though of cautious footsteps. Immediately, they doused their light and stood back in the shadows, weapons at the ready.

As they watched, a portion of the wall sighed and indented slightly, then slid back. From the opening, dim candlelight poured into the room, revealing Morgan carrying the unconscious prince, and Duncan behind him. Even as the two stepped through the doorway, they were aware of the fire burning brightly, felt the presence of others in the shadows.

"Ye demon!" Edgar's voice hissed from the darkness. "What have ye done wi' His Highness?"

The three men stepped into the circle of candlelight and glared defiance at Morgan and Duncan, weapons menacing, their faces dark, masked beneath steel helmets and dark hooded cloaks.

"Have ye nothing to say, ye monster?" Edgar continued furiously. "Stand and defend yerself!"

CHAPTER TEN

*"From whence comes the wonder,
from whence the miracle?"*

THE WORDS of the intruder launched the two men into
action. Duncan dashed his candle to the floor to douse
the light, then tossed Morgan's sword to him. Morgan
had already eased the unconscious Kelson to the floor
at his feet, and now he slung the scabbard from his
blade with a quick, lightning flick of his wrist. At his
side, Duncan drew Kelson's sword and prepared to
fight.

Immediately, the junior of the three attackers engaged Duncan in combat, pressing him back into a
corner. And the remaining two attacked Morgan in
unison with rapier and two-handed broadsword, their
blows ringing out against Morgan's blade like hammer
blows in a forge.

After the initial clash, Morgan proceeded to parry
each thrust of his two opponents easily, methodically,
less concerned now with actually defeating them than
with keeping himself always between them and the

limp form of Kelson behind him. The slender stiletto had again appeared in his left hand, and he was using it to good advantage to deflect an occasional blow from the rapier. But it was, of course, completely ineffectual against the blows of the broadsword which continued to rain down on him.

Also, he was having to refrain from launching a full-scale offensive maneuver. For he dared not take the offensive if that meant leaving Kelson open to attack. Right now, he wasn't really sure who they were after, and he couldn't risk Kelson's life in finding out. He glanced aside and knew that Duncan could not help, either.

In the corner, Duncan was having his own problems keeping abreast of the situation. Kelson's blade was shorter and lighter than those the priest was accustomed to. As a consequence, he was fighting under an extreme handicap: with a blade too light and short against a man who surpassed him in weight, strength, reach, and years' experience.

Not that there was anything lacking in his skill. Duncan was first and foremost a nobleman's son, born and bred to a fine fighting tradition and tempered by many years' experience and training. But these were not the odds he liked. He had only this puny blade to protect him—not even a scrap of mail shirt. People did not often raise steel against a priest, especially of the monsignorial variety.

Undaunted, he continued to press for an opening—and found it!

Apparently, his opponent had also recognized his advantage, and as a result he became lazy, returned from a thrust less quickly than he should have.

It cost him his life. Even as he realized his mistake, Duncan's blade flashed through a weak point in his mail and pierced him to the heart. He crumpled to the floor with a surprised look on his face and quietly died.

Dropping Kelson's bloodied sword, Duncan peered through the gloom, trying to decide which of Morgan's two opponents to take out of the fracas. The decision was not a difficult one, however. If Morgan had to parry many more blows from the two-handed broadsword, there was little doubt as to what the outcome would be.

Moving up stealthily behind the man, Duncan extended both hands before him, palms together, then slowly drew them apart. As he did, a small sphere of green fire hovered in the air there, then drifted unerringly toward the back of the swordsman's head. As it touched the man's helmet, there was a brilliant arc of green fire. The man cried out once, then fell to the floor in a stupor. His fall so unnerved his companion, that Morgan was able to disarm the man easily and hold him at bay.

Outside the door to the apartment, all three could hear the sounds of guardsmen arriving and pounding on the door, their shouts of dismay as they discovered the fate of the guards overpowered by the three intruders. The pounding on the door became insistent.

"Sire!" called a voice, cutting through the outer confusion. "Sire, are you all right? General Morgan, what's happening? Open the door, or we'll have to break it down!"

Morgan gestured urgently toward his captive with the tip of his blade as he edged toward the door, and Duncan nodded. Before the man could react, Duncan slipped alongside him and touched his forehead, giving a low-voiced command. The man's eyes took on a faraway look and he dropped his hands to his sides, no longer trying to resist.

"You did not see me," Duncan whispered, looking

the man deeply in the eyes. "You saw only the prince and His Grace. Do you understand?"

The man nodded slowly.

Duncan dropped his hand and edged toward the balcony doors, nodding to Morgan as he did so. The man would say nothing of his presence now, of that he was certain. It would have been rather difficult to explain just how he happened to be in this room at this hour.

As Morgan shot back the bolt on the door, his stiletto slipped back into its wrist sheath, and he heard a low moan come from Kelson's corner of the room—a sure sign that the boy was coming around. He stepped back into the center of the room as the door burst open, and mentally sent a burst of strength and confidence in Kelson's direction as the room filled with armed men.

A guard captain—the same as in the garden earlier this afternoon—glanced swiftly around the room as his men took custody of Morgan's prisoner, then stalked up to Morgan, his sword extended menacingly.

"Stand where you are, General Morgan, and drop your sword," he said, his own weapon following every move the tall, blond lord made. "Where is His Masjesty?"

Morgan did not need to look around to know that he was surrounded and totally outnumbered. With an apologetic shrug, he let his blade fall to the floor, then turned and stepped back to where Kelson lay. No one tried to stop him as he knelt at the boy's side.

"Are you all right, my prince?" he asked, helping the boy to his feet.

Kelson nodded weakly and steadied himself on Morgan's arm. "I'm all right," he murmured, breathing deeply to steady his wits. "I'm just not used to being attacked in my sleep."

His eyes flashed around the room, taking in the

situation at a glance, and he instinctively sensed that the truth were better not told at this point. These men would never understand. Right now, following Morgan's lead seemed the best plan.

He took another deep breath, then turned to the guard captain. "How did those men get in here, Captain?"

The captain was immediately on the defensive. "I don't know, Sire. Evidently, they overpowered the guard outside. There are three dead, and at least four others gravely wounded."

Kelson nodded, what had happened fairly evident now. "I see. And who are our assailants, Morgan?"

Morgan crossed to the remaining intruder still on his feet and pulled off his helmet and coif. The face behind it glared out with a sudden scowl.

"Lord Edgar of Mathelwaite!" Kelson exclaimed.

"Isn't he one of *your* vassals, General Morgan?" the captain asked, his sword coming up to waist level again.

Morgan detected the note of menace in the man's voice, and was careful to keep his hands in full view as he turned to answer.

"Yes, he's my man, Captain." He turned to gaze patiently at Edgar. "Do you mind telling us what this is all about, Edgar? I trust you have good reason for treason against your King."

Edgar looked confused for a moment, then glanced guiltily at Kelson. "We were only following orders, Yer Grace."

"Whose orders, Edgar?"

Edgar squirmed uncomfortably. "Y—yer orders, M'lord."

"My orders—"

"Morgan ordered you to assassinate the King?" the captain blurted indignantly, his sword moving toward Morgan's throat.

"That's enough!" Kelson ordered, catching hold of the captain's sword and pushing it aside. "Lord Edgar, suppose you be a little more specific."

Edgar shifted his weight nervously, then dropped to his knees and bowed his head, spreading his arms in supplication.

"Please, Sire, forgive me!" he begged. "I did nae mean to do it. None o' us did. Lord Alaric, he *made* us do it. He—he has this power over men. He can make 'em do anything he wants. He—"

"Stop it!" Kelson snapped, his eyes flashing fire.

"Sire," the captain implored, trying to get closer to Morgan, "let me arrest him, *please!* You *know* now that it's true what everyone's been saying about him— that he's a murderer, a monster, a—"

"The man is lying," Kelson said, turning cold Haldane eyes on the captain. "And Morgan is no traitor!"

"Sire, I swear to ye," Edgar began, his eyes wild, beseeching.

"Silence!"

The room was hushed except for the harsh breathing of Edgar, the deep, controlled breathing of Kelson. Kelson looked slowly aside at Morgan, seeking some guidance, but Morgan gave only an almost imperceptible shake of his head. Kelson must extricate them from this situation on his own. Anything Morgan might say or do at this point would only increase the difficulty.

Kelson looked down at Edgar.

"Get up."

As the man did, Kelson scanned the faces around him, addressed all of them.

"You all think it's Morgan who's lying, don't you? And you think that I'm protecting Morgan, that he's deceived me just as you believe he's deceived you." He glanced at Edgar. "But I say that it's this man who lies. I say that Morgan would never have asked any man to take my life. He made a solemn vow to my father, and he is a man of his word."

He looked directly at Morgan as he continued. "No, Edgar lies. And now we must determine why, and for whom. I could ask Morgan to interrogate him. You all know of his Deryni powers, and you know by now that he could force the truth. But because you distrust him, there would always be the suspicion that Morgan controlled the answers too."

He dropped his eyes from Morgan's and stepped closer to Edgar. There was silence as he stared at the accused man.

"Gentlemen, I am my father's son in at least this respect, for I, too, know when a man lies. And I, too, can command the truth!"

He caught Edgar's gaze and held it. "Lord Edgar of Mathelwaite, look at me," he commanded. "Who am I?"

Edgar seemed unable to take his eyes from Kelson's face, and Morgan looked on in amazement. Duncan must have taught the boy to Mind-See!

"Who am I?" Kelson repeated.

"You are Prince Kelson Cinhil Rhys Anthony Haldane, heir apparent to my Lord King Brion," Edgar stated, in a conversational tone.

"And who is that?" Kelson queried, pointing at Morgan.

"Lord General Alaric Anthony Morgan, my liege lord, Sire."

"I see," Kelson said, his eyes narrowing in concentration. "Lord Edgar, did Morgan order you to kill me?"

Edgar answered promptly, without batting an eye. "No, Sire."

The guards shifted uneasily, and a slight murmuring whispered through the room. The captain looked incredulous.

"Then, who *did* order you to kill me, Lord Edgar?"

Edgar's eyes widened, as though some internal struggle were underway deep within him. Then he blurted, "It was not to kill *you* that we came, Sire, but to kill Lord Alaric! An' thus should all murderers die who strike down helpless men in dark places!"

He wrenched himself loose from his guards and flung himself at Morgan, going for his throat, but Morgan sidestepped neatly and controlled him, returned him to the custody of the guards. Edgar continued to struggle in their hands as Kelson held up a hand for silence.

"Explain, Edgar," Kelson snapped, stepping closer to the captive. "Who strikes down helpless men in dark places? What are you talking about?"

"Morgan knows!" the captive spat. "Ask him how young Michael DeForest coughed out his life at the end of a dagger, while guarding in the darker passages o' this palace. Ask if he knew that he botched the job, that young DeForest still had enough strength to smear his murderer's sign on the floor wi' his dyin' blood— the shape o' the Corwyn Gryphon!"

"What?" the captain gasped.

Again, there were murmurs of discussion around the room, louder this time. Stunned, Kelson turned to Morgan once more.

"Do you know what he's talking about?" the boy whispered.

Around him, discussion stopped as all strained to hear what Morgan would say. A dozen swords were still pointing in Morgan's direction, and each had drawn a little closer with Edgar's last statement.

Morgan shook his head. "Probe deeper, Kelson. I have no idea what he's talking about."

"Sure, you don't," a low voice murmured in the background.

Kelson glanced sharply in the direction of the com-

ment, then turned back to Edgar, catching his gaze
and holding it again.

"Lord Edgar, how do you know that this is true?"

Edgar calmed under Kelson's stare. "I saw it wi' my
own eyes, M'lord. Lord Lawrence and Harold Fitz-
martin and I saw it."

"The actual murder, or just the body?" Kelson insisted.

"The body."

Kelson frowned and chewed his lip thoughtfully.
"And just how did you find out about this, Edgar?"

"We—were . . ."

"Go on," Kelson commanded.

"We were—told to go to that place in the corridors," Edgar murmured reluctantly.

"And who told you to go there?" Kelson persisted.
"Who knew about this thing and told you to go there?"

Edgar shuddered. "Please, Sire, dinnae force
me. . . ."

"Who told you to go there?" Kelson demanded, his
eyes beginning to glow from within.

"Sire, I—"

Suddenly, before anyone could stop him, Edgar
whirled and wrenched a dagger from the belt of one of
his captors. And even as Morgan launched himself
across the short space, knowing what was about to
happen, he knew he could not stop it.

By the time Morgan's hands touched Edgar, it was
already too late. For the dagger protruded from deep
in the man's abdomen, and he had slumped over and
begun to fall. Morgan and the stunned guards eased
the body to the floor, and the captain looked down
horrified at what had happened.

"He—he died by his own hand rather than talk,
Sire," the captain whispered, looking apprehensively at
Morgan. "What ungodly power could make a man—"

"Take him out of here!" Kelson ordered curtly.

"And take his friends with him. We will not be disturbed anymore tonight."

He turned away as the guards moved to obey, aware that awed and frightened eyes followed his every move. Morgan stood to one side as the guards began a cursory search of the rest of the apartment, trying to remain as inconspicuous as possible. Then he slipped out to the corridor.

Derry, God help him, was out there somewhere. If he had been following orders, and there was no doubt in Morgan's mind about that, then he had been in the guard detail which was overpowered by the three intruders. Three dead, and at least four gravely wounded, the captain had said. If only Derry was still among the living.

In the corridor, the scene was one of carnage. There seemed to be bodies lying everywhere: some still, some surrounded by guards or surgeons, or both. Attendants were carrying two away, and Morgan scrutinized each as it passed, but neither was Derry.

Anxiously, he searched among the crumpled forms until he saw a flash of the familiar blue cloak over against the wall. A surgeon had just risen from examining a wound in the side of the still figure under the cloak, and he turned a somber face towards Morgan as the general approached.

"I'm sorry, but I'm afraid there's nothing I can do for this man, M'lord," the man said, shaking his head. "He'll be gone in a few minutes. I'd best see to those that can be helped." He turned quickly away, obviously unaware of his patient's identity.

Morgan knelt down beside the still body and pulled aside the fold of cloak which half-covered the face. It was Derry.

As he looked at him, touched his hand, the words of a woman in grey echoed in his mind: *I intend to make*

*you pay . . . and I'll do it by destroying the ones you
love best, one at a time, slowly. . . .*

First it had been Brion, then Lord Ralson, young
Colin of Fianna, his men. And now, Derry was slipping away. *And there was nothing he could do. . . .*

He took one of Derry's limp wrists in his hand,
lifted a slack eyelid. Derry was still alive, but only
barely. A terrible wound had pierced his side, probably
rupturing his spleen and God knew what else. Major
arteries had evidently been severed also, for the wound
pumped bright red blood with every heartbeat.

Morgan pulled a handkerchief from his sleeve and
pressed it hard against the wound, trying to stop the
bleeding and knowing as he tried that it was futile. If
only he could *do* something, could will the entire thing
away, as though it had never happened. If he could
call upon some untapped force, some healing
power . . .

Suddenly, he straightened in astonishment as an idea
came to him. Somewhere, long ago, he had read about
such a healing power—a power which some Deryni
were alleged to have. In the ancient days, there had
been practitioners of that art.

But no. Those had been full Deryni, fully trained, in
total command of the entire arsenal of Deryni power
—not a half-breed like himself. And the times had
been different: an era when men believed in miracles,
and the Powers of Good were not so difficult to guide.
How could he presume?

And yet, if Derry were to have even a slim chance
for survival, if he, Morgan, were to be somehow able
to call up this lost power from the past—God only
knew how . . .

He must try.

Placing his hands lightly on Derry's forehead, he
began to concentrate, to make his mind as empty and

still as possible, using his Gryphon seal as a focal point as he'd done earlier when he had his vision.

He closed his eyes and concentrated on summoning up the healing strength he was searching for, concentrated on making Derry whole again. It was cold in the corridor where he knelt in the shadows, but the sweat began to pour down his face and drip from his chin. Dimly, he was aware of the warm splash as the perspiration touched his hands.

And then it happened. For just an instant, he had the fleeting impression of another pair of hands on top of his, of another presence pouring through him, giving life and strength to the still form beneath his hands.

His eyes flicked open in astonishment. Derry had given a deep sigh. And now, his eyelids trembled and his breathing changed to that of deep sleep.

Fascinated, Morgan removed his hands from the young man's forehead and reached for the handkerchief covering the wound. He paused for just an instant, half-fearing to break the spell, then gingerly removed the handkerchief from the wound.

And the wound was gone, healed, vanished—without a scar or mark to show where it had been! Morgan stared at his hands in disbelief, then hastily checked Derry's bandaged wrist—that, too, healed! He rocked back on his heels, unable to accept what had just occurred.

And then a voice came from behind which turned his blood to ice, raised all the tiny hairs on the back of his neck.

"Well done, Morgan!" the voice said.

CHAPTER ELEVEN

Even as Father, so the Son.

MORGAN WHIRLED defensively on his haunches, half expecting to see the face of his vision again.

But it was no blond apparition of the long-dead Saint Camber who approached, but the smugly self-satisfied form of Bran Coris. With him, Ewan, Nigel, Ian, and a score or more royal courtiers and noblemen strode hurriedly toward the scene of recent carnage. And behind them all came a thoroughly angry Jehana with a pair of her ladies. Bran Coris was the first to arrive.

"Ah, yes. Well done, indeed!" Bran continued. "You've finally finished the job, haven't you? Now you're the only man alive who knows what really happened on that long ride to Rhemuth!"

Morgan stood carefully as the others arrived and gathered in a knot behind Bran, forcing himself to relax and give a civil answer.

"Sorry to disappoint you, Lord Bran," he retorted,

signalling one of the surgeons to come and care for Derry. "But he isn't dead. He has been knocked unconscious but not injured. No doubt an oversight of whoever masterminded this little spectacle tonight." Morgan had no intention of admitting to his newfound talent. It could only serve to arouse further fear and animosity.

Jehana pushed her way through the murmuring onlookers and came to a stop between Lord Ewan and the ever elegant Ian. Morgan had never seen her look lovelier than she did at that moment, her long auburn hair streaming down her back, and he regretted more than ever that he had never been able to make peace with Brion's proud Queen. She had thrown a pale mauve dressing gown over her sleeping garments, and that was clutched to her neck by a pale, slim hand which glittered with the jewels of Brion's ring.

"Your Majesty," Morgan bowed, trying to avoid further friction, "I regret the commotion, especially at this late hour. It was none of my doing."

Jehana's face went hard, and her eyes gleamed like green ice. "None of your doing? Morgan, do you take me for an idiot? Don't you think I know about that guard you murdered in my very house? I think you owe me an explanation before I have you arrested and executed for murder!"

At that moment, Kelson appeared at the door, looking haggard and worn, but very determined.

"Morgan has given sufficient explanation for me, Mother," he said quietly, stepping out of his chambers to stand at Morgan's side. "And there will be no arrests or executions here without my direct order. Is that clear?"

All but Jehana bowed deferentially as Kelson approached, and the boy returned their questioning stares unflinchingly.

"Gentlemen, you wonder at this night's attempt on

my life. So do I," he continued evenly. "And no doubt we shall all be satisfied as to the details in due time." His eyes swept his audience confidently. "But I warn you. Any further attempt to interfere with me in the next hours before my coronation will be considered treasonous. I shall tolerate no further questioning of either Morgan's loyalty or my judgement. Is that clear? Disobey me, and you shall learn just how well my father taught me to be King of Gwynedd."

The onlookers bowed in acknowledgment except for Jehana, who stood her ground and glared at Kelson.

"Would you defy me in something this important, Kelson?" she whispered. "Something I so strongly believe to be wrong?"

Kelson stood firm. "Go back to your chambers, Mother, please. I don't wish to argue with you in front of my court."

When she did not answer immediately, Kelson turned his attention to the guard captain, who had finished his search of the royal apartment and now assembled his men outside the door.

"Captain, I am retiring for the night—again. Will you please see that I am not disturbed? General Morgan will stay with me."

"Yes, Your Majesty," the captain said, snapping to attention.

"And to you, gentlemen, Mother," Kelson continued, "I shall see you all in the morning. In the meantime, I suggest we all get some rest. Tomorrow will be no ordinary day."

Pivoting precisely, he entered the apartment, Morgan close behind him, and the door bolt shot home with a note of finality.

The Queen, after a moment's hesitation, retired resignedly in the direction of her own apartments. And Ian, following the departing group of courtiers and lords, motioned a guard to follow him as he headed down a side corridor.

As the door closed and bolted, Kelson finally collapsed under the strain, clutching at Morgan's cloak as he crumpled in a limp heap at the general's feet. Morgan picked him up, scowling grimly as he carried the boy to the royal bed, and Duncan at last emerged from his hiding place on the balcony.

"Hmmm, it's cold out there," Duncan commented, blowing on his hands as he approached the other side of the bed. "Is he all right?"

"He will be," Morgan said, loosening the boy's collar and beginning to unlace the red velvet doublet. "It cost him a lot to force himself back like that, though. I thought you said he'd sleep until morning."

Duncan felt the boy's forehead, then began unwrapping the wounded hand. "It's a good thing he didn't. You'd have had a hard time explaining things to those guards. It wasn't easy as it was."

He grunted approval, then rebandaged Kelson's hand. Morgan unfastened the boy's cloak and pulled it out from under him, then lifted his shoulders so Duncan could remove the doublet. As he did, Kelson opened his eyes.

"Morgan? Father Duncan?" he questioned weakly.

"We're here, my prince," Morgan replied, laying the boy back on his pillows.

Kelson turned his head right and found Morgan.

"Morgan, did I do all right?" he asked, his voice almost a whisper. "I'm afraid I sounded rather pompous."

"You did just fine," Morgan smiled. "Brion would have been proud of you."

Kelson smiled weakly and turned his eyes toward the ceiling. "I saw him, Morgan. And I heard his voice —before, I mean. He called my name, and then—" he turned his head toward Duncan. "It was like being wrapped in silk, or woven sunlight—no, moonlight. And there was someone else, too, Father Duncan. A man with a shining face and golden hair—but it wasn't you, Morgan. I remember, I was frightened, but then—"

"Hush, now, my prince," Morgan said, reaching across and placing his hand on the boy's forehead. "You must sleep now and rest. Sleep now, my prince. I won't be far away."

As he spoke, Kelson's eyelids fluttered briefly, then closed, and his breathing once again slowed to that of deep slumber. Morgan smiled and smoothed the tousled hair, then helped Duncan pull off the boy's boots. When they had covered him against the night's cold, Duncan blew out all but one of the lights in the sleeping area, then followed Morgan to the fireplace.

Morgan leaned his arms and forehead against the mantle and stared into the flames at his feet.

"Something strange is happening," Morgan whispered as Duncan came up behind him. "I would be willing to *bet* that I know what other face Kelson saw during the ritual."

"Saint Camber?" Duncan replied. He stepped back and stood with hands clasped behind his back as Morgan raised his head to run a weary hand across his eyes.

"Yes," Morgan said. "And here's another thing that'll chill you to the soul. Derry was wounded out there in the corridor. He was near death when I reached him, with a hole in his side big enough to put your fist into. And I healed him!"

"You *what?*"

"I know, it sounds ridiculous," Morgan continued. "But I had this vague recollection about an ancient healing power that some Deryni were supposed to have had in the nether times. And some—wild hope, or something—I don't know—anyway, I had to try it. I didn't think it would work. How could it after so many years, in a Deryni half-breed who has never even been free to use the powers he *has* to the proper degree, much less . . .

"At any rate, I tried. I used my gryphon seal as a point of concentration, the same way I did when I was searching for clues in the library. I had my hands on his forehead, my eyes closed. And then, suddenly, I could feel another Presence with me, another pair of hands resting on mine, power surging through me, yet not really coming from me."

He paused and took a deep breath. "Duncan, I swear by all I hold sacred, I've never seen anything like it. As I opened my eyes—startled out of my wits, believe me—Derry started breathing normally, as though he were just asleep! I uncovered the wound, and it was gone! Vanished with a trace!"

Duncan was staring at his companion open-mouthed.

"I swear it, Duncan," he continued, almost to himself, "he was *healed,* completely, without a mark to show for it. Even his wrist was healed. I—" His voice faltered. "You're the expert on miracles, Father. Suppose you tell *me* what happened."

Duncan recovered his presence of mind sufficiently to close his mouth, then shook his head in disbelief. "I can't explain it, Alaric. You—you think it was the same Presence as in your vision?"

Morgan rubbed his hand across his chin and shook his head. "I don't know. But it's as though someone's putting ideas in my head, ideas over which I have no real control. So far, they've been good ideas, but—hell, Duncan. Maybe we *do* have Camber of Culdi working for us. At this point, I'm ready to believe almost anything, no matter how farfetched." He crossed to the balcony doors and pulled aside the drapes, stood there looking out across the darkened city. "After all, what do a couple of half-breed Deryni know about anything?"

Duncan crossed to the doors and followed Morgan's gaze. "There's got to be some rational explanation, Alaric. Maybe it will all be clear once the power struggle is over."

Morgan nodded. "All right. Dismiss it that way if you like. I have another problem. Did anything else bother you about tonight?"

"You mean Lord Edgar's attack, or his turnabout occupation?"

"Neither," Morgan replied. "That Kelson was able to Truth-Read. I wish you'd told me you taught him to do that. It would have saved me a lot of worrying."

"Me?" Duncan answered, mystified. "You mean, you didn't teach him?"

Morgan let the drape fall back in place and turned to face Duncan aghast. "Surely you jest. I never—" he paused to think. "Is it possible that Brion taught him?"

"Out of the question," Duncan replied. "Brion wasn't Deryni, and only another Deryni could have taught him that."

"Has he ever seen you do it?" Morgan insisted.

"Never! I hadn't made *any* practical demonstrations to Kelson before today. Remember, he didn't even know what I was. Could he have seen you do it?"

"Of course he could have. Dozens of times. But without his father's powers, which he shouldn't be able to use yet. . . . Duncan, I've just had a harrowing thought. Is it possible the boy has Deryni blood?"

Duncan reflected. "I don't see how. Brion was full human. There's absolutely no doubt about that, so— you're not implying that Brion's not his father, are you? That's absurd."

Morgan shook his head distractedly. "No, Brion is his father, all right. You have only to look at him to see that. You don't suppose that Jehana . . ."

His eyes narrowed suspiciously as his voice trailed off. He looked across at Duncan and was heartened to see that his cousin's reaction mirrored his own.

Duncan let out a long sigh of disbelief and shook his head. "The Queen a Deryni? It would certainly explain a lot, if true: her hypersensitivity about Brion's powers, her adamant stand against you, outwardly based on religious fervor. . . . Do you suppose she realizes?"

"Maybe not," Morgan said thoughtfully. "You know as well as I how dangerous it can be to be Deryni. I'm sure there have been many Deryni in the past five or six generations who decided it was safest not to tell their children what they were. And in a world where civil and ecclesiastical law forbid dabbling in the arcane, how are you going to find out? If you've got the Deryni capability and know it, that's one thing. You can always find someone to guide you in its development if you look hard enough.

"But if you don't know what you are, and such queries are highly frowned upon, to say the least, there's not much you can do, is there? I'm not saying that was the case with Jehana, but you can see how easily we could have missed it all these years. There are probably thousands of Deryni who don't know what they are."

"I can't argue with that," Duncan agreed. "Anyway, if Jehana *is* Deryni, that might give us just the edge we need for tomorrow. At least if we've somehow ruined the ritual sequence, there's no telling what Kelson may have on tap from his own resources. Tonight was a splendid example."

Morgan shook his head. "I still don't like it. Kelson's totally untrained. His proficiency was supposed to come with the acquisition of Brion's powers." He paused. "I wonder if even Brion suspected what he was leaving in our laps. At this point, I'm not sure whether to look on it as a curse or a blessing."

Duncan smiled and crossed back to the fireplace. "Did we accept Brion's charge because we thought it would be easy? Or because we loved Brion, love his son—and because it's right?"

Morgan chuckled softly. "All right, Father. No sermons, please. I think you know that my motives match yours rather precisely." He clenched his hands together, unconsciously rubbing the gryphon signet with his thumb. "But you must admit, there's suddenly a whole new flock of variables. Kelson's own possible powers; Jehana— can she stand idly by and watch her son die? And now, a traitor in our very midst, it seems."

"A traitor—?"

"In the palace, at least. And evidently fairly highly placed. You don't think Charissa set up that Edgar episode herself, do you? She's got someone else working with her, all right."

"Well, since you're itemizing, here's something else to worry about," Duncan said. "Suppose Charissa beats Kelson tomorrow?—and it could happen if all our parameters go against us. What happens to Kelson? What happens to the kingdom? And what happens to all those who supported Kelson and Brion, like you?"

"And you, Cousin," Morgan countered, raising an eyebrow. "If Charissa wins, that collar of yours won't be much protection. As Kelson's confessor and my kinsman, you were doubly damned from the start. And your necessary part in tomorrow's festivities will only seal your fate."

"Afraid?" Duncan smiled.

"Hell, yes!" Morgan snorted. "I'd be a fool not to be—and I hope I haven't reached that stage yet. Anyway, we won't solve anything else by further speculation tonight. I don't know about you, but I'm asleep on my feet."

"Amen to that!" Duncan agreed. "Not only that, but

I'm not even supposed to be here. If I hurry, I might be able to get back before I'm missed. Somehow, I don't think my esteemed Archbishop would approve of what I've been up to tonight." He glanced across at the sleeping Kelson, then moved toward the hidden door. "I think I've used more power today than I have in the past ten years!"

"It's good for you. You should do it more often," Morgan grinned, opening the passage and handing Duncan a lighted candle from the mantle.

Duncan's priestly half told him he should ignore the remark, but he could not restrain a small smile as he stepped into the passageway.

"Is there anything you need?" he asked, pausing in the opening. "Kelson should sleep until dawn, but . . ."

"That's what you said the *last* time!" Morgan snorted softly.

"Now, Alaric, you know that wasn't my fault," Duncan whispered in a mock-serious tone. "Besides, I would think you've entertained enough guests for tonight. I'm too tired for any more parties!"

Before Morgan could frame a suitable reply, Duncan had turned and disappeared down the dark stairway. Morgan shook his head and chuckled in appreciation, then closed the hidden door securely. He stared at it absently for a long moment, then turned back to the fireplace.

It had been a long day—a long two weeks. And though the end was now in sight, he knew that the most difficult time was still to come.

He rubbed a weary hand across his eyes and tried to make himself put the worries from his mind. If he was going to be any help to Kelson in the morning, he would have to get some sleep.

He pulled the overstuffed chair from in front of the fireplace to a spot by Kelson's bed, then unclasped his cloak and sank down wearily in the soft cushions. As he touched the chair, a wave of lethargy surrounded him, urging sleep and rest. It was all he could do to make himself pull off his boots and drag the sable-lined cloak over him as a makeshift blanket before sleep claimed him at last.

As consciousness faded, he was dimly aware that Kelson still slept soundly, that all was as it should be in the still, dark chamber, that he would reawaken instantly if anything in that situation should change.

That settled, he slept.

For Lord Ian Howell, however, the long night had just begun. As the tall young lord opened the door to his chambers, he beckoned the guard who had accompanied him to enter also.

"What is your name, my friend?" he asked, closing the door gently behind him.

"John of Elsworth, M'lord," the guard replied crisply.

He was not like the first guard Ian had used for his evil purposes. John of Elsworth was short, stocky, hard, an older man with years of experience in the royal regiment. He was also very strong—which was why Ian had chosen him.

Ian smiled to himself as he crossed to a table in the room and poured himself a glass of wine. "Very good," he said, turning back to face the man. "I have something I want you to do for me now."

"Yes, M'lord," the guard said promptly.

Ian crossed leisurely back to the guard and looked him in the eye. "Look at me, John," he commanded.

The guard's eyes met Ian's, slightly puzzled, and Ian held up his forefinger.

"Do you see my finger?" Ian questioned, slowly moving it toward the man's face.

"Yes, M'lord," the guard replied, his eyes following the finger.

As Ian's finger touched the man's forehead between his eyes, he whispered one word, "Sleep," and the man's eyes closed. It required but a moment more of concentration to establish rapport with his female compatriot many miles away. The aura crackling around him and his unwitting medium cast ghostly shadow-shapes on the tapestried walls.

"Charissa, do you hear me?"

The man's mouth moved, and then spoke in another voice. "I hear."

Ian smiled. "They've been to the crypt as you predicted, my love. Kelson's wearing the Eye of Rom. I don't think anyone else even noticed in all the excitement. I couldn't tell if they'd been successful with the power transfer. The boy was deadly tired, but that's to be expected."

There was a pause, and then the guard replied, his voice deep and resonant, but the tone and inflection that of the Lady Charissa. "Well, he can't have completed the whole power sequence yet. That's always reserved for the coronation or some other important public ceremony. Which means there are several courses we can pursue to further undermine their morale. You know what to do in the cathedral?"

"Of course."

"Good. And be certain there's no mistake who will be blamed. Earlier tonight, I received another admonition from the Camberian Council warning me to stop interfering. Naturally, I don't intend to heed their advice. But it won't hurt to keep them befuddled a while longer. After all, Morgan is half-Deryni. It's even conceivable that the Council could blame the whole thing on him if we plan this properly."

Ian snorted. "The idea of the Council dictating to

the daughter of Marluk is ludicrous anyway. Who does that Coram think he is?"

He received the distinct impression of a smug smile as the voice replied. "No matter, Ian. You'd better get on with your work before you tire your subject beyond recall. His death could arouse the wrong suspicions, and I don't want your cover broken yet."

"Have no fear, my pet," Ian chuckled. "Until later."

"Even until then," the voice replied.

The aura faded and Ian opened his eyes, still keeping his subject under control.

"John of Elsworth, do you hear me?"

"Aye."

Ian shifted his touch to the man's eyelids, pressing on them lightly. "You will remember nothing of what has just happened, John. Is that clear? When I release you, you will recall only that I asked for your escort to my quarters."

The man nodded his head almost imperceptibly.

"Good, then," Ian murmured, dropping his hands. "You will now awake and remember nothing."

As Ian returned to the table and picked up his glass of wine, John of Elsworth's eyes snapped open and he glanced innocently at Ian.

"Is there anything further you require of me, M'lord?"

Ian shook his head and took a swallow from his glass. "No. But if you would be so good as to stand guard outside my door, I'd appreciate it. What with killers stalking the corridors of Castle Rhemuth, I should hate to be murdered in my bed."

"Very good, M'lord," John bowed. "I'll see that no one disturbs you."

Ian raised his glass in acknowledgement, then drained its contents and put it back on the table as the door closed behind John of Elsworth.

Now for the immediate matter at hand: a simple assassination—no more. Granted, it could be a bit messy, and possibly even physically tiring, since there were three involved. But it presented no serious challenge to his talents. Boring, really.

He did lament the fact that he could jump only as far as the cathedral with his remaining power—but that was at most a minor vexation. Charissa would replace the power he used and more as soon as he returned. In fact, all things considered, a short taste of more conventional transportation would probably do him good, help him unwind. There was nothing like a brisk ride in the November night to clear a man's head of the thoughts of killing and put him in the frame of mind for more enjoyable pursuits.

Quickly, he stepped to the center of the room and gathered his cloak around him. Then, murmuring the words of the spell Charissa had taught him, he made the proper pass in the air before him with an outstretched arm—and disappeared.

Later—much later—Ian drew rein in a deeply wooded area in the hills north of Rhemuth. He listened for a long, silent minute, then urged his horse forward at a walk, letting the animal pick its own footing in the dark, moonless night. Snow was falling gently now, and Ian pulled his hooded cloak more closely around himself as he rode through the darkness.

At length, he found himself riding alongside a sheer cliff-face, naked rock to his right and higher than the eye could see. He had ridden for perhaps half a mile when he was suddenly challenged by a gruff voice.

"Who goes there?"

"Lord Ian. I've come to see Her Grace."

Off to the left, someone struck a spark, and then a torch flared in the darkness. The man holding the torch held it aloft and walked slowly toward Ian. And Ian could see at least a half dozen men around him, just within the circle of torchlight. When the man with the torch had almost reached Ian, another man stepped out of the blackness directly ahead of Ian and took hold of his horse's bridle.

"Sorry, M'lord," he said roughly. "We weren't expecting you tonight."

Ian flung back his hood and dismounted, watched as the speaker handed his horse's reins to another man, who led the animal away to hidden stables. Ian began stripping off his gloves and looked around.

"Is our Lady still about?"

"Aye, M'lord," the guard captain replied, touching a portion of the rock wall beside him. "I can't say whether she's expecting you, though."

A portion of the wall withdrew to disclose a passageway into the heart of the cliff, and Ian stepped through, followed by the captain and several guards.

"Oh, she's expecting me," he said with a sly smile which was lost to the guards in the darkness of the passage. He waited until his eyes had adjusted to the darkness, then headed confidently down the long corridor, toward more dim torchlight in the distance.

As Ian walked, he slapped the leather riding gloves gently against the palm of his other hand. His boots echoed hollowly on the marble-paved passageway. The heavy cloak sighed softly as it brushed against the elegantly booted legs. The fine steel of his scabbard gave off muffled pings whenever it glanced off against his boots.

Odd, what strange alliances one sometimes formed in the pursuit of one's goals. He had certainly never planned to join forces with the fiery Charissa. Indeed, that had not even been considered in the beginning. And now, the daughter of the Marluk trusted him almost completely, had agreed to unite their powers in this common goal. Who would have dreamed, a year ago, that he, Ian Howell, would soon be the master of Corwyn?

He smiled to himself as he added another thought on that matter, but he did not allow himself to even sub-vocalize it. Further powers and rule awaited the right man, if he could but take it. And when dealing with the likes of Charissa, it was better not to even think such thoughts. Once Kelson and Morgan were dead, and his holding in Corwyn secure, there would be time enough for other matters. Meanwhile . . .

Silver spurs jangled gaily as he clattered down the granite staircase, and the torches in their wrought bronze holders cast crimson highlights on his chestnut hair, reflecting, perhaps, the even more crimson thoughts of the man who strode by so confidently.

He passed the guardpost and took the precise salute with a studied nonchalance, then approached a pair of golden doors with two tall Moors standing guard.

They made no move to stop him, however. And Ian slipped through the doors without a sound. Leaning back against the ornate handles, he fixed his gaze intently upon the woman who sat brushing her long, pale hair; all thoughts of malice gone, at least for the present.

"Well, Ian?" she queried. Her voice was low, husky, her full lips curved in a slight, sardonic smile.

Ian sauntered toward her with a careless intensity. "It went as I said it would, my pet," he said silkily, brushing a hand across her shoulder as he passed. "Did you expect otherwise?"

He paused to pour red wine from a crystal decanter, filled it once and drained it, then refilled it and carried it to a low table beside the spacious state bed.

"You generally perform according to your talents, Ian," Charissa said, without missing a stroke.

Ian unclasped his heavy cloak and dropped it across

a bench, unbuckled his sword and eased it to the floor as he sank down on the satin-draped bed.

"There will be no further problem tomorrow, then, Ian?" Charissa asked. She laid the silver-backed brush gently on the dresser top and stood, gathering the gossamer folds of her gown about her in a soft azure cloud.

"I think not," Ian smiled, reclining on one elbow and picking up his glass of wine. "Kelson has given orders he's not to be disturbed until morning. If he should make some move before then, however, we'll be informed immediately. I have someone watching." His brown eyes followed her every move hungrily as she glided toward him.

"So, he's given orders he's not to be disturbed, has he?" She rested delicate fingertips on his shoulder and smiled.

"I believe I shall give the same orders."

CHAPTER TWELVE

For surely laughter masks a nervous soul.

THE EARLY MORNING stillness was shattered by a staccato rapping at the door, and Morgan tensed and opened one eye, instantly alert. The brightness of the room indicated it was time to be up and about, and a rapid evaluation of his own condition assured him that the short sleep had been at least adequate. Whatever was about to happen, he was ready for it.

Easing to his feet, he glided to the door and placed a cautious hand on the latch, a quick wrist motion flicking the hilt of his stiletto into his palm. His voice was low as he stood aside and called, "Who's there?"

"Rhodri, the Lord Chamberlain, Your Grace," a voice answered. "The royal wardrobers wish to know when His Majesty will be ready for his bath and robing. It's getting late."

Morgan returned the stiletto to its sheath and shot back the bolt. The door swung open a foot to disclose a stately, white-haired gentleman in deep burgundy velvet, who bowed deferential greeting as Morgan stepped into view.

"Your Grace."

"What time is it, Lord Rhodri?" Morgan asked quietly.

"Past Terce, Your Grace. I would have called you earlier, but I thought both you and His Highness could use the extra sleep. There's still well over an hour before the procession begins."

Morgan smiled. "Thank you, Lord Rhodri. Tell the wardrobers Kelson will be with them shortly. Also, see if you can find my aide, Lord Derry. If I have to go to the coronation looking like this, there'll be no doubt in anybody's mind that I'm precisely the scoundrel I'm rumored to be."

He ran a meaningful hand over the golden stubble on his chin, and the Chamberlain concealed a smile. He and Morgan were friends of long standing, dating from the days shortly after Morgan first came to Brion's court as a page. Rhodri had been chamberlain even then, and the game he and Morgan played was one worn comfortable by the passing of the years. A small, golden-haired boy had stolen Rhodri's heart then, and now he remained just as devoted to the man.

His eyes twinkled in shared understanding as he looked Morgan straight in the eye. "There was never any doubt in anyone's mind, was there, Your Grace?" he replied dryly, his tone not requiring an answer. "And is there anything else Your Grace requires?"

Morgan shook his head, then snapped his fingers as he remembered one final instruction. "Yes. You'd better send for Monsignor McLain. Kelson will want to see him before he leaves for the cathedral."

"Yes, Your Grace," Rhodri bowed.

As Morgan closed the door and rebolted it, he suddenly realized that the room was cold again, so he padded back across the floor on bare feet to stir the remains of the fire and add more wood. When he was satisfied that it was burning properly, he crossed quickly to the balcony doors, dancing gingerly on tiptoes as his bare feet trod the cold flagstones.

As he drew aside the heavy blue satin drapes to let the pale sunlight stream in, he became aware that he was being watched. He turned and smiled at Kelson as he finished securing the drapes, then crossed to the boy's side and sat down.

"Good morning, my prince," he said cheerfully. "How do you feel?"

Kelson sat up in bed and pulled the blankets up around himself. "Hmm, it's cold. And I'm starved. What time is it?"

Morgan laughed and reached across to feel Kelson's forehead, then took the boy's wounded hand and began unwrapping the bandage. "It's not as late as you think, my prince," he chuckled. "Your body squires are drawing your bath and will be ready for you momentarily. And you know you can't eat until after the coronation."

Kelson bounced once on the bed in frustration, then leaned to look at his hand as Morgan removed the bandage. Other than a faint pink puncture mark on either side of his hand, he could see no sign of the previous night's ordeal. And as Morgan bent and manipulated the hand, Kelson was surprised that there was not even any of the tenderness he had expected when he moved it.

He looked up anxiously as Morgan released his hand and discarded the bandage. "Is it all right?"

Morgan slapped the boy's arm reassuringly. "No problems. You're as fit as a fiddle."

Kelson smiled, then poised himself to leave the bed. "Then, there's no reason I should stay in bed, is there?"

"None at all."

Morgan reached across and took Kelson's robe from

the foot of the bed, stood and held it so that the boy could shrug into it. Kelson bundled it around himself and scampered quickly to the fireplace, plopped down on the fur rug as he warmed himself.

"Umm, this feels good," he said, rubbing his hands together briskly and smoothing down his rumpled hair. "What's next?"

Morgan joined him and poked at the fire. "First of all, your bath. They should be about ready for you. And I'll send your wardrobers in to help you dress as soon as they arrive."

Kelson stopped rubbing his hands and wrinkled his nose in distaste. "Devil take it, I can dress myself."

"A king must have dressers on his coronation day," Morgan laughed, taking the boy by the arm and urging him to his feet. "It's tradition. Besides, you're not supposed to clutter up your mind with the mechanics of putting on strange robes when you should be contemplating the responsibilities of kingship."

He propelled Kelson toward the door leading to the dressing room, but the boy paused there and looked back at Morgan suspiciously.

"So I have to have dressers, eh? How many?"

"Oh, six or so, I should imagine," Morgan replied, raising an innocent eyebrow.

"Six!" Kelson said indignantly. "Morgan, I don't need six dressers!"

"Is this a rebellion?" Morgan retorted, unable to control a grin.

He knew how Kelson felt about personal servants —he, too, hated being fussed over. But there were times when it couldn't be avoided. Kelson knew that, and his expression indicated that he realized that fact, too. But there were also signs that Morgan had not had the last word.

As the boy opened the door and started through, he suddenly turned and looked at Morgan with an expression of mock indignation. "I still think," he said haughtily, "that you planned all this deliberately."

"I've been planning deliberately to make you a king," Morgan retorted, his patience wearing thin. "Now, get in there!"

He made a motion as if to chase the boy, and Kelson ducked on through the doorway. The door closed with a note of finality, but not before Kelson had poked his head back through and stuck out his tongue.

Morgan rolled his eyes heavenward in a silent appeal to whatever saint controlled the whims of royal princes. Kelson's maturity of the previous day and of the night seemed to have disappeared entirely. He hoped it was not going to set the tone of the entire day.

Before he could decide on the next course of action, there was another knock on the door.

"Who's there?"

"Derry, M'lord," the familiar voice replied.

Morgan crossed to the door and shot back the bolt to admit Derry. With the young lord were two squires bearing hot water, towels, and fresh clothing. Derry himself looked rested and refreshed in his crisp new livery. The sling was gone from his left arm, mute reminder of the night before.

"I'm glad to see you've fully recovered," Morgan remarked.

"Yes. Strange thing, wasn't it, M'lord?" Derry replied dryly. "I don't suppose you'd like to—"

"Later, Derry," Morgan interrupted, shaking his head slightly as he stood aside to let them enter. "Right now I feel the urgent need of more mundane repairs—such as a hot bath."

"Yes, M'lord," said Derry, taking the hint and gesturing to the two squires accompanying him. "Now if you'll just follow me, gentlemen, I'll show you how His Grace likes things done."

Morgan shook his head and chuckled as Derry took things in hand, then followed them into the room. At least he wouldn't have to show up at the coronation looking like the legendary Wild Man of Torenth now. And explanations to Derry would have to wait until they had some privacy.

Elsewhere in the palace, another was also about his business —one whose day had begun several hours earlier in a place not many miles away. From the arms of an incredibly beautiful and evil woman he had come, borne on the wings of a Deryni spell to complete a specific task and then return.

In an alcove just off one of the main corridors, he bided his time, waiting for just the right passers-by. A fairly large group of pages and squires in formal livery came past, laden with white and golden robes which could only be Kelson's. But these were not the ones he sought this morning.

As the entourage passed, he pretended to be absorbed with a temperamental fastening on his cloak of gold. As soon as they were past, however, he resumed his vigil.

After perhaps ten minutes of this subterfuge, and perhaps three repeats of the cloak ruse, his quarry came into sight as he had known they would: two royal squires carrying a resplendent black velvet cloak and a polished wooden jewel case.

Ian timed his interference perfectly, stepping into their path just as they came abreast of his alcove. The maneuver cost one of them his footing, as had been intended. And then Ian was apologizing profusely and helping the young man to his feet, helping him pick up the baubles and chains which had spilled from the wooden chest.

It never occurred to the young man to check the contents of the chest after the encounter; never occurred to him that the great Lord Ian might have substituted another item for one particularly fine badge of office—that of the King's Champion.

In Kelson's quarters, Morgan gave himself a critical appraisal in the hand mirror as Derry wiped the last traces of soap from his lord's chin and ears. After a bath and a shave, he felt almost like a new man. And sitting here in clean shirt and breeches was more luxury than he could remember for months. It was almost enough to make him appreciate the fortune of his noble birth.

As Derry dismissed the two squires who had been assisting him, Duncan slipped into the room with a silent signal that the young Marcher lord should give no warning. Gliding up quietly behind Morgan, he exchanged places with Derry and continued dusting lint from the white linen shirt.

"Well, well. The prodigal seeks to amend his appearance!"

Morgan whirled in surprise, almost reaching for his weapon, then relaxed and grinned as he realized it was Duncan. With a wave, he dismissed Derry to continue with his other duties, then settled back in his chair as Duncan came around in front of the fireplace.

"I do wish you wouldn't sneak up on me like that," Morgan said. "If Derry hadn't been here, I might have taken off your head before I realized it was you."

Duncan smiled and sat down casually on the arm of another chair. "You would have realized in time," he said quietly. "An uneventful night after I left, I take it?"

Morgan nodded. "What else could have happened?"

"Earthquakes, floods, more miracles?" Duncan shrugged. "Anyway, I have a little surprise for you this morning."

"Are you sure I can stand it?" Morgan asked dubiously. "After some of the surprises I've had in the past twenty-four hours, I'm not sure I'm ready for any more."

"Oh, it isn't really much," Duncan answered with a droll smile. He reached into his cinture and removed something small wrapped in a scrap of velvet, dropped it into Morgan's hand. "Kelson asked me to see that you got this. It seems you're to be his Champion."

"His Champion?" Morgan retorted, his eyes snapping up to stare at Duncan. "How do you know that?"

"Well, after all, Kelson does tell me a few things he doesn't tell you," Duncan said, gazing innocently at the ceiling. "Besides, who did you think it would be, you crazy war horse? Me?"

Morgan laughed delightedly and shook his head, then eagerly unwrapped the scrap of velvet. Inside was a massive signet ring, an oval cabochon-cut onyx etched with the Golden Lion of Gwynedd on its face.

Morgan stared at it in fascination for a moment, then breathed on it and polished it against his sleeve. The gem gleamed like frozen midnight as Morgan slipped it onto his right index finger, then held out both hands, palms down. The Lion of Gwynedd and the Corwyn Gryphon winked gold and green in the light.

"I really didn't expect this," Morgan finally breathed, lowering his hands and standing there sheepishly. "I still don't understand how he did it, either. The office of King's Champion has always been a hereditary post."

He glanced again at the ring, as though still unable to believe, then shook his head lightly.

Duncan smiled and glanced around the room. "Where *is* Kelson, by the way?"

"In the bath," Morgan replied, picking up one of his freshly polished boots and dusting it off with a cloth. "He was a bit—shall I say, 'upset?'—about having to have dressers this morning. He wanted to know why he couldn't dress himself. I implied that this was just one of the trials of kingship he'd have to put up with, and that seemed to satisfy him for the most part."

Duncan picked up Morgan's other boot and chuckled. "When he sees everything he's got to wear today, he'll be very glad he's got those dressers. Many's the time I've been grateful for even one assistant to help me vest for some important ceremony." He gave a weary sigh. "There are always so many little laces and ties."

Morgan snatched his other boot from Duncan and snorted, "Ha! You know you love it!" He began dusting the boot energetically. "By the way, any trouble last night?"

"Only getting to sleep," Duncan replied. He watched as Morgan began pulling on his boots, then picked up his cousin's discarded mail shirt and turned it right-side out. Morgan stuck his head and arms into the mail and settled it over his shoulders, smoothed the light links over the white linen shirt he had donned after his bath.

Over that, he drew on a fine, light-weight shirt of scarlet silk and began lacing it up the front. Duncan laced the sleeves close to his wrists, then held out a black velvet doublet edged with gold embroidery and pearls. Morgan whistled lightly under his breath at the extravagance of the garment, then eased it on without further comment. He adjusted the full, split sleeves to show the scarlet beneath, then held up his arms while Duncan wrapped his waist with a wide, crimson sash.

As he reached for his sword in its worn leather scabbard, clipped it to a ring hidden in the sash, Duncan stepped back to view the overall effect. The priest gave him a long, appraising stare, then shook his head and raised an eyebrow in mock despair.

"Nope, I'm afraid there's simply no getting around it," he muttered. "In spite of everything, I do believe you'll be the most devilishly handsome Champion we've had in a long time!"

"You're absolutely right!" Morgan agreed striking a pose.

"And you will also be the most conceited Champion we've ever had!" his cousin went on.

"What?"

Duncan wagged an indignant finger. "Now, Alaric, remember. I'm your spiritual father. I'm only telling you this for your own good!"

It was no longer possible to maintain a straight face. Morgan was the first to realize that fact, and he promptly dissolved into peals of laughter, hands held helplessly to his sides. Almost simultaneously, Duncan, too, burst out laughing and collapsed weakly in the overstuffed chair, no longer able to control himself.

Presently, a red-liveried attendant poked his head through the doorway to Kelson's dressing room. His expression was very disapproving, for he had heard the laughter even inside, and his tone was cool as he addressed the two young lords.

"Is there anything wrong, Your Grace?"

Morgan managed to control his laughter enough to shake his head and wave the man off, then sobered and called out again. "Is His Highness ready yet? Monsignor McLain has to leave for the cathedral soon."

"I'm ready now, Father," Kelson said, sweeping into the room.

As Morgan straightened, Duncan came to his feet, both of them scarcely able to believe that this white and gold-clad King was the same boy who had knelt with them so frightened the night before.

All in silk and satin, he stood before them like a young angel, the creamy whiteness of his raiment broken only by the subtle play of gold and rubies encrusting the edges. Over the whole was thrown a magnificent ivory cloak, the satin stiff with gold and silver jewelwork and lined in clear crimson.

In his hands he held a pair of spotless kid gloves and a pair of gold-chased silver spurs. His raven head was bare, as befits an uncrowned monarch.

"I see you've been informed of your new title," the boy said, eyeing Morgan's change of garb with approval. "Here," he held out the spurs. "These are for you."

Morgan sank to one knee and bowed his head. "My prince, I'm at a loss for words."

"Nonsense," Kelson retorted. "You'd better not be tongue-tied when I need you most."

He handed the spurs to Morgan and motioned him to rise, then turned to the attendant who still stood in the doorway.

"Giles, do you have the rest of General Morgan's regalia?"

The man bowed and signalled through the doorway, and three more attendants entered, two of them carrying the regalia Ian had intercepted in the corridor earlier that morning. The third carried a wide baldric of red leather, the edges tooled in gold. All three stood at attention in a single line beside their leader.

Kelson turned back to Morgan. "As King's Champion, there are a few items you're required to wear at ceremonials," he said, a slight smile on his face. "I'm sure you won't mind if my dressers help you with them while I speak with my confessor."

As the three dressers swarmed around Morgan with their regalia, the prince motioned Duncan to follow him. They went out on the balcony and closed the doors. Through the glass, they could see the dressers fussing over an annoyed Morgan. Kelson watched the scene for a moment, then turned to Duncan.

"Do you think he'll be terribly upset with me, Father?"

Duncan smiled and shook his head. "I doubt it, my prince. He was too proud when you entered the room to be angry for long."

Kelson smiled fleetingly and looked out over the city, leaning his elbows on the cold stone balcony railing. The chill wind stirred his hair slightly, but the cloak was too heavy to be affected. Overhead, storm clouds raced across the sky, threatening to cover the sun, and the air had grown suddenly damp.

Kelson clasped his arms across his chest and looked down for a long moment, then finally spoke in a low voice.

"Father, what makes a man a King?"

Duncan considered the question for a moment, then joined the boy at the rail.

"I'm not certain anyone can really say, my son," he answered thoughtfully. "It may well be that kings are not so different from ordinary men after all. Except, of course, that they have a graver responsibility. I think you need have little worry on that count."

"But some kings are not ordinary men, Father," Kelson said quietly. "How do they cope with what is demanded of them? And suppose a king finds that he's not extraordinary after all? What does *he* do when the same demands are still made, when—"

"You are not an ordinary man, Kelson," Duncan stated flatly. "And you will be an extraordinary King. Do not doubt it. And never forget it."

Kelson mulled the answer for a long moment, then turned and knelt at the feet of the priest.

"Father, give me your blessing," he whispered, bowing his head. "Extraordinary or not, I'm frightened. And I don't feel at all like a King."

Morgan fussed and fumed as the royal wardrobers swarmed around him, trying hard to stand still and submit gracefully since he knew Kelson could see him from the balcony. It was difficult, however. He was simply ill at ease when surrounded by so many attendants.

Two of the squires were kneeling at his feet, carefully affixing the gilded spurs to his boots, giving the smooth black leather a final polish. The one called Giles took Morgan's sword and handed it to one of his companions, then took the red leather baldric and looped it across Morgan's chest. As he reattached the sword, Morgan breathed a little easier, for he had felt almost naked without his blade. And the slim stiletto in its mail sheath at his wrist would have been little use if any of these men had decided to rid the world of another Deryni.

As Morgan adjusted the hilt of the sword to his liking, Giles went to the wooden jewel chest and took out a dark golden chain of office with pendant badge. He was not permitted the satisfaction of further ceremony, however. For Morgan took the chain from him before he could even try to assist, placed it around his own neck. The sooner he could get through with this, the better he would like it.

The two squires kneeling at his feet gave his boots a final wipe with their cloths, then stood, and a third adjusted the sleeves of his doublet for at least the third time. Then they ushered him before a mirror held by Giles, where the squires of the spurs now held out a magnificent black velvet cloak collared in black fox and lined with deep crimson silk.

Morgan was forced to raise an eyebrow at that, for never before had he worn a garment so resplendent. As the squires fastened it in place on his shoulders, adjusted the chain of office so that the collar did not interfere, Morgan had to admit that the overall effect was impressive.

He was just turning to admire his profile in the mirror when there was a tremendous pounding on the door. Morgan's hand went to the hilt of his sword and the dressers stood back in surprise as the pounding stopped, then resumed again.

"Alaric! Alaric, are you still in there? I've got to talk to you!" It was Nigel's voice.

Morgan reached the door in about four long strides and threw back the bolt. Even as he opened the door, Nigel pushed his way through and closed the door behind him. The royal duke was obviously shaken.

"Where's Kelson?" he asked, his eyes scanning the room anxiously as he moved away from the door. "All of you," he motioned to the dressers, "out!"

As they left, Morgan went to the balcony doors and tapped on the glass. Duncan looked up, saw Morgan's serious expression, Nigel behind, and nodded. As he helped Kelson to his feet, Morgan opened the doors to the balcony and stood aside for prince and priest to enter.

"What is it, Uncle?" Kelson questioned in alarm, seeing the grave expression on Nigel's face and sensing that something of great import was about to be said.

Nigel chewed his lower lip and scowled. How could he tell the boy what he'd just seen? And worse, how could he relate the facts without making them sound like an accusation?

"Kelson," he began, not meeting anyone's eyes, "I have something to tell you that isn't going to be easy—"

"Get to the point," Morgan interrupted.

Nigel nodded and swallowed hard, then began again.

"Very well. Someone broke into Brion's tomb last night."

Kelson glanced quickly at Morgan and Duncan, then back at Nigel. "Go on, Uncle."

Nigel hazarded a glance at Kelson, then looked down in slight dismay, for the boy did not seem surprised at the news. Could it be . . . ?

"Someone broke into the crypt and opened the sepulcher," Nigel continued cautiously. "They stripped him of his jewels and fine robes," his voice broke, "then left him lying cold and naked on the stone floor." His voice became a whisper. "The two guards were found at their posts with their throats neatly slit, with no sign of a struggle. And Rogier—Rogier is dead by the tomb, with his own hand on the dagger and a terrible expression on his face, as though he fought whatever it was that made him do it."

Kelson's face went white and he clutched at Duncan's arm for support. Duncan, too, was very pale, and Morgan glanced uncomfortably at the floor.

"Are you asking whether *we* had anything to do with it, Nigel?" Morgan said quietly.

"You?" Nigel's head snapped up with a start. "God, I know you weren't responsible, Alaric!" He glanced down again and shifted his weight from one foot to the other, even more ill at ease than before. "You know what the others will say, though, don't you?"

"That the cursed Deryni has only reverted to true form," Duncan said quietly. "And it will be almost impossible to prove otherwise, because we *were* at the tomb last night."

Nigel nodded slowly. "I know."

"You know?" Duncan echoed.

Nigel gave a weary sigh, and his shoulders drooped dejectedly. "That's right. And I'm afraid it's not just Alaric who's implicated this time, either. You see, when I told you they found Rogier dead with his own hand on the dagger, I neglected to mention what was in his other hand."

The three hung on Nigel's every word.

"It was a gilded silver crucifix—yours, Duncan!"

CHAPTER THIRTEEN

*"New morn, ring hand. Defender's Sign
shall seal. . . ."*

A gilded silver crucifix—yours, Duncan!

The priest stopped breathing for just an instant.
There could be no appeal from that accusation, for the
crucifix *was* his. He could not deny it. What had gone
into the tomb with Brion on the day of burial was a
matter of record. Just as it was now a matter of record
that the tomb had been ransacked, and that a simple
silver crucifix had been found where it had no right to
be.

Duncan suddenly realized he was holding his breath
and let it out in a long exhalation. The situation put an
entirely different light on things. For now, not only
was he implicated in the various questionable doings
which had been occurring with such regularity, but his
very identity was in jeopardy. As far as he knew, only
Alaric and Kelson were aware of his Deryni heritage,
and he would prefer that it remain that way. But now,
there would be questions concerning his relationship

with Alaric and Kelson. There would be little he could say to explain his part in last night's escapade.

He cleared his throat uncomfortably and finally decided he would have to tell Nigel something. At least he could depend on the duke to keep his secret should it become necessary to tell all.

"We were at the tomb last night, Nigel. And we did open Brion's sepulcher," Duncan began slowly. "I won't even try to deny it." He clasped his hands together uneasily. "When we left, though, the tomb was sealed, and Rogier and the guards were alive. Needless to say, we had no part in their deaths."

Nigel shook his head uncomprehendingly. "But, why, Duncan? Why open the tomb in the first place? That's what I don't understand."

"We ran a far greater risk if we didn't open it," Morgan interjected. "Brion's ritual for Kelson called for something that was buried with him by mistake. We had to have it; nothing else would do. So we had to open the tomb." He glanced at his hands, at the two rings winking there. "As it was, it's a good thing we did. Brion was under a—a shape-changing spell. It had also bound his soul to some degree. We were able to break the spell and free him, though."

"Oh, my God!" Nigel murmured. "And you're sure that's all you did?"

"No," Morgan continued. "We also took what we had come for in the first place: the Eye of Rom. Kelson didn't want to just take it, so Duncan gave him the crucifix to leave in its place. We never dreamed that anyone would reopen the tomb after we'd gone."

"Well, they did," Nigel whispered, shaking his head. "Poor Brion. And poor Kelson. You're all going to be blamed for it, you know, regardless of what you say. Alaric, what are we going to do?"

Before Morgan could reply, there was a pounding at the door, and Nigel's head jerked up apprehensively.

"O Lord, that's probably Jehana! And she's found out about the crucifix. You'd better let her in before she has the door broken down!"

Before anyone else could move to intercept, Kelson glided to the door and slipped the bolt. As expected, an angry Jehana came trouncing through. But Kelson was quick to force the door closed behind her before any of the guards in her company could enter with her. Jehana was so furious, she did not seem to notice that fact, however, for she immediately stalked up to Morgan and Duncan and began to berate them.

"How dare you!" she whispered through clenched teeth. "How dare you turn on him like this! And *you,* Father Duncan!" she whirled on the priest. "You call yourself a man of God. Murderers have no right to that name!"

She whipped out her left hand to disclose Duncan's gilded crucifix, now stained to a deeper, redder hue, and brandished it before the priest's eyes.

"What do you have to say for yourself?" she demanded, never raising her voice from the low, deadly tone in which she had first started. "I defy you to give me a rational explanation for what you've done!"

When Duncan did not answer, she turned her attention back on Morgan, was just about to start on him again when she saw the Eye of Rom glittering darkly in Kelson's right ear. She froze, as though unable to believe what she saw, then turned on Kelson in a cold fury.

"You monster!" she spat. "You misbegotten creature of darkness! You would desecrate your own father's tomb, you would *murder* for this power! Oh, Kelson, see what this foul Deryni curse has brought you to!"

Kelson was speechless, chagrined. How could she believe such a thing of him? How could she have gained such a warped sense of truth, to link him and

Morgan with last night's terrible deed in the cathedral?

"Jehana," Morgan said quietly, "it's not what you think. We were—"

Jehana turned on him in a cold fury. "I don't want to hear about it!" she snapped. "And I forbid you to presume you know what I think about anything, you —you fiend! First you corrupted my husband, perhaps even brought about his death for all I know, now you're trying the same thing with my only son, and Rogier—poor, innocent Rogier, struck down and most wickedly murdered while he guarded the remains of his dead king. . . ." Her voice broke. "Well, you can just take it from there by yourself, Deryni. Because I don't intend to lend even token support to what you're about to do. And as for you Kelson, I wish you'd never been born!"

Kelson went white. "Mother!"

"Don't call me that," she replied, turning her face away from him and edging toward the door. "I want nothing further to do with you. Let Morgan take you to the coronation. I have no wish to see the throne of Gwynedd usurped by a—a . . ."

She began to sob bitterly and buried her face in her hands, her back to Kelson and the others. Kelson started to go to her, to comfort her, but Morgan forbade it with a sharp glance. If there was to be even a slight chance of success, they would have to have Jehana's support, even if given under duress. It was time to play the trump card.

"Jehana?" he called softly.

"Leave me alone!" she sobbed.

Morgan crossed to her side and began speaking to her in a low voice. "Very well, Jehana. I'm through coddling you. We're going to have to get a few things straight right now, and there isn't much time. Kelson is innocent of what you charge him with, and—"

"Save your Deryni lies for someone else, Morgan,"

she replied, wiping her eyes and moving her hand toward the door latch.

Morgan stepped between her and the door and leaned back against the latch, looking her directly in the eye. "Deryni lies, Jehana?" he asked quietly. "You use the term rather profusely, don't you think? Especially for one like you."

Jehana froze, a look of cautious bewilderment on her face. "What do you mean?"

"Don't look so innocent. You know what I'm talking about. I only marvel that I didn't think of it long ago. It would have explained so many things you've done through the years."

"What *are* you talking about?" Jehana demanded, almost backing off in the face of Morgan's confident demeanor.

"Why, your Deryni blood, of course," he said calmly. "Tell me, is it on your mother's side, or your father's side, or both?"

"My Deryni bl—Morgan, you're mad!" she whispered, her eyes wide with fear, betraying the doubt in her own mind.

Morgan smiled slowly. "I don't think so. Kelson has strong Deryni background from somewhere, and we both know it wasn't from Brion."

Jehana forced a laugh. "That's the most ridiculous thing I've ever heard. Why, everyone knows how I feel about the Deryni."

"Some of the most vociferous Deryni haters in history have been Deryni themselves, Jehana, or with some 'taint' of Deryni blood. Those who have studied these things say it comes from buried guilt feelings. It's what happens when a people bottle up their true selves for generations, perhaps; when they deny their true heritage."

"No!" Jehana blurted. "It isn't true. If it were, I would have known!"

"Perhaps you always have, in a way."

"No! I never—"

"Can you prove it?" Morgan replied mildly. "There's a way, you know."

"What?" Jehana whispered, shrinking away from him.

Morgan took her arm, pulled her closer to him. "Let me Mind-See for myself, Jehana. Let me clear up the matter once and for all."

Her eyes grew wide with horror, and she tried to pull away. "No! No, please!"

Morgan did not release his grip. "Are you willing to make a bargain, then?"

"What kind of a bargain?" Jehana whispered.

"Very simple," Morgan continued conversationally. "I think we both know what I'd find if I did Mind-See you. But to spare you that, I'm willing to let you keep your little illusion for a while longer—on one condition."

"Which is?"

"You will come to the coronation and at least support Kelson outwardly. You also will not attempt to interfere in whatever must be done in the course of today's events. Agreed?"

"Is this an ultimatum?" Jehana asked, some of her spirit returning.

"If you wish," Morgan replied calmly. "Which is it to be? Do I Mind-See, or will you cooperate with us, at least for today?"

Jehana dropped her gaze from Morgan and glanced furtively at Kelson. Morgan's threat was a powerful one. And because Jehana had suspected her origin, had considered the possibility of Deryni ancestry, the threat was all the more terrifying. She was not willing to accept it yet. And therefore, the coronation seemed infinitely the lesser of the two evils.

She raised her head, but would not meet Morgan's eyes.

"Very well," she whispered, her voice small and subdued in the quiet room.

"Very well what?" Morgan insisted.

"Very well, I'll go to the coronation," she answered reluctantly.

"And you'll behave yourself? You won't make a scene and embarrass us? I promise you, Jehana, all will be resolved to your satisfaction. You won't be disappointed. Trust us."

"Trust you?" she murmured. "Yes, I suppose I have no choice at this point, have I?" She looked down. "I —I won't make a scene."

Morgan nodded and released her arm. "Thank you, Jehana."

"Don't thank me, Morgan," she murmured, opening the door. "Remember that I am acting under duress, against my better judgement. I have no stomach for what must be done. Now, if you'll excuse me, I'll meet you in the procession later."

At a signal from Morgan, Nigel roused himself and went with Jehana, closing the door softly behind them as he went through. After a short pause, Morgan turned back to Kelson and Duncan and sighed.

"Well, it looks as though we must act on events as they occur from now on. There are no further preparations to make, no safeguards we can take. I'm sorry I had to be so rough with your mother, Kelson, but it was necessary."

"Is there really a chance I'm part Deryni, Morgan?" the boy asked. "Whatever gave you that idea? Or is it just a ruse to get Mother to cooperate?"

Morgan shrugged as he motioned the two to the door. "We don't know for sure, Kelson. There are strong indications that you *are* part Deryni, and under other circumstances I could simply Mind-See you to verify. But I don't think either of us can spare the energy drain at this late date just to satisfy our curiosity. You're far better off to rely on Brion's powers for today."

"I understand," Kelson said.

"Good. Let's begin the procession, then," Morgan concluded. "Duncan?"

"Ready," the priest replied.

"My prince?"

Kelson took a deep breath.

"Let it begin," he said.

Charissa raised her head and took her eyes from the crystal into which she had been gazing.

"So the little Queen is part Deryni," she murmured. "Ian, can't you stop that pacing? You're making me nervous!"

Ian stopped almost in mid-stride and made a half-bow in Charissa's direction. "Sorry, my pet," he replied good-naturedly. "But you know how I detest waiting. I've anticipated this day for many months, now."

"I am aware of that," Charissa said, adjusting the sapphire coronet on her pale hair. "If you will just be patient, though, you will be amply rewarded."

Ian nodded and raised a goblet in toast. "Thank you, love. And what of Jehana? Do you think she *is* Deryni?"

"If she is, I can handle her," Charissa shrugged nonchalantly. "The least of my worries this morning is an untrained Deryni of unknown parentage who won't even acknowledge her ancestry."

Ian stood up and buckled on his sword, then picked up his golden cloak and flung it over his arm.

"Well, I'd best get going, then. The procession will be forming. You're sure you won't let me reveal myself until the last possible minute?"

Charissa smiled wryly. "No, you may not make your entrance with me," she said. "And if you are called upon to assist me openly, it will be to destroy Morgan at all costs. Is that clear?"

"Perfectly, love," Ian said with a wink. He paused with his hand on the door latch. "I'll see you at the church."

When the doors had closed behind Ian, Charissa returned her attention to the crystal on the dresser before her. In it, she could see approximately what Morgan saw—all that lay within the scope of the large stone in the general's badge of office. She caught a glimpse of Kelson in his State coach to Morgan's left, then the view straight ahead, beyond the ears of the black charger Morgan rode.

Soon, they would be at the cathedral. It was time she, too, was on her way.

As Morgan drew rein before the Cathedral of Saint George, he glanced around suspiciously as he had done at least a hundred times during the slow procession to the cathedral. Beside him and slightly ahead, Kelson's open carriage had also come to a halt, and now three bishops and two archbishops were waiting to escort Kelson from the carriage to his place in the new procession being formed.

Archbishops Corrigan and Loris were scowling darkly—Morgan guessed they must have heard about the desecration of the crypt by now—but at least Bishop Arilan was extending a warm smile to his young king. Duncan was standing well back from the archbishops, trying both to be near Kelson to lend him moral support, and to stay well out of reach of his superiors.

As Morgan swung down from the great warhorse, he nodded to Duncan. Then he signalled for Derry, scanned the crowds anxiously as Derry saw him and hurried to his side.

"Trouble?" Derry asked.

"It could be," Morgan replied, jutting his chin in the direction of Kelson and the archbishops. "Have you seen anything out of the ordinary?"

"No sign of Charissa, if that's what you mean, M'lord," Derry said. "The crowd is odd, though. Almost as if they know something's going to happen."

"Well, they're right about that," Morgan retorted. "Something *is*." He scanned the buildings ahead, then gestured for Derry. "Do you see the bell tower adjoining the cathedral? I want you to go up there and keep a lookout. She'll have to bring some troops with her, so she can't just appear. Your warning should give us at least five minutes before she arrives at the cathedral."

"Right," Derry nodded. "When do you think she'll make her move, sir?"

"Probably in about an hour," Morgan said. "If I know Charissa, she'll wait until the coronation is well underway before she interrupts. She knows that we know she's coming, so she'll be counting on our own minds to increase our dread."

"She's accomplishing that already," Derry murmured.

As Derry slipped away to take up his watch, Morgan worked his way over to Duncan, dodging scurrying choir boys and servers, and also doing his best to stay out of sight of Loris and Corrigan.

"What's happening?" he asked in a low voice, as he slipped alongside his cousin.

Duncan raised an eyebrow. "My friend, you will not believe what I'm about to tell you. Corrigan was so upset about what happened in the crypt, he threatened to call the coronation off. Kelson managed to soothe *his* ruffled feathers, and then *Loris* started in. *He* wanted to arrest you, suspend me, and was seriously considering taking Kelson before a heresy tribunal."

"God, what next?" Morgan murmured under his breath, rolling his eyes.

"Don't worry," Duncan continued. "Kelson straightened him out. He threatened to banish him and strip away his temporal powers for even thinking such a thing. And then he hinted to Corrigan that any further dissent and he might end up banished, too. You should have seen old Corrigan. Even the *thought* of Arilan or some other bishop taking over Rhemuth and its estates was enough to scare him speechless."

Morgan let out a sigh of relief. "Do you think they'll cause any more trouble? We don't need a religious confrontation today, on top of everything else."

Duncan shook his head. "I don't think. They backed off muttering indignantly about heresy and other bad things. And I can guarantee they're not happy I'm still in the ceremony. But there isn't much they can do if they want to keep their own positions. Even Loris isn't that much of a fanatic."

"I hope you're right," Morgan said. "I assume you were able to stay out of their way until we arrived."

"Only by means of some judicious shuffling. I'm hoping to avoid that confrontation indefinitely."

An altar boy in gleaming white surplice and red cassock scurried up beside Duncan and tugged at his sleeve urgently, and Duncan moved off to take his place in the procession. Even as he left, a page appeared at Morgan's elbow with the sheathed Sword of State and indicated where Morgan should stand in the line.

As Kelson passed on his way to his appointed place, Morgan tried to flash him an encouraging smile, but the boy was evidently too shaken to notice. Loris and Corrigan were on either side of him, and they glared at Morgan as they passed. But Arilan, behind them, nodded pleasantly to Morgan with a little secret smile which seemed to tell him not to worry.

Damn those archbishops anyway! They had no right to upset the boy this way. He had a lot on his mind— more than any fourteen-year-old should be expected to contend with. And two dour and hostile archbishops were certainly not doing anything to ease the situation.

Someone evidently gave a signal then, for the boys' choir at the head of the column suddenly began singing the processional. The line began to inch ahead: first the choir, then a bevy of altar boys with scrubbed faces and spotlessly clean white surplices over their crimson cassocks, all carrying tall candles in gleaming silver candlesticks.

Behind them came a thurifer swinging pungent incense at the end of a long golden chain, followed by a deacon carrying the heavy gilded cross of the Archbishopric of Rhemuth. Following the cross came the Archbishop himself, resplendent in vestments of white and gold, tall crozier in hand, jewelled miter adding several feet to his height, his face set and grim.

Kelson came next, walking under a golden canopy supported by four scarlet liveried noblemen. He was flanked by Archbishop Loris and Bishop Arilan, both of them in vestments matching Corrigan's, both wearing the tall miters of their offices. They were followed by four more bishops.

After the bishops came Duncan, in his honored place as King's Confessor. He carried the Ring of Fire on a small tray of heavily carved silver. Ring and tray cast brilliant reflections on the snowy lace surplice he wore over his cassock, flashed mirror brightness into his face as he walked.

Morgan followed, carrying the sheathed Sword of State upright before him. And after him, a white-faced and solemn Nigel, bearing the State Crown on its velvet cushion. Behind him, in ranks of two, came Jehana and Ewan, Duke Jared and Lord Kevin McLain, Lord Ian Howell, Lord Bran Coris, and a host of other high noblemen and women who were being honored by their inclusion in the procession. Most, of course, had no idea of the turmoil brewing beneath the surface of this august occasion.

Kelson's thoughts raced as the front of the procession approached the high altar inside the cathedral. He had put the quarrel with Archbishop Corrigan and Loris out of his mind as the least of his worries now, even though he realized that would just give him more time to worry about the other thing. He had seen no sign of the terrible Charissa yet, but he had no doubt she would show up before the ceremony was over.

He knelt at his personal faldstool to the right of the altar, ostensibly to pray while the rest of the procession entered and took their places, but he realized it was useless at this point. He couldn't concentrate on the prayers he should be saying, and he kept glancing to either side through the interlaced fingers covering his eyes.

Where was she?

He wondered briefly if it would have been this way even had there been no threat of the Shadowed One, examined his emotions on the subject, decided it would have been difficult to concentrate under the best of circumstances, immediately felt a little less guilty. Once the ceremony actually started, he promised himself, he would do better.

As the choir finished the processional, and the last of the participants took their places, Arilan and Loris came to either side and stood there expectantly. It was time for the recognition, Kelson knew. Taking a deep breath, he crossed himself, then raised his head and allowed the two prelates to help him to his feet. As they turned him to face the people, Archbishop Corrigan stepped in front of him and took his right hand.

"My Lords," Corrigan's voice rang out clear and sure, "I bring before you Kelson, your unredoubted King. Be ye willing to do homage and service in his behalf?"

"God save King Kelson!" came the affirmation.

With a slight bow toward the congregation, Corrigan gestured toward the altar, and Arilan and Loris escorted the now recognized King up the altar steps. All bowed in unison, and then Corrigan and Kelson ascended the last three steps alone. Firmly, Corrigan placed Kelson's right hand on Holy Scripture, placed his own left hand on top of Kelson's, then began to read the coronation oath.

"My Lord Kelson, are you now willing to take the coronation oath?"

"I am willing," Kelson replied.

Corrigan drew himself up to his full height. "Kelson Cinhil Rhys Anthony Haldane, here before God and men declared and affirmed to be the undisputed heir of our late beloved King Brion, will you solemnly promise and swear to keep the peace in Gwynedd, and to govern its peoples according to our ancient laws and customs?"

"I solemnly promise to do so."

"Will you, to the utmost of your power, cause Law and Justice, in Mercy, to be executed in all your judgements?"

Kelson glanced out at the assembly. "I will."

"And do you pledge that Evil and Wrong-Doing shall be suppressed, and the Laws of God maintained?"

"All this, I pledge," Kelson replied.

As Corrigan placed the coronation oath on the altar, Kelson glanced around again, felt confidence flow back as he caught Morgan's reassuring glance. With a flourish, he scrawled his new signature, *Kelsonus Rex*," then took the document in his left hand and held it aloft, placed his right hand once more on Holy Scripture.

"That which I have here promised, I will perform and keep, so help me God."

He gave the oath into the hands of one of the attending priests, then allowed himself to be led back to the faldstool. As he knelt there again, he caught a stealthy movement to his right, glanced aside and saw Derry glide unobtrusively to Morgan's side and begin conferring in low tones. As the Archbishop's voice echoed through the cathedral in the traditional prayers for the King, Kelson strained to hear what Derry told the tall Deryni Lord, bit his lip in vexation because he could not discern what was being said.

However, the meaning was clear enough. Kelson caught the worried look shot across to Duncan, saw the priest's lips tighten in anger as he realized what Derry had told. Charissa was coming. Derry had sighted her entourage from the bell tower. They had perhaps ten minutes before the ultimate confrontation.

The prayers for the King ended without Kelson having heard a word of them, and the two prelates again led him before the high altar, this time so that he might prostrate himself preparatory to the consecration.

The choir began to sing another anthem as Kelson laid himself prostrate on the carpet before the high altar. The long ivory mantle covered all but his head and the tips of his boots as he lay there. Around him, all his clergy knelt also, their lips moving in prayer.

Kelson clenched his clasped hands even tighter and prayed for strength, feeling the icy touch of terror at the back of his neck, trying to tell himself he would be safe, that he could stand against whatever the Shadowed One chose to try against the rightful King of Gwynedd.

The hymn ended, and the prelates raised Kelson to

his feet and divested him of the ivory mantle. Then, as the four knights with the canopy moved into place, Kelson knelt once more on the altar steps to receive the marks of chrism which would make him the rightly anointed King of Gwynedd.

Morgan watched proudly as Kelson was anointed on head and hands, tried not to be anxious about the presence he knew was even now approaching the cathedral. As the anointing concluded, and the choir broke into the strains of another hymn, Morgan strained to hear what was happening outside, stiffened slightly as the sounds of liturgical ceremony were joined by the ghostly echo of steel-shod hooves ringing cold against the cobbled street.

Kelson rose to be invested with the symbols of his office. Priests fastened the crimson jeweled robe of State around his shoulders, touched his heels with golden spurs. As chain mail clanked against naked steel beyond the heavy doors of the cathedral, Archbishop Corrigan took the Ring of Fire from Duncan, murmured a blessing over it, held it aloft for an instant, slipped it on Kelson's left forefinger.

Then he motioned Morgan forward with the Sword of State.

It was the moment Morgan had been waiting for, for even with the Ring of Fire on Kelson's hand, there could be no magic until Kelson was sealed by the Sign of the Defender. Making his way to Kelson's side, he unsheathed the great sword and gave it into Corrigan's hands, watched anxiously as the Archbishop prayed that the sword be ever used to dispense justice.

Finally, Corrigan presented the sword to Kelson. And Kelson, with an anxious glance at Morgan, touched his lips to the weapon and handed it over to Morgan. As the sword exchanged hands, Kelson touched Morgan's Gryphon seal briefly, then froze in dismay.

For there had been no sensation of power when he touched the seal, no surge of promise fulfilled, no sealing of the force foretold by Brion's ritual verse. His anguished eyes sought Morgan's frantically, and Morgan too felt a sick queasiness rise in his throat.

Somewhere, they had failed! Obviously Morgan's Gryphon was not the Sign of the Defender!

There were loud footsteps outside the cathedral now, and the people grew hushed with fearful expectation. As Corrigan, unaware of what was going on, continued with the investiture, held out the jeweled sceptre of Gwynedd to Kelson, the cathedral doors swung open with a muffled crash, and a gust of icy wind whistled down the nave.

As Morgan turned his head slightly toward the rear of the church, there was no doubt in his mind what he would see. Nor was he disappointed.

He looked—and saw Charissa, Duchess of Tolan, Lady of the Silver Mists, the Shadowed One—silhouetted against the open doorway, veiled in pale grey and blue, shrouded in living mist which twined around her in a sinister aura.

CHAPTER FOURTEEN

"Who, then, is the Defender?"

KELSON DIDN'T even move as the doors crashed back on their hinges, though he yearned to turn his head and look. For even as the sound shattered the silence, he realized that to satisfy his curiosity prematurely might only make him lose his nerve. He had never seen Charissa, and he wasn't sure how he would react.

Kneeling with one's back to the enemy was not generally recommended, either—he knew that too. He was probably taking a terrible chance by remaining in that position while his enemy advanced, and under other circumstances he would never have even considered such a strategic blunder. But since he was helpless anyway, it should make little difference. There was a point where theory had to yield to practicality, and frankly he wasn't sure just what he'd do when he did turn around.

He had to have time to think. If he had to bluff— and that seemed inevitable at this point—he would also have to have some clear purpose in mind beyond mere survival. He didn't think he would freeze up when he faced her—but there was no sense tempting fate. Brion had taught him that years ago.

He heard footsteps echoing down the nave and knew that his adversary approached, that she was not alone. As he stiffened slightly, he saw Morgan's hand creep closer to the hilt of his broadsword. He hazarded a glance to his left and saw that Duncan was signalling the Archbishop to proceed with the ceremony.

Kelson nodded to himself in approval. Duncan was right. The farther along in the ceremony they got, the better were Kelson's legal claims to the throne, and the better were his chances of discovering a way out of his quandary.

Archbishop Corrigan took the jeweled crown of Gwynedd from its velvet pillow and raised it above Kelson's head. The footsteps were much closer now, and Kelson saw Corrigan's eyes flick over his head to the aisle beyond, saw him wet his lips nervously as he started the invocation for coronation. To the right, Jehana's face went pale as the footsteps came to an ominous halt at the transept.

"Bless, we beseech Thee, O Lord—" Corrigan began.

"Stop!" commanded a low, female voice.

Corrigan froze, the crown poised over Kelson's head, then quickly lowered the crown and looked at Kelson apologetically. His glance flicked over Kelson's head again, and then he stepped back. There was the clatter of steel on the sanctuary steps, then silence. Carefully, Kelson rose from his knees to face the intruders.

The significance of the mailed gauntlet on the steps before him was unmistakable, as were the armed men lined up in the aisle behind the woman. Looking down the aisle, Kelson could see at least three dozen war-

riors, some in the black flowing robes of Charissa's
Moorish emirs, the others in more conventional mail
and battle attire. Two of the Moors flanked their mistress to either side, arms folded impassively across
their chests, their faces dark and grim under the black
velvet jubbas.

But it was the woman herself to whom Kelson's attention returned again and again. For she was totally
unlike what he had expected. He had never considered
the possibility before, but Charissa was beautiful!

It was obvious that Charissa had anticipated this
reaction and capitalized on it, quite evident that she
had planned her appearance accordingly, for maximum
effect.

A gown of blued-grey silk flowed from a high, jewelled collar around the ivory neck, and the whole was
covered against the cold by a cloak of deep grey velvet
and fox. The long, pale hair was coiled and braided in
a high coronet at the top of her head, a small sapphire
coronet encircling it. And the entire shining mass was
lightly covered with a gossamer veil of blue which
spilled down her back and softened the determined
expression on her face.

That expression was what finally brought Kelson to
his senses, made him reevaluate his first impression.
For the coiled hair resembled nothing more than a
heavy, golden crown, shrouded slightly in gossamer
blue softness—symbolic in her mind, no doubt, of the
other crown she hoped to wear before the day was
over.

She nodded greeting as Kelson's eyes met hers, then
glanced meaningfully at the mailed gauntlet on the
steps between them. Kelson did not miss the significance of that glance, and suddenly he was coldly
angry. He knew he must hold this creature impotent
—at least until a way of dealing with her could be
found.

"What would you in the House of the Lord?" he demanded quietly, a plan beginning to form. His grey eyes burned with a cold fire reminiscent of the old Brion, and he seemed suddenly to add double the years to his dignity.

Charissa raised one eyebrow, then bowed mockingly. The boy reminded her of Brion twenty years ago, with a presence which was surprisingly mature and commanding for his years. What a pity he would not live to profit from it.

"What do I want?" she asked silkily. "Why, your death, of course, Kelson. Surely you had some inkling. Or didn't your 'Champion' see fit to warn you of the fact?"

She turned to smile sweetly at Morgan, then returned her attention to Kelson. But Kelson was not amused.

"Your insinuation is as unwelcome here as you are," Kelson replied coldly. "Begone before you tax our patience to the breaking point. Armed retinues are not welcome in this House."

Charissa smiled unconcernedly. "Bold words, my noble princeling." She gestured toward the gauntlet. "Unfortunately, you cannot be rid of me that easily. I have challenged your right to rule Gwynedd. Surely you will agree that I cannot now leave until that challenge has been satisfied."

Kelson's gaze flashed grimly to the men behind Charissa, then back to the woman. Charissa, he knew, was trying to goad him into the inevitable duel of magic. But he also knew that without his father's powers, he would fail. Fortunately, there was a way to forestall the battle for a while and still satisfy honor. Meanwhile, perhaps he could gather his wits about him for the decisive confrontation which would eventually follow.

He glanced at Charissa's men again, then made his decision.

"Very well. As King of Gwynedd, we accept your challenge. And under the ancient rules of challenge, our Champion shall fight yours at such time and place as shall be determined at a later date. Is that agreeable?" He was confident that Morgan could easily beat any man in Charissa's entourage.

A flicker of anger crossed Charissa's face for just an instant, but she quickly masked it. She had hoped to leave Morgan unharmed for a while longer, so that he might further suffer as the last of the Haldanes met their deaths today. That was not essential, however. What bothered her more was that Ian might not be able to defeat the Deryni half-breed.

She glanced at the gauntlet again, then nodded. "Well played, Kelson. You have postponed our confrontation for perhaps five minutes, since I still mean to call you out in personal combat."

"Not while our Champion stands!" Kelson interjected.

"That can be remedied," Charissa continued briskly. "First of all, we shall not determine the outcome of this contest at a later date. The time and place are here and now. You have no choice in the matter. Further, I shall not rest my fortunes on any of these who stand with me here. My Champion stands yonder to defend me."

As she gestured toward the right side of the cathedral, Ian stepped from the ranks of the noblemen with a sly grin on his face and glided to Charissa's side. His hand rested lightly on the hilt of his sword as he gazed mildly across the distance between himself and Kelson.

Kelson was astonished at the disclosure of Ian as the betrayer in his midst, for he had always thought of the young Earl as a loyal, if not overenthusiastic, supporter. This explained the strange happenings that had plagued them since Morgan's arrival. With his high rank, Ian would have had no trouble at all setting the Stenrect, killing the guard, massacring the guard detail at Brion's tomb last night.

As he thought about it, he realized that Ian's statements had often tended to encourage the loose talk about Morgan over the past three months. His unfinished statements, his sly innuendoes—of course. In fact, he must also have some Deryni power himself. And motivation was no puzzle. He knew as well as anyone else that Eastmarch bordered Morgan's Corwyn.

None of this showed on Kelson's face, however. Only his eyes narrowed slightly as he turned his attention to Ian, his voice low and dangerous in the stillness.

"You would dare to raise steel against me, Ian? And in this House?"

"Aye, and in a thousand like it," Ian retorted, steel whispering against steel as he drew his blade and bowed silkily. "And now," he gestured with his sword, "will your Champion come down to do battle? Or must I come up and slay him where he stands?"

Cat-quiet, Morgan glided down the chancel steps, drawing his sword as he went. "Save your words for your victory, traitor!" he spat. He scooped up the gauntlet with the tip of his blade and flipped it through the air to land at Charissa's feet.

"I accept your challenge in the name of Kelson Haldane, King of Gwynedd!"

"Don't be too sure!" Ian countered, moving purposefully toward Morgan.

As Charissa's men moved back to give the two room to fight, Ian eyed his opponent thoughtfully, the tip of his blade wandering almost lazily before him as he studied Morgan's every move.

Morgan, too, studied his opponent, his grey eyes

taking in every step, every subtle movement of Ian's burnished blade. He had never crossed swords with Ian before, but obviously the Earl had considerably more skill than he liked people to think he had. There was a careless intensity about the man that put Morgan instantly on guard.

Morgan had no particular qualms about the duel. He was a superb swordsman and knew it. He had never lost a battle in his adult life, and he didn't intend to start now. Still, the uncertainty of Ian's skill and finesse warranted a cautious approach until he knew better what kind of swordsman he was up against. He must win this battle for Kelson, no matter what. Whatever the price, he would pay it.

They had circled long enough. With a savage lunge, Ian sought to penetrate Morgan's defenses in the crucial first seconds of the duel. But Morgan was not fooled. Parrying nimbly, he avoided Ian's blade with ease, tried an attack of his own, then withdrew slightly as he realized it would not, indeed, be an easy fight. Patiently, he threw up a singing net of steel around himself, easily parrying each of Ian's renewed attacks as he studied the Earl's technique.

Suddenly, he saw what he had been looking for and switched immediately to a special offensive maneuver he had been saving for just such a moment. His stroke cut Ian's fine velvet doublet and pinked his opponent in the right shoulder, and the Earl jumped back for just an instant.

Ian was furious at being touched. Though he had always concealed the fact, he considered himself an excellent swordsman. That his maiden battle in public should be marked by a wound, however slight, was something he had not bargained for. He didn't like it at all.

Flinging himself headlong into the foray, Ian returned to the duel, battling now with emotions rather than reason, as Morgan had hoped he would. Finally, he took too long a chance, left himself wider open than he should have. Even as he parried Morgan's first thrust, the general's riposte left him open on the right, and Morgan's blade found a deep sheath in his side.

As the sword drooped in Ian's hand and his face drained of color, Morgan withdrew his blade and stepped back. Ian tottered for a moment, surprise and fear flashing from his eyes, then sank to the floor, sword clattering from paralyzed fingers. As his eyes closed, Morgan tossed his head contemptuously and wiped his blade on Ian's golden cloak, then turned to stroll calmly toward Charissa, sword still in hand.

Charissa's eyes flashed angrily as Morgan approached, but she knew he could not detect what she had seen—a slight movement of the man on the floor behind him.

"Who *now* is ruler of Gwynedd?" Morgan taunted, levelling his sword at her throat.

Behind him, Charissa saw a hand move, saw the flash of Ian's favorite dagger as it sailed from Ian's cocked fist. Her fingers were already moving in a rapid spell as someone yelled, "Morgan!"

As Morgan whirled, the dagger was already in the air, and he squirmed to avoid its shining blade. But even as he tried to dodge, the chain of office around his neck suddenly seemed to move slightly, to coil itself around his neck and choke him, to throw him off balance.

Then the blade was deep in his shoulder and he was stumbling, sword falling from fire-laced fingers to clang on the marble floor with a discordant sound.

As he sank to one knee, Duncan and a pair of other priests rushed to his side. Morgan wrenched the chain of office from his neck with his good hand and flung it across the floor at Charissa, then grimaced against the pain as Duncan and the priests helped him back to the sanctuary and eased him down on the steps. Charissa began to laugh.

"Yes, who now *is* ruler of Gwynedd, my proud friend?" she taunted, as she strolled easily to where Ian still writhed on the floor. "I had thought you better trained than to turn your back on a wounded enemy."

As Kelson, Nigel, and other of Morgan's friends gathered around the wounded general, Charissa glanced down at Ian and prodded him with her toe. When he gave a low moan, she stooped over to look him in the eye.

"Well done, Ian," she whispered. "What a pity you won't be here to see the outcome of our little conspiracy. Your hurt is too great, and I have neither the time nor the spare power to save you."

Ian grimaced with the pain, tried to protest. "Charissa, you promised! You said I would rule Corwyn, that we would—"

"I *am* sorry, my dear, but you didn't quite succeed, did you? A pity, too. You were good at so many other things."

"Charissa, please—"

Charissa put her fingers across his lips. "Now, you know I detest pleading. I can't help you, and that's that. And you can't help yourself either, can you, poor little mortal? I shall miss you, Ian—even though you did think to defeat me eventually."

As Ian tried to speak again, his eyes wide with horror that she knew what he had thought secret, Charissa's other hand moved in another spell. For a few seconds, Ian struggled to breathe, his hand clutching at her cloak in desperation. Then he relaxed, the life gone. Casually, Charissa stood up again.

"Well, Kelson?" she said, the edge of mockery in her voice. "It appears our little duel has decided nothing. My Champion is dead—granted—but yours is so sorely wounded, his fate too is doubtful. It appears I must rechallenge you if I'm to gain satisfaction."

Morgan glanced up sharply at those words, winced as the movement caused him considerable pain. Beads of perspiration dotted his upper lip as Duncan probed the wound with gentle fingers, and Morgan motioned Kelson to lean down closer. Kelson gathered his resplendent crimson cloak over his left arm and knelt by Morgan's side, his eyes grave with concern for the wounded man.

"Kelson," Morgan murmured through clenched teeth, gasping again as Duncan withdrew the dagger and began to bind up the wound. "Kelson, be careful. She'll try to trick you. Your only hope now is to play for time, try to find the key to your own powers. I'm convinced it's got to be here somewhere. We've simply overlooked it."

"I'll try, Alaric," Kelson said.

"I wish we could have helped you more, my prince," Morgan continued. He sank back weakly, half-fainting, and Kelson reached across to touch his hand reassuringly.

"Don't worry."

Kelson stood up, let the crimson velvet of the state cloak fall properly from where it had been gathered over his arm. He felt all eyes on him as he walked the few steps back to the center of the chancel stairs, sensed rather than saw the archbishops and bishops move out of the way behind him, clearing a space around him for the battle they expected to follow next.

He glanced around the nave, noting the tense faces in the congregation, the menace of the armed men still standing in the aisle behind Charissa, caught the wave of quiet confidence coming from Nigel, standing there beside his mother—and Jehana, pale and taut in the awful silence, her hands clenched stiffly at her sides, her eyes feverish, pleading.

"Well, Kelson?" Charissa's low voice echoed through the nave, reverberated in the hushed sanctuary. "You seem to be hesitating, my precocious princeling. What *can* the matter be?" Her full lips curved in a sneer.

Kelson returned her gaze levelly. "It would be best you left now, Charissa," he said quietly. "Our Champion lives, and has defeated yours. Your claim has not been upheld."

Charissa laughed mirthlessly, then shook her head. "I'm afraid it isn't that easy, Kelson. If it wasn't clear, I am rechallenging you to mortal combat here and now —a trial by magic, which is what I wanted from the start, as you're well aware." There was an awed murmuring from the assembly behind her. "You can't avoid it that easily. Your father would have known what I'm talking about."

Kelson flushed slightly, but managed to keep his face impassive. "Our father, through necessity, was more accustomed to killing, Charissa. In that, we will admit, we are not experienced. But there has been enough of killing in the past weeks. We would not willingly add you to that list of the dead."

"Ah," Charissa nodded approvingly, "the Son of the Lion is full of bluster, like his father." She smiled slowly. "But I think the resemblance ends there, perhaps; that our young prince speaks bolder words than he means. One might almost believe he had the power to back up his boldness." Her icy gaze swept him from head to toe and back again. "But of course, we all know that Brion's power died with him on the field of Candor Rhea."

Kelson held his ground. "Did it, Charissa? Did it die?"

Charissa shrugged noncommittally. "Did it? You tell me."

"Are you willing to take the gamble that it did?"

Kelson continued shrewdly. "Our father defeated yours and stripped him of his power. It is reasonable to assume that if we hold King Brion's power, we hold also the secret of yours. And in that case, you would meet the fate of your infamous sire."

"*If* you hold that power," Charissa agreed. "But *I* killed Brion. I think that might just alter the odds, don't you?"

Jehana could no longer restrain herself.

"No!" she cried, running out into the open space between her son and the Deryni sorceress. "No, you can't! Not Kelson! Not Kelson too!

She stood protectively between the two and glared at Charissa, and the sorceress stared back at her for a moment and then laughed.

"Ah, my poor Jehana," she cooed. "It's too late for that now, my dear. It became too late many years ago when you renounced the better part of yourself and settled for being only human. The matter is out of your hands now. Stand aside."

Jehana drew herself up to her full height, and her smoky green eyes grew darker, glittered with a strange light.

"You shall not destroy my son, Charissa!" she whispered icily. "Though I journey even to the gates of Hell, you shall not have him, as God is my witness!"

As Charissa broke into a derisive laugh, Jehana suddenly seemed to blur slightly. The stunned Kelson had been about to seize his mother's arm and remove her from the path of danger, but now he found himself unable to approach closer. As Jehana raised her hands and pointed toward Charissa, long sparks of golden light streamed from her fingertips toward the fearful woman in grey. Suddenly, all the unleashed power of a full Deryni lashed out at the Shadowed One, guided only by the despair of a mother who must try to save her only child, whatever the personal consequences.

But Jehana's power was untrained. The long denial of her Deryni heritage so many years before had left her unskilled in its use, unable to adequately control it or use it to best advantage. And Charissa, in her evil, was all that Jehana had denied herself—full Deryni sorceress, skilled in her art, in complete control of an arsenal of power so great, Jehana had probably never even dreamed of its extent.

Consequently, Charissa was not disturbed by the attack. She recovered immediately from the initial onslaught and wove a defensive net around herself which repelled anything Jehana could summon. Then she began to concentrate on destroying this bastard Deryni who dared to challenge her powers.

The air between the two women glowed. The air crackled as fantastic power was launched and neutralized. Kelson watched wide-eyed as his mother held her own against Charissa for a time. But meanwhile, Duncan and Morgan had already spotted the trap Charissa was laying, and they worked feverishly to deflect the killing force Charissa now directed at her royal adversary.

Then it was over. With a little cry, Jehana crumpled softly to the floor to lie like a sleeping child on the rich carpet of the steps. As Kelson scrambled to her side, Duncan was already kneeling beside her, feeling for a pulse, his mouth going grim and tense as he found what he feared.

With a worried shake of his head he motioned Nigel and Ewan to move her gently to the side, and faint energy crackled lightly around her as they took her to safety. As Duncan helped Kelson to his feet, the boy turned wide, dreading eyes on the priest, and Duncan shook his head.

"She's not dead," the priest whispered, so that only Kelson could hear. "Alaric and I were able to deflect the worst of the power." He glanced aside at where Morgan lay, then let his eyes touch on Jehana.

"As far as I can tell, she's in a binding trance controlled by Charissa. She'll be all right if we can break it. But other than that, only Charissa can release her —either by will, or by her own death. Since the first is unlikely, I'm afraid you're going to have to try for the second. So now you have something else to fight for."

Kelson nodded somberly, his mind reeling in the certain knowledge he had acquired in the past few minutes. He *was* half-Deryni! And if his mother's performance was any indication, he should be able to make use of that fact to at least some extent. After all, he had been trained to accept these powers, to believe in them—even some principles for control. Now if he could just apply some of those principles he'd been taught . . .

And Brion's powers—those should still be available, too. They had obviously overlooked something—in the verse itself, perhaps. Morgan's seal had not been the Defender's Sign. Who, then, *was* the Defender? Now that he thought about it, Morgan *had* been called Protector, not Defender, in the earlier part of the verse. So the Defender had to be someone else. And the Defender's Sign— what could it be?

Charissa returned to her original spot at the foot of the chancel steps and indicated the mailed gauntlet still lying on the floor where Morgan had flung it. There was a grim smile on her lips now, for there was no doubt in her mind that she held the upper hand. Kelson did not have his father's power. For surely he would have used it to protect his own mother if he had had it. The boy was not canny enough to sacrifice Jehana simply for the effect of a later sure victory. Besides, she knew full well that the burst of power which had saved Jehana had never come from the mind of the half-breed Kelson Haldane.

She nodded slightly in Kelson's direction as he took his place at the top of the stairs, and met his gaze levelly.

"And now, Kelson Haldane, son of Brion, will you accept my honorable challenge, to do battle in the ancient and honored manner of our Deryni forbears? Or must I strike out now and slay you where you stand, smite you a martyr, without a fight?

"Come, Kelson. You were full of bragging words before. I call your bluff!"

CHAPTER FIFTEEN

*Now battle joins, the mind of mortal man
cannot conceive.*

KELSON'S MIND raced frantically, turning over every piece of information he had ever encountered regarding Deryni magic, scarching for a clue. As he clasped his hands together, his fingers began absently rubbing the Ring of Fire, and he again turned over the ritual verse: *New morn, ring hand. Defender's Sign shall seal thy force.* . . . Defender's Sign shall seal. . . . Defender's Sign. . . .

Suddenly, Kelson's eyes focused on the floor where Charissa was standing. He had never noticed it before, but there were seals inlaid in the marble floor there in the transept—seals of the saints, seals of—by all the Holy Saints! Could it be?

Trying to control his excitement, he forced his eyes to casually scan the great circle of seals, searching for one he dared not hope was there. If this had been a newer church, he knew he could not have hoped to find it. But Saint George's—by God, there it was! The seal of Saint Camber, he who was long ago called *Defensor Hominum,* the Defender of Man!

Triumphantly, he raised his eyes to sweep the cathedral before him. He had found it! There could be no other answer. They had unwittingly equated Protector and Defender in their first readings of the verse, and almost ruined the entire sequence. But now . . .

He gazed confidently across the space at Charissa, studied her for a long moment before he spoke. Now he must set the stage for what he was about to do.

"You have made the statement that we are afraid to do you battle, Charissa," he said evenly. "You have admitted the murder of King Brion. You have caused one we hold in almost the same reverence to be sorely wounded. And you have gravely injured the mother who made the ultimate effort to try to avert this deed. The time is now past for idle talk." He scanned the assembly confidently.

"Also is the time now past for mercy, which we had thought to offer even in the light of what first happened. And now we warn you, Charissa. We accept your challenge and agree to do you battle, even though it is with some reluctance that we join here in this place. But since you force us to this show of strength, we can guarantee no mercy now, no promise of gentle retribution."

Charissa tossed her head defiantly. "The Shadowed One has no need of your mercy, Kelson. And when such boasts are backed only by bluffs, I can only laugh. Come down, if you are not a coward. I am ready for you."

Kelson regarded her disdainfully for a moment, then glanced over at Morgan and Duncan and nodded slightly. As he reached to his throat and unclasped the heavy, wine-dark cloak, Nigel was suddenly at his side to take it, his anxiety and hope almost tangible in the light of Kelson's new awareness. Kelson flashed an impression of reassurance at his uncle, then turned and walked slowly down the chancel steps. Nigel folded the cloak over his arm, then joined Morgan and Duncan on the right.

As Kelson descended the steps, Charissa withdrew to the far side of the transept, perhaps forty feet away, waited as Kelson stooped to pick up the gauntlet.

Slowly, he stood up, formulating the exact pattern his movements must take to get him to the Camber seal as soon as possible. Out of the corner of his eye, he could see the target area perhaps twenty feet ahead and a little to the left. He began walking toward Charissa with the gauntlet, edging his way slightly to the left so his path would coincide with the seal. Then, just before he stepped onto it, he flung down the gauntlet, ahead and to the right. As it clashed against the marble floor, he stepped onto the seal.

Morgan and Duncan watched the scene with growing apprehension, for the gamble Kelson was taking was against fearsome odds, and with dire consequences. Also, there was some uncertainty as to what the boy had planned. That he had a plan was evident from the glance he had shot them before he descended the stairs. As he approached the seal, they guessed how his reasoning had gone. But as far as they could tell, there was no reaction as Kelson flung down the gauntlet and stepped onto the seal.

Charissa looked disdainfully at the gauntlet for a moment, then caused it to fly to her hand, tossed it to one of her waiting guards. Then she bowed slightly and stepped a few paces closer to Kelson. Never had Kelson looked so terribly young and alone.

"Art thou ready to begin, My Lord Kelson?" Charissa said, the words of long-formulated ritual rolling from her tongue with practised ease.

Kelson nodded. "We are ready, My Lady Charissa."

Charissa smiled and stepped back a few paces,

raised her arms in a low-murmured spell. Instantaneously, a semi-circle of blue fire sprang up behind her, a graven line of sapphire ice which took in half the great circle of saints' signs.

She lowered her arms and stepped back several paces more, then gestured patronizingly to Kelson.

Kelson took a deep breath. Now was the supreme test. For if he could not answer Charissa's spell, it would mean that he had lost the gamble, that the power was truly lost. And he had felt nothing—no reassuring flicker of recognition when he stepped onto the Camber seal. He would not know until he tried his hand at magic for the first time.

Breathing a silent prayer to the renegade saint on whose seal he stood, Kelson raised his arms above his head—a single, fluid movement as he had seen Charissa do.

And unbidden, the words came to his lips—words he had never heard before, a low chant which made the air crackle with power around him in response, which seared a line of crimson fire behind him—a line which bent itself to the semi-circle shape required and joined the two arcs together in a complete circle, half red, half blue.

Kelson controlled a smile as he lowered his arms, felt the power surge through him, became aware of myriads of spells controlling more power than he had dared hope for. All around, he heard the low sigh of relief as his people realized he did, indeed, have the Haldane power.

And that was not all. For deep in the recesses of his mind, he was aware of the fleeting presence of two other entities—Morgan and Duncan. A swift impression of congratulation, confidence, rippled across his mind and washed into the innermost corners, then was gone.

He allowed himself a slight, sardonic smile as Charissa raised an eyebrow in surprise at his response to her spell. But then he forced himself to concentrate on what must now follow as Charissa stretched out her arms and began another incantation. This one was in a tongue he understood, and he listened carefully, mentally pulling forth the response he would make when she finished.

Charissa's voice was low but clear in the stillness of the cathedral.

> By Earth and Water, Fire and Air.
> I conjure powers to flee this Ring
> I clear it now. Let all beware.
> Through here shall pass no living thing.

As Charissa completed the verse, Nigel tugged hard on Duncan's sleeve. "Duncan! Does he know what she's doing? If he completes that spell and merges the two arcs . . ."

"I know," Duncan whispered grimly. "If he does, the circle can't be broken until one of them is dead. That's the way the ancient challenge runs."

"But—"

"It's partly for the safety of the onlookers, Nigel," Morgan added weakly. "Without the confining circle, the spells sometimes tend to get out of hand. They're going to be dealing with fantastic amounts of power today, from many sources. I can guarantee you won't like some of what you see."

"At least we know Kelson has Brion's powers," Duncan added as he watched Kelson spread his arms as Charissa had done. "Kelson was never taught these things."

Kelson's voice was low, steady, as he answered Charissa's spell.

> Inside, all Space and Time suspend.
> From here may nothing outward flee
> Or inward come. The circle ends
> When two are one and one is free.

As Kelson finished, violet fire flared where the two arcs had been, the cold violet line now inscribing an unbroken forty-foot circle where the two must duel. As though on prearranged signal, both combatants then moved to opposite sides of the ring, each standing with perhaps five feet behind them and a stretch of some thirty feet between.

Charissa quickly surveyed the limits of the ring, then bowed slightly. Her voice was slightly hollow in the magical confinement of the dueling stage.

"My Lord Kelson, as Challenged, it is thy right and privilege to claim first blow. Wilt thou claim that right, or must the Challenger proceed?"

Kelson bowed in answer. "My Lady Charissa, as Challenged, it is true that first blow is our right and privilege. However, in the face of so fair a Challenger, we concede the point. The first blow is thine."

As Charissa smiled and bowed, Nigel nudged Duncan again. "What the Devil is he doing?" he demanded in a harsh whisper. "He doesn't dare to give her any more advantage than she's already got."

"That's just it," Duncan murmured. "He *has* to. It's part of the formal dueling rules that a man, even if challenged, concedes the right of first blow to a lady opponent. Kelson agreed to play by the rules, and that's one of them. Don't worry. The first spells are just testing spells."

On the far side of the ring, Charissa stretched her hands out before her, palms together. Then, as she murmured something unintelligible under her breath, she drew her hands apart slowly. As she did, a sphere of blue light could be seen hovering in mid-air before her, slowly growing in size, until it reached human proportions and developed the features of a fighting man.

As soon as the thing's shape had stabilized—blue warrior-thing in blue mail, blazing sword in hand and blue shield on arm—it looked around the circle and spotted Kelson. Then, dripping fire and blue vapors, it cocked its head at the young King and began advancing cautiously across the circle.

Kelson hesitated but for an instant. Then, putting right hand to closed left fist, he drew forth a glowing crimson sword. As the blue warrior-thing came within reach, lightning forked from Kelson's left hand, pinning the blue sword, while the crimson blade lopped off the thing's head. It struck the floor with a hollow sound, and then the apparition and Kelson's weapons vanished. Only a wisp of blue vapor remained.

The people rumbled approval at their young King's prowess, then hushed as Charissa's nimble fingers began moving vexedly in the next spell. Even before she began the incantation, dark mists had begun to swirl around her, a hulking, dragon-shape to form.

> Drathon tall,
> Power come.
> Conquer all,
> Senses numb.

Before she could begin the second verse, Kelson began the counterspell, and the mists began to recede.

> Drathon kill,
> Power fade.
> Senses still
> Conquer shade!

Charissa's eyes darkened menacingly, but she said nothing. She had thought to have an easy victory, but it was obvious the boy knew much more than she'd bargained for. Not that she doubted the outcome of the battle. No upstart boy with new-found powers could beat a full Deryni sorceress who'd been using her powers for years of practice. Still, there was no doubt her puissance was being challenged.

Patiently, for she had the edge in stamina at least, she began the standard testing spells, designed to feel out the weaknesses of her opponent. It would take longer this way, but the outcome, at least, was sure.

Spells flew across the circle: attack and counter, parry and riposte, as those outside the circle watched. Charissa's men stood impassive in the aisle behind their mistress, long used to her activities in magic, concerned only that the duel should take no longer than necessary. There would undoubtedly be physical suppression needed on some parts of the populace once their mistress defeated this upstart prince, and they could hardly wait. Only the half dozen or so Moors watched the contest with any degree of real interest. For their people, too, claimed some acquaintance with magic, and they were always looking for a new spell.

Among others who watched, there were much graver thoughts, however. As Nigel watched the duel, spellbound by the horror of what might happen yet too fascinated to tear his gaze away, Morgan raised his head to look again, then touched Duncan's elbow lightly with his good hand.

"Duncan . . ."

Duncan looked down with concern, for Morgan's face had gone even paler than before, and the lines of pain were etched more deeply yet in the fine features.

"What's wrong? Is the pain worse?"

Morgan clenched his teeth and nodded weakly. "I've lost a lot of blood, Duncan. I can feel my strength draining away. That burst of power we used to save Jehana almost finished me."

Duncan nodded. "What do you want me to do? How can I help?"

Morgan tried to ease himself to a more comfortable position on the hard steps, winced as the movement set his wound on fire again.

"You remember, I told you about healing Derry last night? Well, I've got to try to do it again, this time on myself." He brought his left hand up on his chest so he could see the Gryphon seal. "I think I know the way now, but you're going to have to help me. Support me, reinforce the direction of my thoughts, but don't interfere. I say that last because I think I touch on some areas that are—well, questionable."

Duncan smiled faintly. "Are you trying to tell me you're dealing in heretical alliances, Alaric?"

"Possibly," he murmured.

He glanced wistfully at the dueling area again and smiled as Kelson countered a particularly noxious beast from the nether regions, then shifted his attention to the seal on his left forefinger and began to concentrate. His eyes glazed slightly as he entered the first phase of the Thuryn trance; and as soon as he was well under, Duncan too began to gaze at the seal. The priest entered rapport easily and let his thoughts merge with those of his kinsman, letting himself be carried along the current of Morgan's mind, lending support and strength when called upon. At his very elbow, Nigel was not even aware of the new development.

For Kelson, the time seemed to stretch interminably. And the succession of beasts and beings, real and mythical, which he had both battled and conjured, seemed like a half-remembered nightmare in the dark of some long ago night. Drathons and wyverns, cara-dots with their waving tentacles, gryphons breathing fire, Stenrects like the one he'd seen in the garden, ly-fangs—the list seemed endless. Even now Charissa was conjuring up some new terror that he must thwart.

He straightened slightly and forced himself to pay closer attention, for he suddenly had the distinct impression that Charissa's latest spell was not nearly as routine or academic as the ones before had been.

Even as her fingers moved in the strange new series of passes, Kelson had the chilling impression that this spell was a darker one than those preceding it. He strained to catch all her words as she began the incantation.

> "Spawn of Dagon, Bael's Darling,
> Heed my call, which bids thee here.
> Child of Thunder, hear my order.
> Come: I charge thee to appear.

> "Smite this young ambitious princeling.
> Shroud him in a cloak of flames.
> Help to wrest the usurped power
> Which Charissa justly claims!"

As she spoke, there was a rumbling of thunder in the air before her, and a dense black vapor began to condense into a tall, shadowy form, vaguely manlike in shape, but with scaly hide and long claws and teeth.

As it stood there for an instant, blinking confusedly in the brighter light than that to which it was accustomed, Kelson clasped his hands before him, a chilling sensation rippling around him as he realized he didn't have the proper counterspell at hand. As the creature recovered its wits and began ambling across the circle toward him, he began several spells haltingly and without effect.

Mawing and shrieking its defiance, the creature continued to lumber slowly across the circle, dripping blue vapor and flames as it came, its eyes burning a fiery red which flashed points of light throughout the cathedral.

As the creature reached the half-way point, Kelson began to panic.

CHAPTER SIXTEEN

*You placed on his head, O Lord a crown of
precious stones.
He asked life of You, and You gave it
to him. Psalms 21:3–4*

As THE CREATURE continued to advance, another counterspell suddenly came to mind. Stepping back a few paces, Kelson's lips began to move in the spell, his voice becoming stronger as a feeling of confidence began to replace the panic.

> "Lord of Light, in shining splendor
> Aid me now, if Thou dost hear
> The supplication of Thy servant,
> Battling for his people here.
>
> "Lend me strength to smite this Demon.
> Send it to the depths of Hell.
> Cleanse this circle of the Evil
> Which Charissa doth compell!"

As he completed the verse, Kelson raised both arms high in the air, then pointed decisively to a point but a few feet in front of him, not two strides from where the monster advanced.

Just at that moment, the sun burst from behind the clouds to stream through the high, stained glass windows of the cathedral, casting a brilliant, multi-colored pattern on the floor where Kelson pointed.

As Kelson stood his ground, the monster lurched into the pool of light—and began writhing and exuding streamers of flame and smoke. It shrieked and screamed its rage and pain, thrashed in the color at Kelson's feet, but could not seem to leave the patch of light to get at the young King.

Presently, its thrashing stopped; its shape melted away. And only wisps of pungent blue smoke and flickerings of gold and crimson light played on the floor where the thing had been.

Kelson lowered his hand, the Ring of Fire winked ominously, and the sun chose that moment to go back behind the clouds. As a low sigh of relief rippled through the cathedral, Kelson raised his eyes to meet Charissa's. He stepped forward a few paces to address her, noted ironically that the spot where the monster had died, where he now stood, was the Saint Camber seal. He breathed a silent thank you to who or whatever had aided him.

His eyes were bright with confidence as he spoke.

> "And now, Charissa, this must end.
> I shall no more my powers lend
> To please thy fancy. I defend
> My people, and thy power rend.
>
> "I swear by every Holy Name
> That I shall thwart thy evil aim.
> And further, I refute thy claim
> That Good and Evil are the same.
>
> "Therefore, gird ye for the fray.
> This is the final duel, I say.
> For while I live, the light of day
> Shall cease till thou art done away!"

As he finished his incantation, the cathedral grew dark. And outside the open doors at the end of the aisle, he could see that the skies had, indeed, darkened, even though it was not yet noon.

Charissa swallowed hard, a look of apprehension crossing her face for the first time. She feared this test, but there was no choice. Her fingers began once more to move in the pattern of the acceptance spell.

> Thy boasts are fearsome, little lord,
> But I fear not thy lofty word.
> Threats are easy to afford.
>
> But I, too, weary of this game,
> So I accept thy test of flame.
> Beware! 'Tis *I* who rise to fame!
>
> And when this little farce is done,
> Then death shall come to Brion's son,
> And *I* shall be the ruling one!

With the final word of the incantation, the two halves of the circle suddenly misted over with blue and red auras and became a hemisphere over the two. Where the two colors met, a sparkling violet interface crackled brightly in the darkness—the only light in the cathedral save the candles and vigil lights.

As each combatant stood his ground, the interface began to surge back and forth between the two, giving and gaining as each sought out the other's weaknesses. It seemed a fairly even match for a time. But then the wall of violet fire began moving inexorably toward Charissa.

As the hemisphere slowly turned to crimson, crowding out the blue, a look of fear bordering on terror came on Charissa's face. The deadly interface between her power and Kelson's advanced slowly but unwaveringly, and her eyes grew wide and frightened as she retreated to the limits of her side of the circle. Her shoulders finally encountered the sleek, unyielding surface of the barrier ring and she stopped, unable to go any farther. As the crimson at last engulfed her, she let out a long, agonized scream, edged with fury, which slowly faded as she grew smaller.

Then she was gone. And ring, crimson aura, and hemisphere were gone. And all that remained was a young boy garbed in shining white raiment, standing on the seal of a long-forgotten renegade saint, too dazed from his victory to hear the shouts which rose from the people who had watched and hoped with him.

Outside, the darkness lifted, and the clouds began to roll away.

With the shouts, Morgan opened his eyes and smiled, moved his hand to the wounded shoulder and found it healed. As Morgan looked up in wonder from the thing he had done, Duncan too opened his eyes, glanced at Kelson, then helped Morgan to his feet. Morgan walked to the side of the still dazed Kelson to touch his shoulder gently.

The touch brought Kelson back with a start, and he turned to look at Morgan in astonishment.

"Morgan! How did you—?"

"Not now, my prince," Morgan murmured, gesturing toward the still cheering congregation and smiling. "You have a coronation to complete."

He took Kelson's arm and led him back up the sanctuary steps to where his archbishops waited, stunned and frightened by what they had seen. As the cheering died down, Nigel stepped forward with the royal State cloak and draped it proudly around the young King's shoulders, elation apparent in every line of his body. And Jehana, released from her spell with the death of the Shadowed One, sat up weakly from

her place at the side and stared uncomprehendingly at
her son.

Kelson saw her look, and pulled away from those
who were gathering at the foot of the altar to conclude
the coronation. Gliding easily across the chancel, he
came to a hesitant stop before her, then dropped to
one knee at her feet.

"You risked much for me," he whispered tentatively, half afraid to reach out to her. "Can you forgive
me for going against your wishes?"

With a sob, Jehana reached out and took his hand,
cradled it in hers, held it to her lips. "Please don't ask
me that now," she whispered, tears wetting his hand as
she held it. "Only let me be glad you're alive."

Kelson squeezed her hand, blinking back his own
tears, then pulled away and got to his feet. He smiled
down at her as he backed off a few paces, bowed, then
turned and went back to those waiting for him at the
altar.

As Kelson knelt on the altar steps once more, everyone but the archbishops and bishops drew back and
knelt also. Then Archbishop Corrigan, Archbishop
Loris, and Bishop Arilan elevated the jewelled crown
of Gwynedd, reciting the ancient formula of coronation
as they did.

"Bless, we beseech Thee, O Lord, this crown. And
so sanctify Thy servant, Kelson, upon whose head
Thou dost place it today as a sign of royal majesty.
Grant that he may, by Thy grace, be filled with all
princely virtues. Through the King Eternal, Our Lord,
Who lives and reigns with Thee in the unity of the
Holy Spirit, God forever, Amen."

This is what the people saw and heard.

But to those of Deryni blood, it was rather a different sight. For to them, a fourth figure supported the
crown above Kelson's head—a tall, blond man garbed
in the shining golden raiment of the ancient High Der-

yni Lords. And to those of Deryni blood, there was rather a different message superimposed over the traditional coronation formula. The shining stranger used the ancient Deryni formula, which bespoke quite a different destiny for the brave young King he crowned.

"Kelson Cinhil Rhys Anthony Haldane, I crown thee in the Name of the Almighty One, Who knows all, and in the name of him who was long the Defender of Humankind. Kelson Haldane, thou art King for Human and Deryni Life and Prosperity in thee, King of Gwynedd!"

As the crown touched Kelson's head, the Deryni-seen apparition vanished, and Morgan and all the others stood while Kelson was invested with the rest of his insignae of office.

As they waited for the prelates to finish, Morgan turned slightly to Duncan, whispered in a low tone, "Duncan, did you see what I saw?"

Duncan nodded almost imperceptibly.

"Do you know who it was?" Morgan persisted.

Duncan glanced at him sidelong, then returned his glance to the investiture. The clergy were swearing fealty now, and soon it would all be over.

"Let me guess," Duncan whispered. "It was your mysterious stranger."

This time, it was Morgan's turn to nod. "You don't think it was Camber, do you?"

Duncan shook his head and frowned. "He spoke in the *name* of Camber, which makes it even *more* of a mystery."

Morgan sighed slightly, then straightened his cloak. If he pulled it over just a trifle more, it would nearly cover the jagged hole in his tunic, and the blood down his side.

"I'm glad it wasn't Saint Camber," Morgan whispered, just before mounting the steps to do homage to the new King. "I dislike being the target of Heaven's special favors. It makes me uncomfortable."

With that, he stepped before Kelson and dropped to one knee, let Kelson take his two hands between his own. Morgan's voice rang out strong and clear in the hushed cathedral as he recited the ancient formula.

"I, Alaric, Duke of Corwyn, do become your liege man of life and limb, and of earthly worship; and faith and truth I will bear unto you, to live and die, against all manner of folks. So help me God."

As Morgan rose to receive the royal embrace, other nobles—Nigel, Ewan, Lord Jared, Kevin McLain, Derry—all came to repeat the words of homage, to swear fealty to their new King. Morgan once more took up the Sword of State, holding it naked and upright beside his King, as all the great lords and barons of the land came to swear their allegiance. Then they began to form for the procession from the cathedral.

The ecclesiastics passed on through the transept and began to recess down the aisle. Charissa's retainers had melted into the crowd on her death, and now the throngs proclaimed Kelson with one voice. But as Kelson and his attendants reached the transept, the sun chose that moment to again come out from behind the clouds.

Once again, jewel-toned sunlight streamed through the high stained glass, throwing a pool of color at Kelson's feet. Kelson stopped, and the cathedral became hushed in fearful expectation as they stared at their new young lord. For there had been death before in the colored sunlight.

Kelson glanced up at the window and smiled, glanced around at the hushed sea of faces. Then he stepped calmly into the light.

There was a long sigh of wonder which swept through the still nave then. For there was no death in the sunlight now. The pool of rich sunlight merely sparkled on

Kelson's gems, blazed on his crown like a thousand sunrises.

He turned aside to glance at Morgan and Duncan, motioned them also to step into the light. They obeyed without hesitation.

The light glittered on Morgan's golden hair, on his rich velvet cloak, turned the snowy whiteness of Duncan's surplice to a rainbow of rich color. And then the three continued down the aisle.

As the procession followed, the crowds began jubilant cheering, with heartfelt cries of, "God save King Kelson! Long live the King!"

And the King of Gwynedd went out of that place to show himself to a grateful people.

DEL REY SCIENCE FICTION CLASSICS
FROM BALLANTINE BOOKS

Catch a Rising Star!